The House of Abba

Leslie Musoko

Published by New Generation Publishing in 2013

Copyright © Leslie Musoko 2013

First Edition

www.newgeneration-publishing.com

 New Generation Publishing

The Third book of Divinity Dawns

For those who believe and those who do not

Prologue

Through the skyline Cephas saw the darkness and then the stars. The glow of their shimmering brightness painted the dark night in a beautiful indigo haze. In the yellow, green and blue iridescent colours of the windowpane above, he made out its wings fluttering like the thundering of a herd of wildebeest. He couldn't count how many in total but he was sure that he had seen more than two. They were white, their strong jaw line just about visible in the dark. The horses in a curvet position made such a sound Cephas thought the window would collapse and cave in. He watched from below in the church and then rising slowly above the pews he left.

It was foggy outside and almost impossible to see for any distance. Even more surprising was the fact that it was only twilight and the darkness, which had been conspicuous from the spire skyline had now disappeared. However, he kept to his task passing by the high steel fence that came off from the concrete wall, moving up the hill in search for the entrance. The road had been laid with cobblestones, their grey texture barely visible in the shroud of fog. This was of little concern, he moved with the wind and even at the freezing temperatures that could be perceived from the gloomy weather he felt nothing. His desire was his pursuit to make this new appointment on time. There was strength in the deafening silence, a salient indication of things to come. This was remarkable considering that the ridge was covered in a never-ending myriad of cypress trees. He was guided, led into the courtyard and eventually brought to an area in the park that was fairly isolated compared to others. He noticed a lady talking to a child in the pram. She did not see him, she couldn't. A few people went past him, some even through and he was quiescent, patient, *it* will happen soon. *What ever* had led him to this fountain isolated from the rest of the park was bound to reveal its self any moment now. And suddenly he was there, the appointment, the man with one eye in the centre of his forehead where two would have been under normal circumstances. But these weren't. Cephas opened his hand and the man placed the coin in it and then he was gone. Words were rarely used in this world. Everyone knew what they were supposed to do; instructed to do and fulfilled this without question.

This was a less complicated mission than those he had carried out previously nonetheless a timely assignment. Cephas had come to learn that creatures such as him manifested themselves only when asked to. They changed dimension constantly, fulfilling the purpose of their existence whenever the need arose. In their habitat they were mainly dormant but on those occasions that they were without there was no limit to what they could do, see or accomplish. There were no steps to becoming one of them, you just were. The wind was their comfort. In its waves they became one with their wings flying to places far and beyond yet capable of changing size whenever it was necessary. They were the beings of a universe that time had given up on, that would never die and were given guardianship of one that was terminal. Cephas had been guarding his for many years willing it away from the darkness of its ways and into the virtues of light. Now he was winning and taking over its will. As it fell apart he grew stronger. He had an advantage; he needed no food or water or time to set his body by. Creatures such as him existed without those needs making them immortals and better servants for the guardianship. They were also very few and rare for the unique purpose that they served. Only few of them were awarded the responsibility of being ubiquitous, seeing the livelihood of another while living theirs.

'What is it the *humans* said they missed?'

'Life.'

Yes, *life*. The truth was they were life itself, a pathway that transported mere mortal into immortality. Man became spirit and did that which no one could foresee carrying out death defying missions barely possible to comprehend, their meaning only interpreted by God. This was their haecceity.

I began to stir and Cephas knew he was running out of time. In this soliloquy I had questions.

Dear Father are we allowed to dream? Oh heavenly father are we allowed to dream? If we can would it be as we see it? My bones wither away from not knowing which way it should be. How can I have come this far without knowing? I see the future hear their voices, know their faces but do I have your authority? Oh wretched man that I am wipe off those tears for you are as free as a bird. Search and seek pastures new with impossible dreams and your wish shall be fulfilled. I know very little about this place I find myself in. Who are these people I see before me. Doubt, you lazy soul you pursue your victims into the night and steal away their dreams. I won't let you have mine. No never, I have earned this wish, this place and no one can take it from me, find someone else. A warm hand on this heart of mine feels the vibration of a horse's sternum in full flight. I am weary of my task, not because I cannot do it but whether I have the authority to. Still I have learnt to try and fail rather than not try at all. So come out all of you, come out and see this man who knows not his own name or face, yet knows his future, his past and the present.

When God called upon us in visions we took a new body to see beyond our world, our reality and our humble existence into his. I had been down this road many times over. I couldn't separate man and spirit because they both existed in one body, knew each other intimately than any two people could ever do. Yet I knew that in my best of times I was operating through my spirit and not through the eyes of the man I was. Today I am Cephas and I am both man and spirit. We are one and we live in a new house, in God's house. We call it the House of Abba. This is my story, this is how we got there and this is what it takes to get there.

Part I

Resurrection

Chapter One

Glyfada 2006, on the outskirts of Athens; Cast your mind back to a time when even this splendour would never have been envisaged. Cast your mind back to a time when you weren't even in the running for anything and you would have to agree with me that waking up in this room is a *heaven sent*. I have no bones to bear with you so why the early morning sermon was the ghost that echoed in return. *Because my head aches and the racket out side is driving me insane for one thing*! Then wake up. I turned over in bed and covered my head with the pillow to drown out the noise. My ear lobes were squashed between the folded blades of the sheet and my face now hidden from the earth, sought solace away from mankind. My legs were sprawled beneath the other ends of the sheet. People don't get it, never have and never will. No one needs this before breakfast. No one needs this at this hour. No one *told you* to come; you could have made an excuse. The *dreaded ghost* voices! And then the rapping sound coming from the door, or was it the room next door. I was uncertain, either way I wasn't coming out from beneath the pillows. It couldn't be my room, I was cautious about such things. The night before I had moved the paper flier, the *do not disturb* sign to the handle at the front. When I heard her voice, it appeared to be many millions of miles away from my cave, my solitary confinement and the safest place in these parts at that time of the morning.

'Room service,' the accent was there, strong and distinguishable.

There was a cough followed by a guttural sound. Someone next door was sharing my aches. I wasn't alone in this cave others had made the journey.

'Not now,' said a male voice, a shuffling of feet, a

grunt and then the loud slamming of the door. I was sure the housekeeper's face had been flattened. Choose your fights, don't pick on any one bigger than you, anyone with more pounds behind them than you or worst of all a tired man in the early hours on a Saturday morning. I heard nothing for a short while and then another rapping. She hadn't learnt her *lesson*! Who could blame her it was her job.

I felt the water trickle down my arms. I had to get up. The cave was now uninhabitable, been replaced by a furnace. In a few minutes I would need the fire brigade to cool me down. Oh what *the hell*! One more voice still screaming at me. I had given it my best shot. Soon I was reaching for it without thinking, flipping the pages over to the passage I had been reading the night before. I changed my mind and chose a psalm. I was on my knees my hands clasped before me, my eyes shut, willing my mind away from the present, from the thoughts, from the wrong voices, the ghost voices and unto Cephas, hoping for spirit to reach higher ground, sacrosanct.

Then I was on my feet, moving the curtains aside and staring past the wall at the men that chiseled away in the neighbouring building. The yellow crane moving back and forth behind them like the giant arm of a large creature sent to torment the world and cast shadows in the minds of simple men. Some things never changed you simply had to accept them for what they were. A quick shower would do the trick. It would wash away the cave and weave my thoughts to the present. I was sure I had seen a blue sky above the yellow creature, I was sure it offered better terms and conditions for my current bearings. One way or the other I was going to find out.

I snapped the door shut to my room and stored the key card in my wallet. I was already in a better mood, heralding to what lay ahead. I had chosen to travel light, using the side pocket in my trousers for my wallet and leaving my mobile phone behind as the battery was flat. I walked down the narrow corridor side stepping the cleaner's trolley and sparing a glance into the room she attended to. Rays of sunlight streamed through the blinds and bore a bright shadow in the dimly lit hallway. No one could argue that I wasn't in the Mediterranean; it was conducive to good weather and masked whatever misappropriations had befallen one. We had chosen a good day to explore Athens and I was grinning like an excited child before opening my present. It was good having these vices, the breathless shoreline of Marseille in ninety-one, the towering cathedrals of Cologne four years later. Ploys that taunted and provoked the whimsical mind, wet palms and goose bumps that were unspoken niblets of code; the product of a misspent youth in a chalice of irrepressible desire.

I turned right unto the stairway and followed the sounds coming up from the foyer. The walls were hardly thin in this part of the world. On the contrary they had been built by men who wrought metal as though they were gleaning bee's wax. It was the howling of a brigade preparing for a stampede with no thought for others who had endured the night. John's hotel could hardly be classed as the talk of the town but for some reason there seemed to be more commotion than was usual for this time of day on a Saturday morning.

'Ah there he is come and help us,' my Chinese colleague said smiling. 'I stand here now for more than two hours talking and nothing,' he continued, looking in my direction as I came down the stairs. He then proceeded to chat rapidly in Cantonese to the group of six that had taken up most of the entrance, his numerous gestures indicating that he may have been involved one way or the other. I forged my way past the picket, avoiding the vase of the shrub at the foot of the stairs and heading directly to the reception desk to enquire about the commotion. Perhaps it was better to start there and avoid the group for now. I had no understanding of Cantonese and trying to decipher what was being said would be downright erroneous and obtuse.

'Do you know these people?' the anxious lady behind the counter said, her blue eyes locking with mine as she searched for some assurance in a fellow westerner. Her black hair was worn loosely at shoulder length. She could have been in her mid forties but could be taken for someone much older as the flaccid skin under her arms hung disparagingly beneath her freckled tan; the macula beneath her left eye now a prominent birthmark. Her broad neck was covered in a chain of opal beads that reached the crest of her strapless white blouse.

'I do,' I replied.

'Good. Then you can explain to them what I have been trying to all morning. Tell them that the cleaner found the door open and the room in a mess. She immediately called for my attention and I called the police. Those men you see in the corner are detectives and they are here to enquire about what happened. They have already looked in the room but no one can tell if anything is missing,' she blurted out, allowing herself no time to pause just in case she was again rattled by the cluster of Chinese men and women in her foyer. She immediately returned to her duties, the bangles on her hands ringing in synchrony as she began filing the papers on the desk into the room number slots behind her. She hadn't allowed me to speak or give any indication that I had absorbed her outburst. She had assumed I would understand, pick up the mantle and run with it. Perhaps it was something in the water today or I woke up on the wrong side of the bed.

I couldn't answer immediately, allowing myself time to examine the detectives that talked a few metres away from the entrance that led to the bar. Their cheap suits looked as though they had been slept in; it was a casual day in the office, probably one unwarranted for. There was nothing to diagnose from their body language other than a forgone conclusion of utter boredom. I sympathized and echoed their thoughts. Who needed this, why me and *why now*? It was a Saturday morning that had come too soon and given the mayhem in proceedings, heading to the bar would probably have seemed a more palpable consideration.

'I do not understand. Why are the detectives here and what is going on?' I asked trying to gain some degree of control in my environment. I needed to assert myself, dismiss the urge to walk away, *run* and chase the adventure that beckoned.

'One of the guest, yes, the gentleman standing over there says that something was stolen from his room but I am confused because he checked in last night and no one has been into the room except this morning when the cleaner discovered the place in a mess.'

'So what was taken?'

'I don't know. I cannot understand a word he is saying. Every time I ask him a question all his colleagues intervene and I cannot understand his accent.'

'Do you want me to try?'

'Please do because I called the detectives and we have been going round in circles all morning. I still have a lot of work to do and this is stopping other guests from checking in,' she answered, looking apologetically in the direction of other supposed guests that occupied the plush seats in the lounge almost resigned to the fact that it would be a while before there was any change in events. There were passports strewn on her desk and I could hear a dot matrix printer in the back office screaming out the paper work to go with them. Alarms bells were going off at full tenor. *Stay and you become a victim*! *Run* and life would offer you a pasture of freedom. *Remember* the blue sky of hope above the dreaded crane, run I say, run!

I nodded in defeat and walked to the group of my colleagues quickly isolating Lung who had approached me at the foot of the stairs.

Present Day, Mougins, South of France; It was difficult starring at one's reflection in the mirror without looking beyond and seeing what could have been had things been different. The only difference this time was the alternate to what they were wasn't the preferred choice. I'm here now and that's what matters those times are passed. Hailey cleared the smudge of toothpaste from the corner of her mouth. Hadn't her mum always told her that first impressions counted, or had it been someone else. She couldn't tell. She had made her first impression the night before still it didn't take away the fact that she always had to look her best. Given the elegance of her surroundings what was there to think about.

'I give you this girl you certainly can pick them. How did you find this one?' She whispered quietly to herself as she saw the sparkle from the bright light overhead reflected in her eyes.

Her oval shaped face hadn't lost any of its youth. Twenty-eight was a good age to be hitting one's prime in their career. You had seen some of the world and picked up a few things along the way. However there was the youthful desire that burned within for what you wished. No offence to the early twenties but still it took confidence and self esteem to find this point in one's career and that did not come with poppy-eyed excitement. It came with guts, hard work and a bit of luck. She had found hers to be exact she had made hers.

Rays of the bright sunlight were already pouring in through the large window behind her. She would take in the vast expanse of the garden and then sit by the pool. She wouldn't swim yet unless invited to. Sarai had said she had free access to any part of the villa. It would steady her pen, weave her wand into conjuring a good story for the magazine. Susan waited, New York waited and then who knew perhaps even the stars.

She walked back into the large bedroom and took off the bathrobe that had been provided. She slipped into an open yellow top and pulled on jeans shorts. It was casual attire in these parts. That too was something her host had insisted upon. Her tape recorder was on the dresser. Her note book not too far either. Sarai had said she hadn't made any plans for the day. They would have some breakfast by the pool after her early morning swim and then take things from there. It was time she learned more about the woman. It was time she began putting the pieces together for this story.

Glyfada. I approached the group listening to the voices fight each other in my head. It was not all bad, at least I had somewhere to start; I knew Lung. Lung Yuen was considered the honcho for things in the group having had the most experience outside China. There were the small benefits that came with this, you got a say in deciding which countries you went to. For Lung it had been North America and Europe, he had lived in Mexico for almost two years and in England for under a year. He had a small family, a wife and son and from what I knew of the man he was less rattled than most under most circumstances. I knew if there were any answers to be found in this chaos he would be a good place to start.

'Lung what's going on?'

'She not tell you?' Lung Jun Yuen asked as he turned to face me.

'You tell me. She sounds perplexed.'

'I *go out* this morning to walk and when I return I find my musical set is missing.'

'You had a musical set in the room?'

'Yes. *I travel* with it from England, it's a Sony player. As we are here for two weeks I think I might need it you know.'

'Was your room broken into?'

'I don't know I *just come* back I check my things and find that my musical set has gone. So I called the reception and she called the detectives but up till now we have heard nothing.'

'Okay let me speak to the detectives and find out what is happening,' I replied.

It looked like my morning in Athens was about to take a kick in the teeth as there were more pressing matters to attend to in the Johns Hotel on Pandoras Avenue. At this point I began to regret not charging my phone the night before. With hindsight I would be in a position to warn the friends that waited for me in Athens. However there was some small consolation, I wasn't late at my peril, I attended to a good course, they would understand and they would have done the same in my place. I had worked with Lung for almost six months; he had become a friend and had supported me during my visit in Shenzhen. Lung had offered precious names of friends in homeland China that had helped me during my stay there. There was no doubt now that it was my turn to repay the favour.

'Excuse me are you the detectives for the robbery?'

I asked.

'Who are you?' replied one of the men roughly, a thin Greek with a charred moustache that turned to face me. His drooping shoulders now a pair of troughs that had managed to crock his jacket. His face harnessed a grizzly beard and looked like it had been begrudged much needed sleep. His appraisal of me wasn't friendly.

'A colleague of the Chinese man Lung over there. The man who reported that something was stolen,' I said addressing both men. I understood their frustration. It was obvious that the mayhem of matters at hand had taken over and the men were waiting for the chance to get out of there.

'Well we checked the room already and we made a few calls to the office but other than that it does not look like a break in,' the second detective interjected, a little embarrassed by the attitude of his partner. He was lighter in complexion and presumably a better receptacle of his surroundings, a lapdog unaffected by the chagrin of his comrade. He gave a few years to his partner and was the livelier of the two with an eagerness to impress.

'We have made a report and have called it in but...' his charred moustache partner shrugged as he stubbed his half smoked cigarette into an ashtray. It looked like he was now following his partner's lead and being polite, reappraising me and realizing immediately that I could be more of an influence than he had first assessed. Perhaps I was the elusive ticket he needed to get out of the place.

'Can we take a look again?' I said. 'I would like to see the room for myself.'

'Sure.' The detectives nodded and we walked back towards Lung.

'Lung, I would like to take a look at your room and

see what happened. The detectives are not sure whether it was a robbery.' I said.

'Why? They think I lie that my player was stolen.'

'Well, that's what we are trying to find out. I just think that they do not understand what happened but maybe we can all go up to your room and take a look before we decide. I guess it would help if we talked up there,' I said lightly, my voice calm and now a tad persuasive. If Lung knew how desperately I wished to escape through the revolving doors to the beckoning Athens he wouldn't have bothered with this concern for derision.

Lung Jun Yuen shook his head disapprovingly and then uttered something in Cantonese to the group before turning in the direction of the stairs. I had just come down them hoping and wishing for more, it was a shame I was returning so soon under these circumstances.

Mougins. 'How did you two meet?' Hailey asked.

Sarai was silent as she considered the girl's question. She could have given her the simple answer as it really was, perspicuous, as most natural things were. However he had told her different, he had told her that the way she felt when he first held her in his arms was a long time feeling that they had both known and felt before they met. It was evident that the present, future and past where all one when we accepted that the impossible was made possible with God. We had to be patient to see the future, wise when we acknowledged the present and without regret looking back into our past. They were entwined. That would be the truth. That would explain everything to this girl but she would have to start somewhere simpler in order for the girl to understand.

'I suppose we first set eyes on each other on the

dance floor.'

Hailey grinned.

'But who saw who first? I mean did you see him or was it the other way round?' she asked, her excitement within immediately taking a turn for curiousity.

'I chose my husband. And you can quote me on that, he wouldn't deny it either.'

'Then you saw him first.'

'I saw him first.'

'But why, there must have been many other men in the room, why him and why then?'

Sarai was silent again as she tried to remember. The confluence of these two rivers was a mantra played in a world apart from the one Hailey inhabited. Was this a secret or had she been provided a carnet to reveal to the world the deluge of hidden truths for the mystery that was the man she had married. Cephas was different to anyone she had ever met. He had said that the reason why she chose him was because he had been searching for her. He had said that the true person in her was always searching for the true person in him and those choices were made long before they manifested themselves in our reality. It had been his way from day one, teaching and showing her a world that existed beyond her own. It was the most bizarre thing as he described the moment they had first met to her how things had played out, how much he already knew of what had happened even before the real thing had come to pass.

'Yes there were other men in the room, many, some more handsome than others, others more affluent, each capable of giving something different to a woman. My husband was there and I was attracted to him. Still when he held me in his arms I couldn't say now that it was just this alone that brought us together. It is not how he looked or what he had. It just felt as though we

21

came into the room together even before we met and so it was the most natural thing that I should be with him.'

'And you went to him.'

'And I went to him.'

There had been a tall blonde lady in the room leaning closely to Cephas as they danced. She spotted him immediately and walked up to them. She had touched his hand lightly already feeling his presence, their centers entwined in a world far beyond the one they existed in. She knew that he wouldn't hesitate, Her intuition coming alive like a tigress protecting hers. The other woman had not objected and then Cephas had turned and looked at her with his dark eyes curious and searching her face. He kept her in his sights as they danced his eyes never leaving her. She loved those eyes she loved the way in which they said there was no one else but her. Soon he was talking, asking her what she did and where she was from. Time stood still as they moved on the dance floor. It was as if they had been restrained for many years locked away from one another to avoid an inevitable reunion and then finally their time had come, a moment they both wished for. A few weeks later, he had said before this happened it had already been. That was Cephas.

'And I went to him,' Sarai said again quietly and closed her eyes. The lotion was working magic for these few days that she had taken off to focus on the article. The sun, the pool and even the sound of the waves coming from the sea not far off were causing a stir within her. You couldn't argue with the beauty of this magic. She had wanted a place like this and with Cephas by her side this was the dream life she was now living.

Glyfada. The room was in disarray when we got there. There were piles of clothes scattered in every available corner and with the odour slightly nauseating it was a pile of charcoals about to go up in flames; a cyclone couldn't have done enough damage. It was as if the place had been visited by species from an alien planet making a roundtrip and discovering that they had lost something. I came to an abrupt halt just outside the door, undecided whether to proceed any further and for the first time I began to understand the tremors in the receptionist's voice. Perhaps I should have stuck to my first counsel and ran while the going was good. We were all about to get gangrened and I had been chosen as leader. Man was the founder of cleanliness. Man was the highest species and elected to live above animals. *Man did not live in this room*! There was no absolute criterion in life for how people lived but it became immediately apparent that perhaps Lung should have thought a little bit more about the state of the place before inviting us back to it.

'Is this how you found the room?' I asked. The door to the small patio was open and there was washing hanging on the railings. A half filled suitcase lay open on the floor with men's underwear hanging on the chair facing the dresser. The only untouched bit in the room was the bedside lamps and the ceiling. I knew that even those would get their turn it was just a matter of time. If ever an intruder had been in the place I was sure his trail would have been long gone.

'No. These are not my things. You know I share with another person and these are his things. He also do laundry. But my musical set was on the table and it is missing.' Lung said. His eyes were impassive and unperturbed by the disorder, his voice sounding as a matter of fact and relinquishing no excuse for the mess.

'This is why we cannot make sense of it all. I mean there is more than one person living in this room and look at the state of the place. How can we tell if there aren't others?' the charred moustache detective shrugged. His hands were on his hips, his dark rimmed eyes staring bewilderedly around him. I knew the feeling, animals belonged to a cage and not to this room. Perhaps he felt police time should not be thrown away chasing shadows beneath refuse. It was obvious that Lung and who ever he shared the room with were an untidy pair that wasted police time.

I said nothing. Outside the yellow monster had its pincers digging incessantly. I would not falter; my troth has to be maintained under all conditions, especially those that are unfavourable. It would work, is *working*. My prayer would get me through the day; there is hope, the *blue sky* above. Charred moustache's words were not far off the mark. The man had a point. Perhaps being described as sloven would be putting things mildly for whoever was the other guest. These were *new* business rules, company *pledges* - make money by letting your workers become menagerie. Instill in them parsimony and you would rip the benefits of a global evolution. The fact remained that the reason for Lung sharing the room with another was something only the company could answer for. It was the frugal nature of things and the burden placed on the Chinese employees. It was an insidious gaol that gnarled its occupants from within and passed on its traits to those around them. However even under these circumstances there was no explanation for the dearth in sanitation. The laundry on the railings outside only reinforced the detective's opinion.

Step away from it! *Trawl* with patience! Silence, and then I was listening, everything else shut out. I was quiet for a while, poised as I took in my surroundings waiting for *something*, waiting for the *voice*, waiting for God. A heartbeat away was directions, I had to wait, listen for his guidance.

When it came it was low, it was far away from everything that had happened all morning but it was there.

Check the door.

Just like that, the silent ringing from beyond, an undertone, amidst the distractions and chaos I had to be wise and not fooled by the obfuscations. I was no detective but I had come to know the way of the world, it was always able to mask what mattered.

Suddenly I felt the throbbing! The sensation evident and unmindful of my surroundings, my pounding heart was racing out of proportion, I knew this feeling; albeit staring through the bleak eyes of a corpse in another world. Man was weak and could not exist in the world beyond, spirit wasn't. The white horses, their fully stretched wings and then the churchyard, glimpses! *No! Not now! Do not deviate, it's not time yet! Some things came sooner than others!* I wished I was elsewhere. I wished the Lord would unveil the mystery behind the identity of the *man with one eye*, Cephas's vision, but it wasn't time, God's *time*. The fervent pounding had caught me off guard. I had to be patient, it would come soon. Matters at hand were less interesting but more pressing. In an instant of time that passed for the thought to come through as the men in the room waited for my next move I said,

'Let's take a look at the door just incase we find signs of a break in. I assume you both had key cards and so did the cleaner. At least this could narrow our suspicion to just a few.'

We gathered around the entrance of the room. The door now ajar, looked okay but under closer examination, especially at the scuncheon in the doorframe were metal met metal it was obvious that the door had been tampered with. The klepht hadn't been thorough. The clasp was slightly disengaged from its initial bearing, something that could have been easily missed because the door opened and shut as normal. However under careful scrutiny it became apparent that Lung's recollection of events had not been a fable. His room had been broken into and although he shared it with another it had been neither of them or the cleaner that had taken the player. It had to be an intruder, maybe someone who had noticed him bring it in the night before. The hotel had a bar, an excellent restaurant and a swimming pool that was used not only by houseguests but also by visitors from outside. It could have been anyone.

'Was it expensive?' I asked.

'It was. I only bought it two days ago for this trip,' Lung said.

'He would like to file a report,' I said turning my attention again to the detectives. 'You can see the damage that has been done to the door. Include this in your report, maybe he can get some sought of compensation for his loss. I shall speak to the receptionist and tell her that the room was broken into.'

'Okay we agree. The first time we checked we did not see the damage in the door,' charred moustache muttered under his breath, his face embellishing the worried look of a man who had hoped for less and got more.

'We would make a report and call the station,' lapdog wagged with more gusto.

'I understand, the room is mucky and the door looks fine but then again it isn't so....' I explained letting them fill in the blanks and left.

As I descended the stairs I felt lighter and happier. The drowsiness of the morning was completely gone. The blue sky, hope, it lingered in the distance. Maybe it was time to really begin the day and see Athens.

Chapter Two

Pandoras Street led to Metaxa Street, which opened up to Vas Gergiou Avenue at the Kritis Square on the east side of the gulf and the B' marina to the west. The trams followed the railing up A' Voula Beach past Metaxa Street in to Vas Gergiou Avenue and then unto Poseidonos Street to allow their passengers the best view of the Saronic Gulf. They then headed west up Poseidonos Street to Piraeus Athens leaving the bay and moving inland north into ancient Greece. This made John's hotel the ideal location for guests who wished to explore Greater Athens. One could spend as much as half an hour taking in the stunning scenery of the gulf before the run into the city centre.

I walked up the small street listening to the alarm of the car parked outside the small super market at the corner of the street. It seemed as though no sooner had one chaotic event ended than another was immediately ready to take its place. This time I wasn't going to be a victim. I'd already had my bellyful for one morning. The birds were out in full and chirping away in the trees. There was plenty to espy in this one way street than most, the espalier climbed the walls uncontrollably; the verges were ruderal amidst a pile of waste land that had been dumped on the side of the street. There were weeds growing out of the drainage holes and an overgrowth on the sidewalk that seemed to have lost its bearings. I toyed with the idea of living in this city all year round. It had the sun, the beaches and the greenery to go along with it. Then there were those trees I had seen. I would use the walkway past them all year round without the slightest cause for concern. It wasn't too far from the hotel and a side road that some colleagues and I had discovered on the route back from our offices. The scenery there was breathtaking. The houses, large mansions surrounded by high fenced walls that one could only dream of. I could feed on this for a year and if I was lucky take a holiday to a winter resort to balance things out. The food wasn't bad either. The restaurants catered for all sorts but then there was no harm in cooking. I'd choose to and with all the vegetables available to man it could just work. It was something to think about. Then there was the language to think about, this could be the deal breaker; the rattlesnake that hampered an almost perfect setting. I understood none of it.

I crossed the street unfazed by the refulgence of the sunlight, my mind already in gear as to where I had planned to meet some friends. They would be at the acropolis. We had planned to eat out. Then it was anyone's guess what would happen next.

I watched her approach the tram stop in a languid stroll with her eyes downwards and her hands clutching her bag close to her chest. She looked isolated, enveloped by her surroundings. I knew the look, had carried it myself a while back. It gravitated towards a calling for familiarity. You felt exposed away from what and whom you knew and relied upon to make you feel real. You wanted to run and hide from the world yet you allowed bravery take precedence. I didn't have to be in her shoes to know.

I watched her reach for water in her tow sack and then turned my attention to the rendezvous ahead. Maybe I had seen her some place before but there was no need to dwell on it, she was obviously in her own world without the need for my intrusion.

'Is this the right ticket to buy?' she asked.

I reined my thoughts back to the present and looked at her. She was small in statue, young maybe in her early twenties. Not plain but neither pretty, however in her brown eyes I could see something.

'Where are you going to?'

'To the city, to town, to Athens.'

'Then that is the right ticket.'

'Thank you,' she said and sat down. She wore a small sleeveless yellow and white blouse over a black Jaquess skirt and there were droplets of perspiration on her forehead. She brushed them aside with her bare arms, they couldn't have been there because she talked to a stranger; she had been out earlier, it was the weather we were having.

'Are you staying in John's hotel?' I asked making conversation.

'Yes,' she said and then looked up the tramline for any signs of it. I followed her eyes. We could use the air-conditioned interior of the tram. If and when it decided to reveal its square metal frame it would converge on us from the left snaking its path through the cluster of trees to emerge on Vas Georgiou Avenue.

'I just want to see Athens before I leave,' she continued. 'This is my last time before I go back to China.'

'You have been here long?'

'Only two weeks. I arrange everything for the new director. I am also interpreter to help the new director from China settle here.'

'And he is settled now I guess.'

'Yes, maybe good for him but not for me because now I have to go back.'

'And you don't want to.'

She sighed and looked down at her white trainers. I could read the thoughts, was she going to be a collocutor to our light discussion or not? You had doubts, you questioned yourself; do I talk to a stranger or not? In the end you had no choice in order to survive. They provided hope, gave you a way out from your solitary confinement.

'This company gave me the opportunity to travel, to visit Europe. Okay I do not know many Chinese over here, well maybe one or two. But this is not what I want to do. In university I studied journalism. I hoped it would take me around the world, to the places I wished to see. But now I do this.'

I could sympathize with her. Most people rarely did what they studied in college or what they had their hearts set on. It was tough finding out this the hard way but she had time on her side. For most people they had hit middle age and beyond before they decided to change careers, this girl had yet to hit her prime.

'Maybe you still will. This is just the start,' I offered.

'I hope so because I am very bored of this job. I call my mum everyday and talk about what I want to do. This country is nice but when I have to do the work that I do all day, well it is difficult.'

It was getting hotter by the minute. The episode in the hotel had delayed my exit that meant that I was not only running late but it was also approaching midday. It was lovely weather but sweating in it was not what I had intended. I hoped the tram would turn up anytime soon for both our sakes as the small shade we sat in was no camouflage for what was above. I looked with purpose towards the hidden bend of the tramline willing it on to show itself. I felt sorry for my young acquaintance yet I knew that it was still too early for her to feel the world on her shoulders. Allow yourself a few more years or else you could run yourself weary to the ground. I had to think of something to say, maybe words of comfort if any could come to mind. She was pouring her heart out to a stranger it was the least I could do.

'It must be difficult here though; I mean there aren't many people that speak English, even in the offices.

How have you coped all this while?' I threw into the box.

'I can handle it. I don't mind being alone here without friends because I visit places. There is so much to see in Glyfada and many different people. Sometimes I just visit the beach. I like it here away from China even though most of my colleagues would say they prefer to be back home. I am different I do not need to be with my family, I like to travel you know, to become a journalist. My problem is this job. It is boring.'

'You may get your chance some day, you sound determined.'

'I try and try but in China no opportunities as over in Europe. I apply even when I am in university for the chance but nothing,' she said, again allowing herself to look up the tramline. The sun was relentless. We were now baking and had been joined by three other passengers, an old lady and a small boy who spoke to each other in Greek and another man that paced the length of the tram stop in his shorts. The boy tugged at the old lady's skirt continuously as he spoke. Eventually she seemed resigned and reached into her handbag and took out whatever he seemed to be pestering her about. The child's eyes brightened as he removed the lollipop wrapping and tossed it into his mouth. He let go of her skirt immediately, his face suddenly becoming animated and his small body primed for take off. And as he put his thoughts into motion she grabbed at his arm pulling him back to her side.

The girl reached into her bag and retrieved a small bottle of water and sipped a little.

'You know in China there are so many students for so few opportunities especially a career in journalism.'

I listened. I could imagine her frustration. There was

no doubt that there were more careers for those occupations that were technology driven. China was developing rapidly but careers such as the one that this girl had her heart set on usually came on the backdrop of others. My own travels in life had revealed a few things to me. Some careers took others to carry them along. The reason for journalists to prosper in a country such as China would require the existence of other professions, ones with more affluence that could allow a different kind of social development. Weeks earlier I had listened to a financial advisor on CNN talk of *Chimerica* it was supposed to be a phrase conned for trade agreements between the two countries. If this was the way forward then perhaps there was still hope for this girl. However I knew being cautious would be prudent before readily accepting western values so easily. If you lived in the West you naturally assumed that your democratic right entitled you to freedom of speech. This was refreshing but information flowed both ways and this meant when you did not need to hear bad or irrelevant news it was present at your doorstep and a means by which your thought process could be manipulated. There were flaws in a western society that most people could not identify in the first instance especially those that had come from restricted regimes or cultures. Maybe xenophobic paranoia was being severe when associated with China's current propaganda but then from what I had observed lately on television and the internet perhaps change streamlined in this fashion was something that could be worked on. We had been rewarded with various avenues for the press and information distribution but then those same avenues brought us a cultural decline that none of us could stem the flow of.

No system was perfect and none was sufficient on its own to be relied upon. We made it what it was.

I had no doubts that the girl's fortunes would probably change for the better abroad given her enthusiasm and drive. I couldn't see her waiting for an evolution of significant proportions in China. It wasn't going to happen overnight. There were the other small details to put into consideration, such as freedom of speech. Glasnost had not changed Russia from its former values it was hard to tell whether an economic evolution would make any difference to China.

'I am sure you would be a journalist one day.' I said.

'I think I will too,' she replied, her voice sounding livelier than when she had first spoken. We were there for one another. God had a reason for not letting any one man survive his chores alone. In the grand scheme of things I didn't know whether what I had said would make a difference but I had done it.

Finally we heard its noise and then spotted it only a stop away from ours. There would be air-condition in the tram, we would be able to cool off, maybe because we would be moving things would feel different. I hoped for the girl's sake that they did.

Mougins. Hailey swam with swift breaststrokes from one end of the pool to the next as Sarai watched from beneath the large umbrella. The morning had gone much better than she could ever have imagined. Sarai was easy to work with and there was a truth in her every sentence. Most people interviewed for these stories were interested in one thing only, getting their picture on the front cover of the magazine and making their popularity known worldwide. Sarai was different. It was as if she wanted more from the article, wanted to relive a moment and tell her story to none other than herself.

How two weeks could make all the difference. It

was hard to imagine that she was the same person cutting through the warm blue water in these pleasant surroundings when only a couple of weeks ago she was staring blandly at the stars through a small opening in a tent which she shared with two other girls as they tried to cover a story in Mexico. There was an audience for the Hispanic population back in the States and Rezance Magazine had decided to open its doors to reach it. Susan wanted her magazine to be number one on every woman's mind. The two girls and her had pursued the story of a baroness and her husband into the hills and were storing away in a tent to reconstruct the hard times the baroness had faced before life had changed for the better. She could feel the dust particles as the wind blew hard on their tent. High in the sky where the stars that glittered and told very little of what fortune lay ahead. She had lain there in the evening light and wished for more, asked for better. Perseverance was a word she had come to know personally over the few years she had spent on earth. Their story was completed within a week and they were back in the safety of their cubicles within the office. She had barely read through her unopened mail when she was summoned into Susan's office.

The place was something out of the future. Susan had put all her ideas into this haven she had created for herself with a colourful hysteria that only she could understand. There was modern art, designer chairs and vases that one only saw in the museum. It should have been an honour to be called into Susan's office instead she always found herself using this time to imagine how differently she would decorate the room if she was in charge. Her haven won't be this futuristic hemisphere. It would be something down to earth with a little touch of herself and the places she had been to.

'So you did it, gal,' Susan said, her large green eyes

shining beneath the bolds of makeup that she was wearing. She was a large woman without being fat with curvaceous features and a presence that was always domineering. There were rumours that she had started the magazine with a small fortune she had inherited from her parents after moving to New York from Texas. She called everyone gal and had this smile that made you at ease yet spoke volumes of what she expected of you. Today Hailey could not take her eyes off the watch she was wearing. She had seen something like it on her travels, maybe in the airport. Being into watches meant those were things she never missed. It had to be Swiss cut and not less than four thousand dollars.

I'll get one of those some day. I'd wear a dress with less colour to go with it, and allow the watch to show its elegance, she thought to herself. Her expression remained that of the attentive stewardess awaiting her master's next orders.

'You did it didn't you. The ad you placed got answered,' Susan said smiling.

Before heading out to Mexico, Hailey had asked permission from Susan to place an advert in their international section of the magazine. It had read,

'If you have a story to tell, something that you wanted the world to know, something different then contact me.'

She had expected many replies and had gotten a few but hadn't followed up on them, as they were mostly local. She wanted something different, something away from the US. She had confided in Susan that unless it was from someone abroad there was no point in letting her know of it. She wanted Europe. She had been there at one point in her life liked the sun and the yellow sand and wished to return now that her career seemed to be taking a turn for the better.

'I got a call from a woman today. She is in Mougins, somewhere in the South of France and wishes to have you write about her.'

Hailey could barely contain her delight. South of France was close enough and even better. She would remember the seas, those hours by herself again and then maybe she would have an article and a great story to tell.

'Well gal, are you speechless or are you going to tell me what makes you different from everyone else here?' Susan joked.

Joke all you want Susan, but come see me now she thought as she completed another length of the pool and climbed out to sit on the edge allowing her legs to stay in the water. Sarai lay beneath the large umbrella wearing large sunglasses. It was hard to tell whether her eyes were open and watching. I'll ask her something different this time maybe a little about her past, something before now, before this place, she thought.

Sarai watched as Hailey made the short walk from the pool to where she sat with interest. She looked pretty fit. There was hardly any fat on her. She wasn't exactly pretty but anyone could tell that she did take care of herself. When she reached the recliners, Sarai said,

'You're not American.' It was a statement and not a question.

' No I'm not.' Hailey said quietly, her earlier smile disappearing and her joy taking a turn for the rational and the reality of the journey it had taken to get to this place.

'So tell me Hailey, what part of China are you from?'

Glyfada. I spotted the stunning architecture of the

Parthenon on the hill as the tram pulled to its stop on the overpass. Even from that distance it stood out, solemn, picturesque, inviting. I climbed out and took long strides down the bridge. I would have to be apologetic when I get there; the episode in the hotel earlier on wasn't my fault. It was a despairing situation impugned upon me and I had coped.

I turned left and headed down the enormous boulevard in the direction of the Parthenon, increasing my pace. The welcome shade from the green leaves of the tall trees was much needed shelter to my burning back and neck. Across the road a woman slowly put her child in the back seat of a Volvo wagon. I kept my instincts alert taking in as much of the scenery as I could. I had no map so small details counted. Any signs that could help direct me to my destination could not be missed. At the end of the road I came to a pedestrian crossing. Once again I was back at the mercy of the unyielding sunlight, my back feeling the full force of the heat and waited to cross. There were trams to avoid and four lanes of traffic in both directions. It was nothing that I hadn't seen before. My focus was the small road that branched off the wider street across from where I stood. Its path led up hill. This was what I needed. I needed to be climbing if I was going to beat time and meet my friends at the acropolis.

The path snaked, curving up hill past a small shop and then a local estaminet. There were a few tourists in it already sampling the local varieties. It was an effective way to kick start the day before the full force of the evening took over. The signs indicated that the acropolis was somewhere at the top of the hill. A group of people trudged in that direction, maybe even to the Parthenon; it was the only stunning sight above the hill. I followed. A quarter of an hour later the road led us to the foot of a graveled path with a high fence and then we stopped. At this height the boulevard below looked miniature, the cars parked by its sidewalks now obscured under the shade of the trees. It was a complete transformation and it felt as if we were at a cliffs edge staring down towards Athens. We had been climbing steeply with most of the people perspiring now and it was incredible to think how far we had come in such a short time. The scenery was breathtaking and I gasped, adjusting my footing on the rock scree to get a better look. Perhaps I wasn't as fit as I used to be or the view was just paralytic. Athens certainly stood up to its reputation and I felt reluctant to steal my eyes away from it.

However matters at hand beckoned, the group had come to a standstill, the chatter was louder, apprehensive, direction was needed. Our thoughts were being questioned; this couldn't be the entrance to the acropolis. There was no one there, no adoring crowds, travelers, noise, just silence and the occasional chirp from the birds in the trees. I could see ridges at different heights, encased in cemented paths that made circles around the hill but no direct route to the Parthenon at the top. How was I going to get up there? It looked as though our trek had discovered the staffage, perhaps even the rear entrance but not the main attraction of the landscape. There were one or two people walking on the path and the group in front had stopped to ask for directions. I listened quietly hoping to hear what would be said. The new arrivals on the path a man and his wife could not help as they were also lost and searched for the entrance to the acropolis.

Instinctively I checked my watch, it had just gone past one. My friends had to wait. I hoped that they had guessed that I was lost. Suddenly I heard voices, people talking to me. More tourists had emerged from one of the tracks on the hillside. Four Japanese men stood before me wearing khaki shorts, white short-sleeved jerseys and black pouches around their waists. The first man on the track with glasses whom I presumed was leading the rest spoke.

'Do you know how we can get to the top? We have already been that way, but there is nothing, it just leads into a forest,' the man said pointing in the direction that they had come from. He used his hand to shield the bright sunlight from his eyes.

'It's a dead end,' another member of his group said and then opened a map he had retrieved from his knapsack meanwhile saying something else in Japanese to another of the party.

I looked across the street, a man worked on his vehicle, wiping away undeterred by the heat.

'I don't know where the main entrance is but maybe the man across the street might know, he looks like a local,' I suggested. Some of the other tourists had already extracted themselves from the group with the same intention. They approached the man across the street and began asking for directions.

'I don't know why they do not put better signs up,' the man was saying when we got within hearing distance. He had a green shirt wrapped around his waist. His bronze chest was bare and exposed a glowing tan from many years of basking in the heat. It looked as though it had now become part of the landscape visible for all to see. He said something in Greek to the elderly woman that sat in the shade of the house. She was munching on something and nodded continuously, probably agreeing with his assessment, the dewlap under her neck rising and falling with each nod. We were obviously not the first of many for the day. He said something to the member of the leading party and I assumed that these were directions to the acropolis and followed suite. They were, the next turning only a short walk from were we had been standing was the entrance. It had been hidden from our view behind the trees. It could have been easily missed and with the landscape so well corroded the trees had managed to disguise the fact that there could be anything other than plain forest beyond them.

I could hear a light cheer from my Japanese comrades as they took in the scenery of hordes of people climbing the steps that led into the acropolis. It was amazing how the hillside was also able to shunt the noise of the crowd from the back of the hill. I bought a ticket and begun the long climb up the steps. My friends were somewhere up there I thought and probably terribly agitated.

Shenzhen, China 2005; For Hsu, Bacaio Gardens was the furthest she'd been outside the village of Yong Ding in the Fujian Province. It was convalescence from what looked like a life that wouldn't change any time soon. Now she felt like the fish she had played with as a child in the swamps just beyond the fields where she had watched her parents work for endless hours during the day. She had picked the fish out of the water and tossed them in the air and just when they were thinking life was over for them she had tossed them back into the water. She tried the same for the crowing frogs but didn't get that much excitement from it. Either way she knew they experienced a change of habitat, which was what she desperately needed in her solitary existence. Her father was Hakka, and considered a pillar of society but that didn't make much of a difference to her. She was the older of two girls and knew her fate was sewn to become the wife of a handsome suitor in the village long before she was born. There was just one problem, marriage and settling in that village were the two furthest things from her mind at anytime. She knew the sun rose and settled somewhere further than the village of Yong Ding. She knew more people than those living in her village could see the bright oval moon that appeared in the sky overnight.

As the bus pulled into the courtyard she alighted from it allowing herself the freedom of absorbing the flavours of some of the roasted pork and noodles that came searing through the local market nearby. The food might have been the same as that in her village, as the privileged few could afford but the town was different in every respect. She knew she deserved to be in this place for standing firm in her aspirations despite the challenges she faced back home. Hsu had quickly decided what her priorities where from fourth grade. You had to if you did not want to become the loyal wife that joined the rest of the farmers in the field. She worked harder then anyone else on whatever bits and pieces she could garner from the small box they called a television in their home. She learned broken English quickly and encouraged her little sister to do the same. She made it a habit to say a few words to her father and mother each day. They would see it in me she thought. They would recognize a girl who isn't a farmer but someone more. High school was the highest form of education for most girls from the village. This hadn't been the case with Hsu. Having gained the recognition that she desired so adamantly she was sent to university and it was then that she chose journalism as the career she would like to settle in. She hadn't perfected her English but knew that there were very few words she didn't know of.

There were people coming out of the main gates of Bacaio Gardens as she walked in the opposite direction. There were young men and women chatting excitedly in the early evening as they walked around offices that felt more like a university campus. Hsu watched excitedly and followed the rest of the group she had arrived with as they moved towards a reception assembly area. Soon there was silence as the leader called for their attention. He was saying something to them, probably of importance but she could barely hear. Soon she saw papers being handed around and eventually she received one. It was an itinerary that they all had to have in order to become residents of the Gardens. The list covered a single page. It had the much-needed campus ID card which most young grads could give their lives for. It was said that people with ID from these offices where given a carte blanche in the main cities. They were respected by many in down town Shenzhen, their prowess in attaining these cards considered worthy of their efforts. There were other useful details like who to call for medical aid, where to eat and the price of things.

As Hsu concentrated on the paper before her she heard the leader start another announcement and once more the flow of papers coming again towards her. This list was different. There was a long list of names in it but what caught her attention this time was that they were all foreign. She listened as intently as she could to hear what the leader of the group was saying.

'Over here in Shenzhen it is mandatory to have a foreign name. We employ foreign workers and now and then we may have to work abroad. We all have to pick a foreign name from the list. This would become our new name and we would use it when abroad.'

Hsu was puzzled as she caught the words. So it wasn't just her environment that was changing, it looked as if her name too was something that would go. The moon certainly shone beyond the village of Yong Ding. It looked like it had plans for her further than she could have imagined.

She prised herself from the past with some difficulty

as she examined the names on the list. Her ball pen was in her mouth as she quickly scanned the names one after the other. There were Spanish names, Austrian names and even French names. Soon she found something she new no one would regard and she circled it with her pen. I'll call myself Hailey, she thought, not many people will choose this name. When I am a journalist, I'll be famous and so would Hailey, maybe just then I would let them meet Hsu.

Chapter Three

Glyfada; I prided myself in believing that I had come through the first test unscathed. Entry into the spiritual world required one to have a better understanding of themselves and their surroundings. In spite of the heartache it took to visit the past, my woes and throes were now behind me. I hadn't run away from them, I had run to them. The spiritual world had taught me that longsuffering was part of its syllables. This part of the curriculum taught you patience, perseverance, tolerance and compassion for your fellow man. It softened the edges to arrogance, pride and lust for what was worldly. Like anyone else out there I had my flaws but I couldn't say that they were in excess when it came to arrogance or pride. I was glad that from an early age one of my heroes in the bible had been king Solomon. God had granted me grace in wisdom and in understanding his word when I opened his holy book. This curtailed my temperament and despite my ambition and the aspirations that fueled my carnal existence I knew God's word was final.

The second part of my odyssey required me to understand the hidden mysteries behind the word of God and proclaim his name as I had been taught. In this class courage was a necessity. The world did not welcome you with open hands when you decided to proclaim the name of our saviour. The bible was specific on this topic, if the Lord had not been accepted then what more of his followers. I did not expect much as my own journey led me into places of visions and dreams far beyond my comprehension. There was no beginning or ending to what one could learn about the Lord. The truth was there was only one thing we all needed in order to know our maker and that was faith. Faith was the summons, the beckoning and on it centered our strength. By faith did men of the past make the impossible possible, risk their lives and fulfill the works of God. When I took on this next part of my journey I knew this was the ingredient I would need in order to survive. In this too from what the Lord had shown me I fared well. My faith had led me to the furthest corners of the earth and I had come back from where others had said I wouldn't. There were realms to see beyond that which the eye could comprehend. There were the actions of a man with good intentions and those of a man with Christ. Good intentions as best as one could accept them in our world meant very little unless they obeyed the word of God. If the Lord is the way the truth and the life and there is no bad in him then how could the good that man offered surpass his? When the true meaning of these words descended upon us it spurred us to yet pursue another understanding, heaven on earth. There was only one way for this to be possible and that was by the resurrection. Christ had said he was the resurrection and no man came to the father except by him. As a Christian it was easy saying those words because one believed in God. Yet we all had a responsibility for saying them. In the bible we were taught to make immortal our mortality. Grow in spirit such that we weren't broken by the woes of our earth. Saying these words without a second thought was easy when the going was good. Perhaps I had been through longsuffering and called upon God to save me. However what did it take to see the world of the spirit, what did it take to be Cephas and leave the world behind to pursue that of our Lord's. Now I had a new journey and a purpose to fulfill. Perhaps it started in Cephas's vision in the church or it had started long before I was conceived. I didn't know what lay ahead, still I knew I had to walk the path and see where it took me.

'There are different types of people. Don't worry. I already mentioned to the guys here that you won't take as long as everyone else. You would visit one or two of the places and within no time you would be out,' Ramon giggled.

'So tell us, what did you see? What is of interest to you?' Jens asked.

I could sense the light tension in the air as I stood before my friends and colleagues. The child in us whimpered when we were pushed to the limit. I knew that Ramon my Portuguese colleague and now close friend could forgive me easily. The same could not be said for Jens. The words from his mouth were completely different to the tension that surrounded him. His flat head and enormous torso implied that the jokes would be on him, it was apparent that he had reversed the situation overnight. I could sense that the gaping hole in his potbelly hadn't been put there by him. It had been as a result of trusting people and I was the fall guy he had put that trust in recently. It was obvious to us all that he was hungry and thirsty and it looked as though the only thing preventing his blonde hair from going up in flames was the silly hat he had chosen to wear. He didn't care that its white colour matched nothing else on his huge torso. One thing was for certain, he wasn't moving from the stone he now looked enshrined upon unless we were talking food and beer.

'Statues,' I replied. It was sad that I couldn't give my friends more than they deserved. The Parthenon which may have been an incredible sight at one time and even stunning from the tram below now appeared to be transformed under closer examination. It was littered with debris, areas of it coned off from tourists as builders tried to restore its originality. A hideous sight of blue tarpaulin covered part of the scaffolding and support trestles. I had waited for something to happen, nothing did; there was no response from my body, the earth did not move, no rain or clouds.

'That all?' Jens propped.

'Yep,' I shrugged.

'You certainly are a hard man to please,' Ramon said and burst out laughing. 'I told Jens that you would go into the first place take one look and walk straight out. Then you would pretend to look across the town at Athens and within ten minutes you would be out. I know you my friend, I do more than most people,' Ramon continued and laughed even louder.

'Okay you are right, there's not much I could do except look at the statues. They may have meant a lot sometime before but now I felt nothing,' I agreed.

'You're a real pain in the ass, you know that! You kept us waiting here for you for almost two straight hours and then when you show up you talk about statues. See guys I told you what he was about,' Ramon laughed. 'No heart my friend, just no heart.'

'I felt nothing, what do you want me to say? I took a look at the building and its statues, thought of ancient Greek civilization but after that nothing. Maybe on reflection it might mean more but here and now well, just nothing.'

'It's okay my friend I knew you did your best to appreciate centuries of Greek ancestry, it's just not for you,' Ramon conceded all the time shaking his head and grinning widely in the heat of the sun.

It's not spiritual. The whisper so silent in the noise of the crowd and yet I could hear its echo like the ringing of a bell tower. *It's what others relish, it's who they are, you aren't - you seek something else.*

'Well if that's all then we should get something to eat, I am starving, yah?' Jens said. It was evident that the small talk wasn't fulfilling his desires and I had used up all the good blood within him. Now he looked upon us with green eyes that were intense and uncompromising, a large cat that foraged the forest for wild boar. His round stomach just about contained in the orange shirt and khaki shorts he was wearing. No one dared argue. When he got to his feet standing at akimbo his calf muscles glistened in the sun challenging the pillars on which the Parthenon stood. There was a stern look in his eyes, the cats fangs visible for all to see, I had seen this look too before in a man, disgust; he was indifferent to Ramon's comments whether he agreed with them or not. It was obvious that he disliked this debonair attitude. He disliked the way in which he chose to speak freely at all times to anyone. He felt Ramon's teasing was something more derogatory and needed to be silenced. Whether we agreed with his menacing stare or not, his suggestion for lunch was one readily accepted.

We descended the steps to the acropolis, filing past the next flock of sheep that sought pastures in its confines. All the time I held my tongue acknowledging the importance of the balance in this friendship. Contrary to Jens I admired Ramon's blithe. It weathered an otherwise dull encounter and unbeknown to most there was some truth in his words. I had taken a look at the caryatid and had been unable to understand why flocks of people gathered at its plinth with a voracious appetite to read the history. They canonized the statue building upon what they read at the base of its structure. I had felt nothing, no reminiscence, none of the subtle memories as I had hoped for, merely an observation of a statue in well-designed architecture. It had been disappointing considering how much I had looked forward to it.

Perhaps it was the build up as was often the case, the thought itself surpassing the real thing face to face. I had no complaints; I was outdoors and where I wanted to be. Besides Ramon's comments never went down lightly. Although aware of most things he deferred to the direct approach and it was the tendency of the group to put that down to the Latin in him. The truth was subtlety was not his strong suit. He embroidered a characteristic that some of the older members of the group found exhausting, quite simply too much energy. However it was much needed. It had been the source for most of our exploits. He was the instigator, the catalyst that pushed for adventure, sought the unusual places and demanded something more. In his own way Ramon's perception had hit the nail on the head. The statues didn't do much for me as there had to be more, something else.

'Okay Jens, lets go eat something and maybe drown in a few ouzos!' Ramon said grabbing me by the arm with a sly grin. There was no harm in a bit of sarcasm, he was certain that I could handle it.

'One of these days Jens would wring your neck.'

'Why, don't you think the guys need ouzos?' Ramon quibbled.

'I know they do pal, you are right, just keep it down,' I said laughing at Ramon's expression. He had pulled a wry smile on a silly face under his dark glasses. It was like school all over again, men returning to the playground to sort out their differences.

'Then stop telling me to pipe down my friend, I am only stating the fact,' Ramon said.

'Well go state it some place else, these boys are not interested in your facts! Just because we like to laugh at each other doesn't mean that our jokes are worth their while.'

'You give me too much credit, way too much.'

'And you underestimate these boys pal, really badly. Have you forgotten how we almost got our heads blown up yesterday when we talked about

49

management?'

We had reached the foot of the steps and were walking downhill towards the city. Although enveloped in the cross wires of events at hand I knew my presence in Athens was no coincidence. There had to be more within the magnificent architecture and beautiful merchandise below. It was a beautiful silhouette that demanded more of its observer. *When would it come? How would I know?* Others had asked those questions and now it was my turn. No one could tell what was happening in the mystery of my spiritual world many miles away. I was two people, the man who listened to the lively banter amongst his friends and the other, Cephas the spirit that searched beyond the realms of my reality into his own. I had received a talisman but understood nothing of what it meant. I was the son that desired answers from the Father, the Lord. My friends were the pincers that serrated the edge, their witty combat stimulants for something bigger; far-reaching and more desirable. I was an employee in the world but wished for the sublime. However I would have to be patient, wait and abide by the insightful repartee that was a common occurrence between my friends. I had come close to losing my head the day before while treading on dangerous waters by explaining our positions as defined by the company. The assignment of power as most of the guys had come to discover, was only an illusion within this particular company. We had been recruited as managers with the understanding that this title was an entelechy. For most of us it was the basis for moving from our previous jobs, however we were to find within a matter of days that this was merely a façade.

'Yes, we are all managing ourselves, that's my point isn't it?' Ramon commented weaving his magic wand back from my deixis to the present. We walked by the houses that I had passed on my way uphill. Gone were the deeply tanned man and old lady and for the first time that day I took a closer look at the architecture on the hillside. The houses were all on one floor with their walls stained with fawn sand from the road. They straddled alongside one another making it possible for us passersby to peer into the backyard of some of them. There were patios decorated with ceramic tiles. Their owners providing recliners that overlooked the city, it was the perfect view whilst basking in the heat.

'Well your point almost got us into trouble yesterday as some folks think they are managing others,' I offered benignly.

'Good for them, they are in for a shock and by the way I still think they need ouzos!' Ramon said and laughed even louder.

In the short time that we had been in Greece we had come to discover that *ouzo* was the ideal derision. It was piquant, a Greek aperitif that was often taken before a hefty meal. Only it had become apparent that some members of the team had taken a more fervent liking to it. They had bonded with the culture and were now ordering ouzos on every occasion more than was necessary. Ramon and I found this amusing and unfortunately to the detriment of other members of our party because of our comments. I was able to refrain from going too far, unfortunately the same couldn't be said for Ramon.

Greece means more, remember Thessalonica. I was silent and listening. The restaurant that we had elected to go to could be seen in the distance. I straggled quietly alongside Ramon a few steps behind the others. I could now hear the voice of Cephas within me clearly, skirling through and reminding me that my stay in Greece was not a parade. Greece was important, it was ancient - it was one of the first to receive the message.

It had history with the guardians, those who carried the message of our heavenly father, the message of God. It had something else; this was what I had to listen for. Cephas knew this, could feel it and was poised in my thoughts, waiting and then tugging at the restraints. *"Do not quench prophesy."* The Lord's words, God's words, these words from the book of Thessalonians. They meant something, a foundation of steel to a spiritual landscape. They were directed to me revealing that it meant more to be in Greece than observing defaced statues. Cephas could feel it now and he needed me to feel the same.

I knew little of what could be happening but I was certain that he would wait and sooner or later I too would understand.

Mougins; The object of this interview was not just for the present but to retrace her steps back into her past if that was necessary, if that added salt to the meal. It was unmindful of time what was of interest was the recollection, everything counted, mattered if it added substance. Hailey's request to know more about Sarai's past had taken her back to the summer of 1995. Back then Sarai lived in Epsom, Surrey with her parents. This particular afternoon was important and one of those stored in Sarai's memory because it had spurned some sort of self-discovery. Hailey was churning up the article seeking to quote Sarai from the past, her time in university as Sarai tried to recollect.

'Just say it in your own words. Sometimes our readers love this part of the article it proves that our guests are human.' Hailey grinned.

Sarai nodded as she searched for the appropriate words.

'I could hear the rain outside, my mother rustling pans and making changes to her kitchen yet I stood paralyzed before the mirror. I had just turned nineteen and it was my first long vacation from university. You don't miss Loughborough, I thought. No you can't, the change of scenery will do you some good. One needs a vacation from the countryside to a bit of city life. Yet what could one say for the weather? Here I was thinking summer is the pits in this country, if all one has to do is stay home because of this damn weather. I could have gone to Wimbledon to shop or even walked down the high road to pick up some flowers yet my best bet of making it through that day unscathed was to stand before that mirror and wonder what makes my life tick. I continued staring at myself in the mirror. You could imagine at that age my body was changing, my black hair was a little shiny with coats of brown because of the occasional sunlight but still I had no tan because the sun barely lasted long enough for me to have enough time under it. I looked fuller in a red top over faded blue jeans that appeared to be a little too colourful at the time. It is amazing the kind of things that one would notice as a girl. Still I expected that old mirror that had been there since I could remember to tell me the same great news that it had always done in the past. I had stood in that same spot with my dolls during the day excited to see my face each time my mother would lend me her make up and at night I would lie scared in bed wondering about what scary creature lurked behind it.'

'I think we have all had that sort of experience in our lives one time or another,' Hailey said relating to what her host was telling her. She knew the juicy stuff was to come but so far she was happy with what Sarai was offering. It meant no one was alone before the dreaded mirror. We all looked at the changes and more.

Sarai reached for her glass of water before continuing.

'How come people always say, I won't leave a certain place for another? How come they always say, it doesn't have this or that? How come they say they'd feel lost if they weren't around familiar surroundings? Can you believe that I had all these questions running through my head at the time? Suddenly I began answering my own questions with others. Don't these people know that it is they that make the place what it is? Don't they understand that any place is as bland as the next unless we feel different from within ourselves? I may have been naïve in my assessment of things back then but as far back as I could remember even as a child I enjoyed the vacations that my parents and I took to various places. It wasn't because of the change of scenery or the people I met but rather what those places had brought out in me. I then began to realize that it was I that made the difference. It was I who made the place different for me. No one could change how I felt about a place or anything for that matter except I was willing to accept that it was I who wanted it to be different. That day as I walked away from the mirror and tucked my car keys in my jeans I knew that the rain would not stop me from having fun. I would go to Wimbledon as planned and I would shop like crazy as need be. First I would make a couple of pit-stops to pick up a friend or two because my day would need this to reach those dizzy heights that lay in waiting.'

Both women were silent for a short while as Hailey considered what Sarai had just told her. An introspective discovery to find that any changes in our lives first began with us would be inspiration for many people. She could not deny the fact that she had also felt the same, two days earlier when Sarai had enquired about her past. Then it had been her turn to talk of her choices and how she had taken the name Hailey. Out of nowhere Sarai had asked her what part of China she was from and then she had spilled her guts or some of it about Yong Ding. Her village was exotic if one compared it to all the other places she had been to. The fields and the lives that those people had been through, were still going through was something that she rarely found anywhere else in the world. Even the type of facilities that were available to one in Yong Ding made one humble to their reality and what life had to offer. Still all this did not matter if you came from there. It was just another regular day in life and boring as hell unless you could see what it brought out in you. Sarai was right in her assessment of things, it was us that made the difference that changed how we felt about a place because it was only from within that we could truly make those changes. Sarai had asked her why she didn't want to be called Hsu and she had replied that it wasn't that she didn't want to be but for now Hailey was necessary for what she had to accomplish in life. She had no doubt in her mind that Hsu would return when it was time and when she could face her. Hsu was personal, the person she was, whom she didn't like sharing, her treasure. Shenzhen had given her Hailey to share with the world and accomplish dreams and aspirations. She couldn't guarantee anything for now but maybe Sarai would meet Hsu, very few people had but she was quickly warming to her host.

'Then your mirror did talk to you,' she said willing herself back to the present.

'You can say it certainly did back then,' Sarai replied and smiled.

'I would remember to quote you on that,' Hailey said.

This was the kind of bonding she wished for with all the people in her articles. It looked like on all fronts she was scoring maximum points. So far Susan was pleased with her progress to date. It was important to keep her on her side if she wanted to spend more time in France. If she got on well with her host then this particular job may just turn out to be a pleasant holiday. Sarai had mentioned that they would be going out today. She wasn't sure what was planned but she hoped for a pleasant surprise.

Glyfada. 'You are having only an ice tea? What a shame you should be having a beer it would put hairs on your chest especially in this good weather,' Jens said sipping at his beer and wiping of the white moustache that he had been rewarded with. He sighed contentedly and his nostrils flared, he was finally home. There were beads of sweat trickling down his forehead, the dark markings of grime beneath his armpits evidence of the trek we had made.

'I don't drink beer. I never really liked the taste,' I replied.

'My friend here only drinks wine or sophisticated drinks, I should know I order them for him,' Ramon glozed in my favour.

'Drink beer it's good for you. Hey barman tell him that it is good for him will you, it is the only way he would get a Greek girl!' Jens scorned ignoring Ramon, fangs glistened then turbulence. The slight look of anguish in his eyes indicating that he should mind his own business as his comments weren't directed at him.

'Yes, your friend is right. If you want a pretty Greek girl then you must order a beer. Only boys drink soft drinks like wine. You want to show you're a man then beer is the thing,' the short waiter said while propping up his thumps close to his chest.

'Women here, they go for strong men, they see you drinking fanta, coca cola, ice tea, no good they think he boy not man. You like Greek women?' the waiter asked.

'Sure I do,' I responded.

'Then you ask for beer. You see that girl out there, you cannot go to her with your glass of ice tea, you go with your beer and you stand a chance,' he confided, bending his head as if to be heard only by the party at the table. Most of the group laughed and waited for my response. Ramon smiled and looked enquiringly at me. It was as if a direct attack at me was intended for him.

'You say that but as I look out there the girls are looking at me and none of these beer bellies so I doubt if they stand a chance,' I said and laughed.

'Aha, you cheeky man, but I like you I can introduce you to some of the girls,' the waiter grinned.

'You can? Well maybe I *can* introduce you to some of the girls because I am sure that if I go out there I would certainly do better than you,' I smiled, what did the man expect he was wearing a red girth on a white fustanella, which was hardly the pull of the century.

'Aye where did you find this guy I like him. He laugh at everything,' the waiter gurned.

'Yes, he is one of us, he is special,' Jens replied and laughed, wiping drops of sweat off his forehead in the process.

'Maybe it is a lot easier when the shoe is on the other foot. The man can laugh when a joke is directed at someone else but crumbles when I mention a few words to him,' Ramon whispered to me.

'Holster thy sabre, let him be, he needs this, it gives him confidence,' I whispered back.

'Tell me now, seriously why don't you drink beer?' Jens asked. 'It would be difficult to handle the clients in Germany and you would suffer my friend. They would ask you to drink with them until you fall especially in Hamburg,' he persisted.

'He can handle anything that is thrown at him. You should have been in China with this man. I reckon things are even stranger there than you Germans but he handled them pretty good,' Charles said. He had been listening in the background to all that was said laughing and barely commenting as he ordered his lunch. He was from Holland and like Ramon had been in Shenzhen when I was there.

I listened as the conversation slowly drifted away from me and towards the exploits of the group during our stay a few months ago back in China. I watched an old man and old lady walk by. The man was doing his best to cover his wife under the parasol. Across the road a bus pulled in and more people alighted. There was plenty of activity in the train station on the other side of the square with some of it coming our way. I had not been entirely wrong with what I said to the waiter, maybe just a touch arrogant. The truth was I had already been approached by a couple of girls supporting their local charity. They sold calendars that had spawned from a college nearby. The girls had isolated me before turning their attention to everyone else that sat outside the restaurant. No one had commented except for a few sly winks being thrown in my direction. Perhaps beer wasn't the ply needed to lure the girls after all. I had been honest about not liking beer for the taste and did not go near strong alcohol because it did not agree with me. There had been a time, there had been another life, a much different life when all this, what was before me what was happening to me could never have been imagined or was possible. My friends knew nothing of this. Those friends of the past, where were they now? People would have said that I had changed a lot, much older but some things never changed, one's thoughts, one's spirit, Cephas.

It was 1981, West Africa and I was a child that had found his way into his Mum's bed because I had fallen

58

ill from the toil of events earlier on in the day. I gulped down medicine, happy to be in safe hands after the predicament of my day. Back then I was friends with a much older boy from school, one almost twelve years my senior. It was the natural thing to seek a role model and an older brother to look up to. I had sought refuge in this man. That day I left school torn with excitement to see him. I barged into his room only to find myself staring at two pairs of feet beneath his covers. The larger pair of the feet had waved at me, my friend's, they indicated that I should go away and return later. I had vanished from the scene fascinated with wonder. At that age most things seemed like a mirage, the closer you got to them the further away they became. Later that day my friend had explained the mechanics of the process, the mirage became even more of a certainty; the rift between youth and adulthood a gaping black hole. However there had been some consolation when he asked me to join him for a drink and I accepted, eager to prove my worth.

I followed him escaping the clutches and security from home and headed via the back streets to a lively part of the town. We entered a bar and before long my friend had many girls around him. He was a senior in the school and naturally drew the attention. I was in his proximity so they came for me too and my head moved to the clouds. There was no harm in venturing out for the night to see how real men lived even though I was only eleven. I was introduced as a younger brother and welcomed the attention. The drinks had come and then there was *palm wine*. It was no pushover even for adults and I took a sip or two and then was given my own glass. Unlike most who knew what they were doing, I drank fast and more was added. It was sweet and easy to swallow until I felt the after effects kick in. I was asked to stand up and fell straight down in a heap as most of the bar laughed. I laughed back stupidly from my position of authority, completely lethargic and passed out. When I came to I was being dragged from the bar, half carried by my friend. The next time I woke up I was lying in bed, sprawled in a pool of retch listening to my mum scream at my friend. It had been a tough lesson to take at that age. There were things I liked about becoming a man, there were things I liked about my friend's life but there were other things I knew would not be the path to follow. It was simple I could not hold my liquor.

Yes, my new friends could mock me all they wanted but I won't fall for the same old ploy. My system may have grown and developed to be stronger and more resilient but I could still feel that horrid taste. It was wise to stick to the alcohol that I preferred and in the quantities that I could manage. My mission required me to have a clear head, they didn't know that but I felt it.

We left the restaurant and walked in the direction of an ancient burial sight. There were rocks almost the size of boulders and we crossed them to peer down into the pit. It looked like a massive hole where bodies had been thrown in and covered with soil. My friends talked and I watched. The sound of a scooter caught my attention and I was distracted for a while as the boy sped along the narrow passage we stood in almost hitting some of the tourists that were coming our way. It was early evening in Athens and the sun was slowly vanishing into the hillside. Finally a brisk wind that was much needed to cool off the heat from the day and then changes.

I shuddered.

A different crowd was now prominent in the streets. There was a profusion of loose clothing, cotton shirts and white trousers for the men. The younger women wore short blouses, décolleté; the trend to expose tanned cleavage and stomach obvious while the older women had resorted to free flowing summer dresses. Canopies had been erected in the centre of the small square with candles lit at the centre of each table. I could smell charbroil as waiters rushed to keep up with the new business. There were more couples, less groups and I watched, curious. Maybe the ancients of Greece had this same time to themselves.

"Do not quench prophesy."

It was there again and prominent, this time I could hear it clearly, distinctly. It was the Lord's voice he was talking and through the spirit I was listening. I had to go in, be the good thought within, Cephas, to hear, to acquiesce and to accept what the Lord had planned for me. Greece meant more, so did the book of Thessalonians, I had to go deeper if I wanted to understand these words. It was clear that the spirit remained the cord that linked past, present and future. There had been other visions, clear like day and night and in them were answers. I had to open up and see them to understand.

Chapter Four

Mougins. Sarai slowed down as she saw the traffic building up just beneath the arc on the A8 autoroute just before Promenade des Anglais outside Nice. Nice was her treat for Hailey. It was her time away from home, from her husband and children. Sarai needed this freedom to put the story together for the magazine. She missed them dearly but a girl had to use all the time alone that was available to her.

'Hailey you must be used to traffic back in New York, right? I bet this is nothing to you,' She said making light conversation.

'It is better not to own a car in New York,' Hailey replied. 'I've always taken cabs if I needed to travel by car it makes life less complicated over there.'

'Where do you live? I mean where in New York?'

'I'm somewhere in Manhattan. If you know the place then it is off Frederick Douglass Boulevard just before Central Park.'

'Yes, I think I know it, then not so far from one end of 6th Avenue. You must be closer to the north of Central Park. I have to say though that I've always found it easy to manouevre through the streets of New York. It's a grid system with street numbers. Not the case here, when you get lost you really do.'

'You've driven over there?'

'Yes. Been there on my own and now we occasionally visit with my husband. I love the way everyone always seems so busy and on the move. It is interesting to have one of those busy days in New York. Coming back here then makes all the difference.'

'That's one thing I accept in my life these days. I take change as a constant to whatever happens to me. It seems that something is always new whether it is music or the economy there is always some kind of movement in life,' Hailey replied.

They were crawling behind almost stagnant traffic into Nice. She spotted the holiday travelers with large luggage holders on top of the cars. Nice was opening into a beautiful city and she thought of her home in New York. Just now she had confided a personal opinion to Sarai. Change was inevitable. We couldn't avoid it in our lives. It was there whether we accepted it or not. There was always something new to learn, something different happening around us. Daylight eventually became night and the dawn of a new day meant the passing of time. If we adjusted to this then we had conquered most of the difficulties that we struggled to accept in our lives. New York offered change in so many ways. It felt like the capital of it with the number of people that passed through its streets each year.

'You know what you say about change is interesting although I have to say sometimes I feel that if we take a deeper look to what happens around us it is hard to see anything new from what has already been.'

'How do you mean?' Hailey asked.

'Well I just feel that we all seem to do what has already been done in the past. We go to work and then home and then maybe vacation. We have ambition, failure, doubt, love, jealousy and all the other facets available to man but still what remains truth is that people of the past had these available to them too. Perhaps change is constant but what I'd add to that is, it is for the material things but not for those that aren't,' Sarai said.

'But then that makes life boring. If all that we have is what has been then what is the point of what we do, unless we believe that it makes a difference?' Hailey asked. She was now truly curious. The traffic was now flowing and Sarai was again driving at a reasonable speed as she cruised on the popular Route Carlifornie looking for somewhere to park. Sarai was turning out to be the alchemist. One minute Hailey thought she was interviewing a heiress of some sort and the next she was finding herself lost by a chemistry of perspectives.

'I'm not saying change doesn't happen, I'm just saying if we look into more detail of what happens there is nothing really new that hasn't been already done. We still retain the human facets of greed, lust, desire, love and many others even though we can say today that perhaps global communication and technology as a whole have come a long way.'

Sarai pulled into a spot just outside a boutique that sold bags and hit the button for the convertible's hood to close. Soon the women were climbing out with their handbags greeted by a welcoming committee of stares from passersby.

'I know, but what then do we live for if we cannot make a difference?'

'Well we all have our doubts and our shortcomings. We all wonder when we shall have the next buck or make that difference in the job. We wonder about love, war and all the other uncertainties that are put before us. One thing we should all rest assured is that those people who were before us also wondered about these things yet they managed to pull through. They came out on the other side. If they did as we do and made it then we should know that we would also do as they did and succeed. I think our journey in life is one geared towards self-discovery rather than merely changing our society. In other words we change society to know ourselves better. We may learn something new about ourselves, still the truth is it has always been in us in spite of the fact that we are just discovering it for the first time. I don't think the changes in society create this in us. I think they were there before the changes, we just didn't know about them. '

Sarai pushed open the door to the boutique and strolled in. There was a hidden responsibility being the wife of a mysterious man. You became one with him and thought alike. There was one constant that we could all fall back on through these changes. This was our Lord and savior Jesus Christ and God. Solomon had said there is nothing new under the sun. Each generation went through changes yet the God of Abraham was still the same God of Isaac and Jacob. He kept us real. He made us have no doubt that we would succeed in our endeavours. If we ever wondered about change then God was our past, present and future it was through him that we got the reassurances.

It was time to treat Hailey to the finer things in Nice. Perhaps add a little change to her life still whenever she could it was not a crime to pass on some of the wisdom that she had gained from coming to God. Nice had the scenery to go with the fashion. They would do some shopping and then take in the sights. There was a Cathedral just outside Nice pretty old and famous. She would take Hailey there. It was a place that Cephas and the kids loved. It was peaceful and she would share this with Hailey.

Glyfada. I was blessed. God loved me and for all reasons unknown to me he also gave me visions and allowed me to see beyond my years into those further on. My visions happened at random and usually in the early hours of the morning. I became spirit, Cephas and took flight into a world beyond mine. On this occasion once more I did not know where I was headed for. All I knew was to keep a record of events and hope that God revealed the truth to me some day. They were my prophesy, they would help me understand.

There was some light in the room as Cephas

emerged, he sailed to a height above the bed and then dived at tremendous speed towards an unseen hole in the wall and close to the floor. It was just about wide enough for a small mouse to crawl through. He flew through it at blinding speed, drawn into the vortex and then emerged at an isolated car park. There were many unoccupied spaces as he again rose to mid height. He was being directed, waiting for what would happen next. With his wings fully stretched he tore through the park and headed for the concourse in the other side of the building. He was moving fast and invisible to everyone. Soon he had cleared that building and headed for the meet. It was something that had been arranged he was merely the spirit directed to the appointment to fulfill the mission.

They were already out of school when he got there. The children emerged, several of them walking alongside each other and chatting excitedly no doubt about their day, their plans and playtime. He waited, hovering as they went past him. And then suddenly he was moving again towards a pair. The boy and girl were the only children amidst the crowd that saw him. They immediately ran towards him with their hands open and hugged him. This was possible because God allowed it to be. The Lord had made the spirit visible to these children and malleable to their touch. Cephas hugged them as if he had known them from before. Then he looked around without speaking but knowing that there was one missing. There was no need for words for the others as if sensing his questions told him without speaking that the third child was around the corner in the playground. Cephas did not know what to expect. He rose up again above the two and glided slowly in the wind. Around the corner he came to a park with all the toys and playhouses as was available to toddlers. He flew slowly down until the small boy saw him and then he too hugged him and held on to him. Cephas held on awhile, it was his mission he was fulfilling the requirements asked of him by the Lord, by God.

I was breathless waking out of it, my body was screaming out to Cephas,

'What does this mean?'

The window was shutting down soon he would be gone, it would be over, spirit would go back to being man and I would be lost again in my world. Who were these children and what impact would this vision have in my life. There were so many questions and still that deafening tone from beyond, 'Remember Thessalonica…' I needed answers to this mystery. Greece meant more than the beautiful landscapes and I would have to dig deeper and work harder. I hadn't come to Athens just like that it had started somewhere.

People came to us at different times in our lives. Some stayed and became a part of it others didn't. Several months earlier Ramon Eswaldo Barbeiri had pursued an appointment in his beloved city Lisbon in Portugal. It was the first time that he had made any connection with his prospective colleagues and the first time he had ever considered visiting China. After confirming the details of his flight he had hung up and checked his messages. It was always difficult leaving his mum like this. She depended on having him nearby. He was her strength, a pillar through tough times.

There was a text message from his girlfriend Maria,

'Eu peguei o jantar,' it read in Portuguese - I have got dinner.

'Eu devo chegar ai em dez minutos - I shall be there in 10min,' he replied. The night was clear, the evening warm and his thoughts fresh and spiraling to cities far beyond. Perhaps Beijing was an option but it seemed miles away from the coast. Then there was Hong Kong to consider, either way he was going to visit one of them; both if time would allow it.

The cobblestones offered a slippery climb but he was filled with optimism. It was not everyday that one considered a trip to China. He wished Maria could come along but all things considered he would be meeting new people and sometimes it wasn't so bad that they spent time apart; the reunion was often something to look forward to. It would be a different culture but this was where his worldly insight served dividends. He was open to all people and had the personality of a man that was willing to try anything for fun. The short walk past the Jeronimos Monastery allowed him to see the 25 de Abril bridge and then further up the hill the Cristo Rei Statue. China would offer other symbols he felt, even a different perspective to life. His mother had confided in him when he was a boy that he was destined for great things. She had been in his corner when he had come home from school with his uniform torn after being bludgeoned by others who couldn't stand his shrewd streak, now he was reaping the rewards.

With his hands in his pockets he slowly climbed the hill to his new apartment. He would miss the beach, his mum and time spent with Maria. They had been working none stop on the apartment for over five weeks. The painting was almost complete even though the plumbing and heating system still needed to go in. They would have to wait a while for this. He was out of pocket, his finances and those of Maria now stretched in the prepayments they had made for furniture. They had picked out the wood together but Maria had chosen the design. She was the savant of the family and he the hunter. He had found the place that she liked knowing without hesitation what she would want. The equivalent was true on her part when it came to the furniture, her choice had been remarkable and there was no doubt in his mind that they were perfect together. She was a child hood sweet heart and even after so many years he had never strayed.

When he entered the apartment Maria was already in her painting overalls. The floor was covered with old sheets from his Mum's place and she was stroking away with a paintbrush in the second room. On the floor in the center of the living room was a small stool and on it was the food she had purchased. They would have to settle for burgers and fries as they had no cooking equipment yet in place. This too was another burden that had almost pushed his bank account into the red. It looked like the much-admired architecture from the Manueline ornate style wasn't about to make a reappearance any time soon. Nonetheless he had to give credit to the girl. She had made the effort for their last time together in the apartment before his journey. There were wine glasses and a bottle.

He walked up to her and grabbed her from behind bending her backwards and giving her a long kiss. He allowed his face to linger for a while close to hers as he feasted upon the L'acoste fragrance she was wearing with the fresh tint of paint that blended in. There were few things worthwhile in life, she certainly was one of them and looked the part. Her head tie adding even more to the femininity that she exuded.

'What was that for?' she asked when she eventually got the chance to come up for air.

'Are you complaining?' he replied looking around the room for his overalls.

'No. Hey, just for your information I phoned the plumbers and it looks like they would be able to give us a quotation for the work in three weeks. That gives us some time right?' she said admiring the man she loved.

He was dressed in black slacks, a white shirt and some light brown shoes.

'It does give us time. But you know we have to take it slow, I don't want to rush this place,' he replied taking off his shoes and getting into his overalls.

'I know, I know I was just being proactive.'

'Well then let's eat woman because I'm famished!' he said widening his eyes and smiling broadly at her.

They took up residence on the floor and Maria shared the portions of fries in the bag. Ramon poured out the wine and raised his glass.

'To us.'

'To us,' she replied and took a sip.

'Have you picked out the curtains for the rooms yet?' he asked looking at the large bay window that overlooked the seaside and the bridge. There were beams of lights from cars crossing the bridge and those of houses miles away barely visible in the dark.

'I'm thinking Venetian blinds to start with until we can build up some capital.'

'One day this place would all be different and we would have our own home,' he replied as he reached for more fries.

'How was your mother?' she asked looking enquiringly at him.

'A bit sad but understanding.'

'Three weeks is a long time,' she said and then as an after thought, 'Make sure you take a lot of pictures. I want to see the places that you visit to see if they are the same as those that I visited when I went there. And make sure you visit Beijing, there is nothing like the Great Wall.'

'Hey I want you to see something,' he said scrambling to his feet and walking to his rucksack in the other room. He returned with a folder and again squatted beside her.

'I got my itinerary today and thought you might want to see it. It appears I am not the only one invited on this trip. There are several others from different countries. Here take a look at the list, isn't it something?'

Maria perused through the list of names slowly. Ramon had been right. There were managers from different parts of the world invited to China. It might have been a conference or something similar, she thought. The backgrounds of these people could be astonishing.

'I can see two names here from Nigeria. Brings back memories doesn't it? Maybe you could have something to say to them about your trip there,' she observed.

She was right Ramon thought. Lagos in 2002 spoke volumes of its own in the history of Ramon Eswaldo Barbeiri. He was willing to consent that living in a land as the only white man that could be seen at times in a room sent waves through your spine that set your hair on end. He had learnt of his own vulnerabilities, he had learnt of his boundaries, learnt that they could be extended proportionately if the will was there. They had. No body could be a patzer and expect to survive in Africa. You haggled for pittance knowing that it was practice for when the big fish came into play. He considered himself street smart in Europe and a man that could handle most situations until he hit Lagos. There was paucity for scruples like he had never felt before and you got beaten down unless you were willing to stand your ground and fight for what was yours. The taxi drivers stole from you, the shops stole from you and even the banks stole from you, there was no end to it. He had developed a scabrous layer on body and in mind by the time he boarded the flight out of the place. Before leaving Lisbon he thought his hardest task would be what he had been sent to do in

Lagos. He thought the students wouldn't listen, wouldn't understand him. That had been the least of his worries. They not only listened they sympathized and came to his rescue more than once.

'I see names from Algeria, Syria, Indonesia and even countries from South America such as Brazil and Argentina. At least you would get a chance to speak Portuguese to your Brazilian comrades,' Maria said and smiled.

'I know,' he replied. He was looking down the list at the countries as well and the email addresses used for correspondence. There was a column that represented the length of time that each individual had spent with the company. On average most had been with the company longer than a year; some even longer, especially for the employees outside Europe.

'It looks like they've all been with the company for quite some time. And here is me thinking that my six months in the place was a lifetime,' he commented.

'Not quite, the Europeans haven't been as long with the company as the others,' Maria said.

'You are right. Hey look at this, France and Holland just eight months only two more than me.'

'Look at UK, maybe there is a mistake. I thought you said that this meeting was for managers that had been with the company for more than six months?' She asked looking curiously at him.

'I did. It looks like the UK representative has only been there for one week. That's strange. And take a look at his email address too. It's not the company's address, he must have just joined.'

It was bizarre that the UK representative had only been with the company for a week and already had been invited to this meeting. This certainly went against protocol as everyone else had been there for at least six months. Ramon was now curious, he had to meet this

UK representative and find out why he had been invited. This was no ordinary company, it was Chinese and loyalty played a big part in getting one ahead. You weren't offered a free ride because of your background. In his short time with the company he hadn't been able to get a single thing to happen his way unless he pushed and probed and even then it was his loyalty and friendship with his manager that made the difference. What could this representative have said or done to get this far so quickly and so soon. Ramon knew he now had another mission in China. He would get details, information - perhaps this would help him back home in Portugal, either way he needed to find out. He hated loose ends.

The old road was barely visible in the dark with weeds covered in dust growing through the tyre tracks. There were pebbles of different sizes to navigate and a brush that needed to be restrained, as it grew undeterred across the path. The crickets were out to play but on this occasion they weren't alone. Their heels could be heard tapping against the pebbles as they flaunted their colourful frocks beneath the bright sky full moon, encouraging everyone around them to follow in pursuit. They walked a few metres ahead of their boyfriends. And as each new face arrived on the track there was a cheer followed by side cheek kisses. Maybe it was a wedding or birthday party of sorts because everyone seemed to know each other. Ramon and I walked gingerly behind, the prospect of sampling a night out away from familiar surroundings spurring every step.

'Do you think we could gate crash this party?' Ramon asked.

'We have to try. It's too late to turn back we are already here,' I answered.

'Man I have more confidence with you along. This

is not something I would do alone,' Ramon grimaced, wiping his moist palms on his jeans.

'Me too.'

'Then let's get it over and done with I hope they ask us no questions at the gate.'

'They won't if we appear to know a few of these people.'

'Do you speak any Greek?' he enquired.

'Nope.' I didn't know a single word.

'Then our chances are bad. I was able to read a few words today because I remembered things like alpha, beta and theta from school. But stringing the words together could be a different story.'

'Be brave pal, we survived China were you couldn't string three letters together so what more of this place.'

'You have a point my friend we did survive China didn't we? Boy that place was crazy,' Ramon replied nervously and shivered the anxiety in his voice barely audible now that we had drawn closer to the entrance and music. China had told a different story. I had only been with the company for a week when my manager had insisted on me representing the UK at a manager's conference in China. It was an appealing prospect, as I had always wanted to visit China. I had been to this part of the world before but had missed out on China. I took the opportunity with open hands, after all we were all managers and it was an opportunity to enjoy the finer things in life whilst being in this position of authority. After the first day of the conference Ramon had come up to me wanting to know how it was possible that I had come to China only having been in the company for a week. Before long he was telling me about himself, his new home in Portugal and why we must always stick together. I couldn't argue with him, as we seemed to agree on most things, especially our urgency for adventure.

'That's the understatement of the century,' I offered, China was hard to forget.

'Anyway let's get this over and done with, if nothing comes of it we can join the rest of the gang in the snooker room. At least we would have a story to tell them.'

'Boy, I love these adventures.'

We crawled tentatively towards the entrance of the club. The music was European and blaring so loud it could be heard for miles down the long street of Vas Georgiou Avenue. Behind the club the waves could be heard reaching up from the gulf and pounding against the embankment. The beach that had hosted thousands of people during the day was now a dark mass of endless sand, deserted and awaiting daybreak. Things had turned around to suit the nightlife with a flurry of wine bars and clubs all open and drawing the masses that had flocked to the beach during the day.

The women got in first then it was the turn of their boyfriends. After the bouncers had run their hands over the pockets of the men they got in too. Finally it was the moment we had been anticipating. Maybe it was our night, a full moon in the Metonic cycle or the meltemi deciding to grant us our wishes, whichever the case time would tell.

Ramon and I took a step forward.

Sarai picked herself up from the ground helped by her Dad for the third time that afternoon. The skies were dull and it looked like bad weather was on the horizon. The truth was there was bad weather already circulating within her. At four it was difficult to understand why a two-wheeled bicycle could be so different from a tricycle. She couldn't remember anyone teaching her how to ride the old tricycle but with the bicycle she'd have to say without her Dad things would certainly have been worse. They had been at it all morning and the best she could do was a straight line before she was sprawled on the pavement and adjusting her helmet. There had been tears the first time when she felt the bruising on her palms and then her dad had explained to her the process of falling down and getting up stronger. He said falling down was part of the process of learning to ride it was the getting up and starting all over again that was the difficult part. It had made little sense at the time but still she had followed his lead determined to ride and prove to him that her Christmas present was worthwhile.

'Cephas is a prophet, and a prophet bears his cross.' She let the words escape from her lips as the women sat waiting for their meal to be served. She sat facing the east side of the square, the panicle of flowers that hung from the restaurant just blocking some of her view of the city clock. It was easy reaching Promenade du Palais once one got on Promenade des Anglais. At this time of day Place du Palais was busy with all the screens for movies and theatres in the square attracting a vast audience. Time and again she had insisted on Cephas bringing her to the square to watch old black and white movies in the theatres. It never was his preferred choice of movie but sometimes a girl had to get her way.

As she turned her attention back to Hailey she began to notice the effects of what her words had done. Hailey was confused. What had began like any ordinary tale was turning out to be one that was more mysterious than she could have anticipated. She had flown over 8000 miles to a place she hadn't been before with the hope of writing about another rich lady that probably had a sob story in the past. One who wanted to extend her affluence to a new part of the world but she was in for a surprise.

'In order to know my husband I had to follow him deep into places I never thought existed.'

Hailey's recorder was running. It was almost noon and the sun was high above them. This was not the script she had been asked to put forward for the magazine. This was something out of an alien manual. Where was this woman leading her to?

Sarai let Hailey absorb her words while she thought of how it had happened, how one of her voyages into the world of her mysterious husband had happened. They had been lying in bed. It was a Thursday morning and she had taken the time off to be with him. She lay in his arms as he worked his fingers through hers. She was enjoying this moment away from work.

'One of our children is going to have a problem when he reaches seventeen.'

Her body went cold in his warmth and she tried to pull away from him, get away from this man that she now thought in her mind was clearly insane! However she couldn't he had anticipated this knew what would happen and held her tightly making sure she couldn't escape. She panted.

'How can you say that when we don't even have children? How can you say that when you don't even know if we would have kids? How can you wish this on any one let alone your own kids? You are insane!' She screamed as she fought him to let go of her.

'But I haven't finished my darling. You have to let me finish before you accuse me of being this insane person.' Cephas responded quietly.

Sarai was quiet as she felt the cool Mediterranean breeze from the French Riviera flow through their bedroom window. She was again calm in his arms and listening. She knew a little about Cephas's way. She knew about his relationship with God and the deep spiritual person that he was. However he had never pressured her to follow him into his world. He kept this away from her and just shared some basics. She never pushed because she was too busy in the office. Their time together had always been about fun, traveling and making love. They were the couple that had it all without worries and complaints. Yet she knew that one day she would have to see this side of him. She would have to know her husband better and see this world that he loved so much and said he was from. This time she won't be too busy to talk. After all she had taken the time off to be with him. This time she would listen to what he had to say and then draw her own conclusions. One thing they had agreed upon was that he won't change who she was. If she was to come into this world of his then she would do so willingly. She could give him that at least. She would listen.

'Okay darling what do you have to say for yourself. It had better be good because no child of mine is going to suffer.' She said this with all the energy she had. She would fight him all the way to his world and beyond if that is what it took.

'You must have heard about Abraham having to sacrifice his son as a test from God to show his faithfulness?' Cephas said.

'Yes. ' Sarai replied.

'Well if you ever read the stories in the bible then you shall see that each prophet has a cross to bear as Christ did.'

Sarai was quiet. Cephas considered himself a prophet. He would talk about things that would come to pass, visions of places he had been to. He even said he knew they would be together before they had met. Most times she listened but immediately put this at the back of her mind and focused on the man before her, the one she knew and loved. Today was different he was venturing into territory that mattered more than the ordinary. Her children would mean everything to her. She knew this from young so why would he say something like this. What was his point?

' Before you become a true prophet of God you must first learn how to walk on water as Christ did.' Cephas said.

'You are my wife so it is my duty to teach you how this is done.'

The room was silent as the long white curtains that led into the large double windows of the patio doors blew in the wind. I had a choice of men. In my job I had met many. I had met rich and poor men, handsome and ordinary. Some good others bad. I am educated, rich and don't need a man to support me. I come from a good home so why on earth out of all the choices that life presented to me did I have to fall in love with Cephas. Sarai felt herself listening to this voice that haunted her from the depths of her mind. There was some truth to what Cephas in his clairvoyant madness had said to her a while back. They were meant to be to serve a purpose. She couldn't think of any logical explanation why she loved him so much and why despite his spiritual world she just wanted to be with him and no one else.

Hailey was now spellbound. They were walking through the cathedral and she felt as though her feet were above water. Perhaps it wasn't the story she came to write or the typical story of boy meets girl and wealth follows. However she was as intrigued as ever. The restaurant was over. The meal a light salad for both women now wearing thin as she heard the aching cries coming from within. Yet she would not pull herself to utter a word. Sarai was doing all the talking bearing out heart and soul of her relationship. Intimate moments were what her readers died for. They fed upon this like tarantulas on their prey. She was the mother of the ocean and she was bringing food to them. She knew Sarai was a romantic, their home said it all. However knowing this detail of one's life made another think that there was more to life than met the eye. She so wished for her to carry on. Tell her some more about the time that she decided to follow Cephas into his world. She didn't know why Sarai had chosen the cathedral for their day out but one thing was certain to her it was perfect for the story she was going to write. She wouldn't say a word, let alone accommodate the thought for food. She'd listen and then listen some more until Sarai decided otherwise.

'Do you want to know what my husband said to me next?'

Hailey said nothing. It hadn't been a question. It was an after thought. It was Sarai reliving a moment by herself. She could have been a statue in the cathedral. She could have been a tree outside waiting for the rain to replenish its nutrients. Or she could have just been herself silent and waiting with baited breath to learn how to walk on water and understand what most of the world did not.

'He said drown.'

Glyfada. It was the second time he cursed with furore that night and we all laughed.

'My partner doesn't seem to like this game,' Charles said.

'More like the game doesn't seem to like your partner,' Ramon replied.

'Maybe he should try bar football with Jens, that looks a lot easier,' I added.

'I don't think he would do well there either,' Charles said laughing as his partner at the pool table missed the black ball and handed victory to Ramon and

I.

Charles sipped again on the bottle and Ramon nudged me mischievously.

'He's at it again,' Ramon whispered. 'I bet he cuddles unto an ouzo tonight,' he chuckled.

'Let the man have his day, he's got plenty on his mind,' I responded.

I had known Charles for almost as long as I'd known Ramon. We checked in at the Chu Kong Passenger Transport Co. in Hong Kong International Airport in Lantau, electing to board the Shekou route departing to mainland China. I had followed the directions from the flight attendant, past the terminal E1 transfer area, the AVSECO security checkpoint and taken the lifts to level 4, Gate 10 where I could board the ferry. Although it was quite a distance from the Arrival Corridor it was worth the walk. Having been cooked up for the past fourteen hours in cattle class on Cathay Pacific from London Heathrow I felt that my days in life had shortened considerably. It wasn't any ordinary cattle class it was built for leprechauns. When I alighted from the plane I got the impression that I had shrunk several feet. Reaching Hong Kong was a blessing in itself.

Gate 10 was vacated when I got there apart from a young Nigerian lady that approached me in the lifts. She offered her assistance knowing immediately that we were both headed to Shenzhen. In her own words she had passed through that terminal several times already in search for her luggage. She didn't speak Cantonese but had diagnosed the arrival times of others destined for her employers. I was grateful for the company. Before long, Charles joined us. He did not approach us at the terminal but waited until we were on board the ferry. It had been reasonably empty for a Saturday, allowing conversations to be louder than usual especially those that weren't Cantonese. I was talking to the woman three rows in front of Charles when he had introduced himself asking if we could all share a cab together to Baicao Garden where our offices were. It had been one of those moments away from home, away from everything else but the pounding of waves in the fog shrouded South China seas. I had grazed on the forage, accepting that the taipan had traveled these waters a while back before my time and now I was doing the same. It was something one read in books, one imagined as a boy, God had been kind to me.

My new friends had plenty to say, Charles more than the girl. That day I learnt that Charles was a man with a lot on his mind. He had a young daughter and a very sick wife back home. She needed him at all times to assist her with the little things as she was on constant medication. They had married in Thailand were things had been a lot easier when Charles was posted in Bangkok. Now they were different. Since moving to Amsterdam his wife's illness had taken a turn for the worse and with little or no family support for her, the strain had become almost unbearable at times.

In China Charles talked endlessly about his family. Glyfada may have been a different location but the people were the same. Maybe meeting Charles back then across the China seas made me believe that we shared some history that allowed for some sympathy to his need for alcohol. Trust was something that most people shied away from in the modern world, the hefty levy to pay - a risk no one was willing to take. I was a good listener and Charles talked. Now he needed his ouzo and no one would begrudge him this, the man needed a way to forget.

'Tell me again why you guys are still here?' Charles sneered as he leaned awkwardly on one of the shelves that had been placed in the large snooker room for player's drinks. 'Laugh all you want but we just won this game and the last one. No amount of teasing would put us off,' I replied focusing on my next shot as I cued over the baize.

'Yes but I want to hear why you two missed out on a date in Athens and are sharing our humble company for the night,' Charles continued, placing his bottle on the shelf and putting his hands in his jeans pockets. The large smoke filled room was now crowded as more people flocked to the tables and waited their turn.

'We have other nights still my friend,' Ramon said.

'I hope you have more success, maybe the same luck you are having in this game,' Charles gurgled.

'Well we should have got in. I still can't believe how close we were. We had made good progress until they started talking to us in Greek and then we looked at one another in horror as we could not understand what was said and then the bouncers threw us out. It was a sad thing because I am sure the party could have used our company,' Ramon answered.

'Dream on. These are not easy prey like China, boys. You have to do better than throwing your charm around, you have to speak the *linga*,' Charles gurned.

'We do, it's just not Greek,' Ramon grinned.

Chapter Five

Nice. Neither woman had heard of 'Our lady of seven sorrows' until they walked into the interior of the Baroque of Basilique-Cathédrale Sainte-Marie and Sainte-Réparate de Nice located in the old town of Nice. Hailey for one was learning that this was the name which the Blessed Mary was referred to in relation to the sorrows in her life. Hailey knew that the Catholic church had given names to the blessed Mary in part to her sufferings and joys. She was no great believer nor did she discount the existence of God but she knew that as she listened to Sarai's story it was hard not to stay intrigued to see where it all led to. There were those that said God was a pleasant fiction created by man to make man seek comfort from difficult times. There were those that argued otherwise. She never bothered with the politics of it. Hailey had chosen to live her life with the cards that had been dealt before her. She had survived the poverty of Yong Ding village and changed her name successfully this was good enough for now. Perhaps other paths lay before her and she would pursue either side of this discussion one day. For now she was content being the writer, the storyteller and it seemed as though Sarai had one to tell.

'He did not immediately tell me how I could drown,' Sarai said as she stared at the towering height of the ceiling in the Cathedral. Hailey listened, urging her to continue.

'He said that even before we met he had traveled a lot. He sought cities that the ancient greats had been to. It was his desire to be in these places to meet other people to learn from them and be a part of them. Cephas wanted to see what others before him had seen. He was in Athens, Rome and many other places that the prophets had visited. He couldn't tell me why but it was just something he needed to do. He said his visions were random, blending in with the trips he made showing him more of himself, who he would become and the life he would lead,' Sarai said.

'How did you take this, I mean what were you thinking all this while as he spoke?' Hailey asked. Man was a being that could be dimidiated. Most times the good half was enough for many of us. Learning about the other side, the peculiar half that strayed into unknown territory often made us change our opinions about each other. Hailey was curious.

'I knew what I had married into when I met Cephas. There was a greater whole to consider something more than what we were as individuals. We could still be ourselves but we also knew we had a commitment to one another.'

Hailey said nothing, waiting. Or maybe man wasn't really two people, as she had first assessed but rather one. We made a choice of whom we wanted to relate to. It was wiser making our choice of being with a person based on who they were rather than who we wanted them to be. It looked as though Sarai had more to say, she would wait.

'He said that there had been some tough times and some great moments still there was this question that lingered in his mind. He said God taught the prophet how to drown. You convulsed and stuttered. You were short of breath and then you sunk. As you did you began asking yourself all sorts of questions of what you had or did not have. Each question brought more questions and extended your self-examination. This brought you further into the depths of the ocean. You gave up hope for rescue because you knew there was no one coming. The light above slowly faded away as you choked in the salt of the seawater. He said that this was drowning,' Sarai said.

'Sounds scary, dark and melancholy, were you concerned?' Hailey asked.

Sarai said nothing as she went back to the moment she had shared with Cephas. It wasn't sad or depressing. There was something different she had felt. Like as if she was floating, drifting like a flotsam carried away by the waves. He had played with her fingers at the time, running his through hers as he held her in his arms. She was breathing lightly against his chest, holding on to him as he talked, carrying her deeper and further into his world. She could hear the trees outside, the birds and most of all his heart beat. The slow pounding intense and next to her almost as though it were her own. He talked about drowning as though he was seducing a mermaid, teaching her to visit the depths of the ocean and allow her mind to do the thinking.

'No it wasn't scary, dark or depressive but rather light as if I could take off into the distance, fly if I wanted to,' She replied.

'He said there was no hope in drowning except what awaited your body at the bottom of the black ocean. He said this was what drowning felt like.'

Any moment now Hailey thought. Any moment now these large trumpets within the Cathedral are going to blare at us and I would join you in this hypogeum that you take me to. It was amazing how cool it was in the interior of the Cathedral as opposed to the refulgent sunlight outside. Hailey shuddered inwardly as she absorbed the full impact of Sarai's words. She is not the oracle but I have to listen because somewhere down the line I shall get what I need.

'He said that God teaches us how to drown through longsuffering. He gives us truly bad days when nothing matters. When we shall question his existence and ask ourselves why we came to be. It is the first test we must pass to walk on water. If we can learn how to drown then we have a chance. In other words if we accept our longsuffering as part of our existence then we can overcome the fear of facing it.'

Sarai had kept her thoughts to herself at the time. Cephas was going where her dad had taken her many years before. If we learned how to fall off the bike then we could learn how to ride it. It made sense that to swim we learnt how to breath under water. It could have been the same concept. She had learned how to swim in this way. His next words had put things into perspective.

'The next thing he said to me was that the next step was to learn how to die.' She said the words to Hailey like a woman discovering for the first time that she was capable of more than she had ever thought. Pillow talk was between two people, intimate and kept away from the rest of the world because although it may have sounded natural between the two people who shared and bonded, it was absolute madness before others. Perhaps she was there and beyond, it was a risk she had to take. She had called the magazine and Hailey was here, there was no turning back. She had to go all the way and see what happened.

'You have got to know that by this time I didn't know what to say to Cephas. I could just listen to his voice as he told me how I had to learn to die. It was scary but I wanted to know all of it. I needed to be a part of him and see this side of a world that I had never known,' She continued.

'How was he? Was he calm? I mean talking about death in this way is not normal?' Hailey asked.

'I would have thought the same if the room was cold or I felt empty. However there seemed to be something else as if any moment soon the sun would descend through the darkness, come out in the night as opposed to its natural time in daylight.' She replied.

'He said that death leaves behind. Death loses, death gives up something for good. Death lets go of. After you learn how to drown you must learn how to die. When you fall deep into the ocean, you must give up what you had and believe that it would not be any more. When you give this up you find death.' Sarai said.

She was now looking at Hailey looking into the girls eyes whispering those unspoken words and appealing to her wisdom to understand that Cephas wasn't crazy, that there was more to come, that this discussion had a purpose, it served for something more.

'At the time all I could think of was that this is not like riding a bike. You fell and then you got up. This looked more like you fell and continued to without any hope of recovery. I remember asking him in a very shaky voice when I had the courage to look at his face whether in this process, one lost everything and everyone,' She said. To her amazement Cephas had been waiting for her to look to him and his gaze was loving for in the deepness of his eyes she saw something else. There was no sadness, there was only warmth, and for whatever reason unknown to her she felt herself chanting within. She couldn't tell what the song was but it was there.

'What did he say?' Hailey asked. Why would anyone wish to say this to someone they loved?

'He said yes you lose everything and everyone. Nothing stays the same.'

She hadn't let it go she had asked him other questions. There were emotions she was feeling and wanting to know why they were so different from the natural ones any human being would be feeling.

'Then how come I don't feel sad. Even though you are telling me that in death I lose everything and everyone ?' she had asked. Why did his eyes reveal something else even though he talked about death as the loss of all? Why was he so calm about something so terminal? Why did she trust him?

Cephas had assured her, he said thinking of a thing was not necessarily the same as living it. We cried when people died because we felt the pain and loss but thinking about this of ourselves was difficult and hard to imagine a sadness for what had not yet been.

'How do you mean ?' she had asked pushing and probing wanting to find out more.

'Well ask yourself this question, how can you thirst when you have water, how can you hunger when you have food or how do you hate when you are surrounded by love? The fact is as hard as we try we cannot be sad for a death that has not happened. We can worry but we cannot cry for our own death because we are not dead,' he had replied.

'But we can cry for others that die or are dying?' she asked.

'Yes because we feel sorrow for them.'

'But we can also cry that we have a terminal disease and know that we are going to die.' She was again probing, needing answers for what she could not comprehend.

'True if we fight to hang on to life. However hanging on to life doesn't necessarily mean hanging on to everything that we have got. It can also mean starting a new life. Why can we not hang on to the hope of another existence a better one with those that we love.' He had said.

She hadn't understood what he was saying. He spoke in riddles. One minute he said death made you leave everything behind, naturally you will be out of your mind if you were not sad after losing this. The next he talked of a better time with others, was this a fantasy? If so then what could explain her emotions, they weren't in synchrony with the discussion. She was calm in spite of all the questions.

'But hows that possible we haven't been there yet so how do we know it would be okay or that it even exists? We cry for what we have because we know of it and what it has given us. We hang on to what we have because we come to love it and what it offers despite the heartaches. We know it is real. If death takes us away from this then this is reason enough to be sad.' She had replied.

'That's the thing my darling. This is why I must bring you to the third step of walking on water and that is beyond death. The truth is we do know what is going to happen and we have been to this place beyond death. This is why even now as I tell you about death you do not feel sad or see it in my eyes.'

Athens. We wandered downhill and then turned right following the narrow stairway into the dimly lit taverna. The waiter was at hand greeting us and smiling obsequiously, it was a rare occasion to get customers this late.

'You guys like fish, right?' she said.

'We like everything,' Ramon replied.

'Good because I have to repay you both for a glorious time in China. What would the other girls think if I say you came to Athens and I did not take you out?' Erica continued.

'They have probably forgotten about us by now. It has been a while you know,' I replied.

'I doubt it. I keep in touch with them even though you don't and they always talk about the time in that club and our trip out in Shenzhen. Celeste remembers you, she mentions you time and again,' Erica said.

'Oh you mean the girl from Turkey?' Ramon asked

as he reached into the bowl for more peanuts.

The *Mata Hari*, the whirlwind, I knew who she referred to. It had been the time of my priesthood, memories, time alone with God.

'That's the one. Do you know that we flew home together? We had to stop over somewhere in the Middle East I can't remember now. She is a nice girl,' Erica said.

'You are all nice girls that is why we came to see you,' Ramon said.

'I must say this company is much more pleasant than what we have been sharing lately,' I added. The change was necessary. I liked the team that had flown into Athens for the course. We all had different backgrounds from our various countries. Yet because we were all managers and men it just seemed as though the room suffered from egos being put to the test. It was nice to be with someone different and away from it all.

'Yep I second that. Don't get us wrong we love the guys but now and again it would be good to see some place else other than Glyfada and the snooker room,' Ramon said with a slight quiver.

'Oh but Glyfada is a nice place. Over here we call it the area with new money, the up and coming place for young entrepreneurs,' Erica replied.

'Yeah, that's why they escorted us out of the club last night,' I interjected.

'Why what happened? You probably looked like outsiders, don't take it personal,' Erica answered.

'It's hard not to considering that we were looking forward to enjoying ourselves away from the office were we had been all day!' Ramon said while refilling everyone's glass with wine.

'Never mind you're here now so *stop complaining*!' I whispered harshly with a small giggle.

'Yes stop complaining!' Ramon and Erica saluted in unison raising their glasses. It was a joke shared by most people that worked for the company. They were always deemed to be complaining as far as the senior management were concerned.

'By the way when is Rufus joining us? At the rate at which I am adding this wine there won't be much left if he doesn't show up soon,' Ramon said almost looking apologetically at us.

'Never mind, we can drink white now and order red for dinner. He would be here soon he told me to keep you guys entertained.'

'And you are going about it in the right way. Fish is a welcome break for me from the souvlakis,' I said.

'Oh by the way did I mention that there is a special drink that Rufus wants you both to try? But then you Ramon, a man who knows his drinks has probably had that one before,' Erica winked at him.

'What is it?' Ramon asked.

'Agua ardiendo. It's called hot water. But it's anything but hot water, more like a strong vodka,' Erica said.

'I have had it, now there's a drink for you my friend. But I think a better description for it would be firewater,' he said smiling at me. 'Sorry guy, this is a lot stronger than caipirinha. I know you love your Brazilian cocktails but this baby has a kick to it that would make your throat boil.'

'Yep, I have had my fair share of what drinks I should try and shouldn't in the last few days,' I replied. This subject was now trite. 'I just hope this firewater doesn't finish me off.'

Celeste was the Mata Hari, the whirlwind that had taken Shenzhen like a storm. She had been my companion under the neon lighted streets. She had played her part unequivocally as I evoked and revealed the mystery behind the hidden words, spiritual words spoken by the Lord, the Father. It was the second step in my indoctrination, fulfilling the wishes of the Lord. Erica was the Athenian, a blonde bombshell that had also been present chatting away with others, Ramon one of them. It was how our group evolved the first time we all met. Then I paid little attention to what was happening around me, my mind focused on the task ahead. When I eventually returned to London I had been exhausted, the revelations a journey I couldn't have imagined. Then as if in the balance of things my wit dropped, nutrients evaporated, I felt abandoned, my spiritual side moving in a direction that left me asking foolish questions. The circumstances were completely overturned, not by bad judgment, just the way things were, had to be, for me to grow. The highs and lows of the spiritual world caught up to me. Like everything in life after the feast came the emptiness and for me it was helplessness and exasperation. I needed to dig deep from within. Search for my spirit, Cephas, the *voice*, a vortex that opened and shut, gnawing; a fawn for support beyond reason, especially when answers were needed.

God had answered my prayers. In the bible it was written,

"And there are also many other things which Jesus did, the which if they should be written every one, I suppose that even the world itself could not contain the books that should be written." I had asked for one of those stories, one specific to my needs and the Lord obliged in a dream.

"My son I would tell you a story. Once upon a time there lived a young man in a house on top of a hill. One night this young man was walking through the rooms of the house bored of being in the same place day in day out. After a while he thought he should make himself

useful and began cleaning his room. But he had to go out to get a brush to sweep after tidying, unfortunately when he returned he found that his mum had dumped a load of washing on the bed and some dirty clothes on the floor. The young man asked his mum why she had done this and she explained to him that since his room looked tidy she had decided to sort out the laundry there. She won't take too long and soon it would be back to how it was. The young man thought nothing of it. The only problem was he was still bored and now with no outlet.

Eventually it was 1AM in the morning and the house was now quiet as everyone was in bed. The young man became restless. He could not sleep and decided to go for a walk. He walked for a while until he got into the town centre and the buzzing nightlife. There were people everywhere. This was better than lying in bed doing nothing at least here there was plenty to see. Suddenly out of nowhere appeared a dog. This dog had hair all over its face and began to follow the young man barking loudly at him. He noticed that the dog had three legs and he smiled at it. However the dog barked louder forcing him to standstill in the crowded street. Why had this three legged hairy creature selected him to torment? And then the dog spoke and shouted at him,

'Go home it is late you should not be out at this time.' The young man did not argue with the dog but consented. He began to walk back home but when he got to the foot of the hill, the path that linked the town with his house, the road had disappeared. He looked everywhere for it without success. Then came a young prostitute who smiled at him invitingly, she was very pretty but he resisted her. Eventually he saw several other people also looking for this path. He heard a few of them say they knew of a back way, a shorter route and the young man followed, curious to see where this

would lead to. As the people walked behind the houses in search of the path they walked past a fire station. It was a huge house and there where two guards sitting at the front. Some of the people walked by and a small number stopped to ask the guards for direction."

Dreams were another means of communication to the Lord. It hadn't always been the case with me but this one was different. I had a vivid memory of it, living through the eyes of the young man and facing each obstacle strewn in his path. It had been another time and place but the Lord's words had meant so much then.

'How much longer have you guys got in Athens?' Erica asked cutting through my reverie.

'About another week,' Ramon replied.

'I think there is plenty more for you to see, we could do something else some other time,' she said.

I could hear their voices a million miles away as they tried to cajole me to the present. Little did they know that spirit had taken over man. It was so easy in life to write off a dream as a factor of one's imagination. Not all dreams served a purpose but those that did always made one stop and think of what could be.

'Didn't you visit London sometime in December last year?' Ramon asked.

'I did,' Erica answered.

'Tell me what it's like I still haven't been.'

'You are asking the wrong person, you should ask your friend, he lives there.'

'When I want to ask this type of questions I never turn to him, you tell me.'

'It rains all the time, more than most cities I have been to but the night life is something else.'

I listened blindly and returned their smiles but offered no words. The red brick in the restaurant was bare, the place sparsely furnished. The few tables in the room were dispersed evenly and covered in bistre, some of their wooden surfaces sitting on trestles of metal. The trellis on the wall had plants festooned in vertical and horizontal directions making irregular patterns as they groped the hanging lamps. I seeped some of the frascati and listened quietly. I had listened quietly some place else when the Lord had spoken. It had been another disparate story and a parable from the spiritual world. I hadn't expected anything then but had received plenty. I had been guessing all the time the outcome of the dream. *What fate would befall the young man? Who was the dog?* My dream hadn't ended abruptly. The Lord had told me the story to the end.

"*As the people and the young man stood before the guards at the fire station asking for directions, one of the guards had answered the people. He knew of no such path that led up the hill. The people persisted and the guard said the only road he could think of was through the fire station but he wasn't allowed to let them all through. He then took a few of them and led them through the door of the fire station. The young man watched for a while until the people disappeared out of sight with the first guard. Soon he was left alone with another man waiting in the dark, the others who had been denied passage had walked off. The young man could hear others coming up behind him. He approached the second guard and asked if he could also be let through the building. The guard said,*

'*Well for you there is no problem you can go through.' The young man looked to the other man that had waited in the dark and asked the guard if he could come too. The guard had let him pass stipulating the terms, 'The other man did not have the same right through the fire station as the young man but was also allowed passage.'*

When they entered the building they saw the first guard leading the small group of people ahead of them. The fire station was nothing like he had seen before. There were pipes running everywhere, diagonally, perpendicularly and connected to different stairs. It was like a maze. The man he had entered with began following the same path taken by the first guard and the other people. At first the young man walked behind looking around the house, admiringly and then as they descended the stairs like the others he stopped. He remembered that firemen often slid down poles. This way they traveled faster to get to the fire trucks. He told himself that he would use this method instead of the stairs because it was much quicker and fun. So as the rest of the people descended the stairs in the building he climbed unto one of the poles and begun sliding down. He went in a spiral pattern down the pole until he reached the bottom and then realized that when he tried to get off the pole his weight could not keep him on the ground. He discovered that his feet could not touch the ground and no matter how hard he tried every time he attempted to do so he felt as if he was going to fly off.

At this time he took a closer look at the fire station to discover that it was like nothing he had seen before. There were people sitting down at tables eating while others did several different things in the background. The place seemed to go on forever. Soon he spotted the other people still being led by the second guard. At this point the young man decided to grab unto another pole to see what would happen. It had the same effect; he would slide down it for miles in a different direction in the huge building and then when he tried to get off he would find himself flying off. He could not understand how all the people he had come in with could walk and he couldn't. He wondered whether the others would report him to the guards, he was abusing their kindness by mistreating the facilities. However no one seemed to care. Suddenly he stopped and remembered something."

I had been quiet listening to the voice of the Lord, waiting to learn, to understand the fate of the young man and the Lord had said,

"My son, do you wish to understand the moral to this story?"

'I do,' I had answered.

And the Lord had said,

"Now hear the wisdom of this parable and remember it. The young man is you. You read the bible over and over until you got tired. Then you decided to do something different. Now do you remember Balaam in the Old Testament?"

'I do,' I had replied. And the Lord had said,

"I am God as I directed the ass to drop Balaam off so did I direct the dog to send you home."

'The prostitute lord, what does this mean?' I had asked. And the Lord had said,

"Do you remember the parable of the ten brides and the lamps? Well again your persistence paid off because you listened to the dog, you found the fire station and were not distracted by the prostitute, temptation. And as you are blessed by me of the many that came forward you are among the few that are chosen."

'In the fire house father, why were the people sitting? What does this mean?' I had asked. And the Lord had said,

"Do you remember the sons of Zebedee who asked for a place beside Christ in my house? Well you are the same that is why unlike the other people who walk in my house you have the freedom to fly and not be led."

'Thank you father,' were the only words left to say.

A parable had been revealed and I had learnt that God would come to my rescue in my time of need. I had sought comfort in helplessness and exasperation and God's word had prevailed.

Nice, France. Hailey sat down on one of the pews beside Sarai as they stared blindly ahead of them. There was more beyond death and she had to be patient knowing that Sarai was going back to the moment, digging up this time she had shared with Cephas.

Sarai was somewhere else in the past staring at the pattern in the ceiling of their bedroom. Her head leaning on Cephas's arm as she tried to think of what he had just said. They had been to the place beyond death. Could her eyes see further than what Cephas had just put her through, explained to her? What was beyond this remarkable pattern of their ceiling roof? There was a blue sky high above and yes the sun. Then there were stars more than a billion light years away only visible in the dark and beyond that who could tell. Had she been to what no one could tell? She hadn't grown up going to Sunday school regularly but she knew God and had faith. However this was truly new to her. She was now using her imagination and what she too had read once upon a time in the bible to put herself in this place that Cephas referred to as beyond death.

'His next words were, you can't get there by astral or spiritual projection my darling. You can't get there through your imagination. Your eyes cannot see that far and your imagination is flawed, he said to me.' She looked at Hailey. Hailey's arm rested on the backrest of the pew. Her watch said 10am, naturally she hadn't bothered to change to European time. Sarai knew it was almost 4pm in the afternoon. They would have to start thinking of getting home.

'What happened next?' Hailey asked.

'I asked him if he was reading my mind?' she said, 'how could he know what I was thinking? He said that he wasn't. He said he didn't have to, that he'd be thinking the same thing as I was if he was in my shoes and someone just told him what he had said to me.' Sarai replied. She turned again forward facing the pulpit. The interior of Sainte-Réparate de Nice was decorated with a reverence of what it represented. It's pulchritude was majestic inviting you into its ensconce. Although it was meant to represent the lady of sorrows no one could feel enervated in this interior. Perhaps this was what Cephas was talking about in their discussion. She had asked him other questions.

'Then how do we get to know that we have been to this place you refer to as beyond death?'

'First let us look at what we have, what God has told us. He says before we were conceived in our mother's womb he knew us he knew what we would become,' he replied.

'I think the story of the prophet Jeremiah?' she asked.

'Correct. I think here God is telling us of what we were before we came into being.'

'But how do I remember that I have been with God when I can't remember being born as a baby?'

'Do you think you just came to be when your parents made you? What God teaches us is that we came to being when he created us and being in our Mothers womb was God giving us to her. So before we were this flesh and bone that we see we were already with God,' he replied benignly.

'I still can't see it,' Sarai had said. She had seen something in his eyes, felt at peace when he had talked about death yet she couldn't explain it. It was the same as this he talked of something that she knew was a comfort but she just did not understand what he was saying.

'I would ask you a hypothetical question then, how do you know that when you get out of bed you will go downstairs and have something to eat in the kitchen?' he had asked.

'Well first of all I went shopping yesterday and know for certain that I bought some of my favourite biscuits so I could have some.'

'How do you know that someone hasn't been downstairs and eaten them?'

'I know because its just you and me in the house and I know that you haven't been down there since last night. I know this because I closed up yesterday and I saw them last.'

'Are you certain by fact or hope?'

'Fact because I put them there and hope because I pray that I find them and I'm not going crazy talking to you,' she had smiled.

'What if I say I crept downstairs and ate them while you were asleep,' Cephas said.

'Then I would be certain by faith that I hoped you did not go down there and eat them because that is what I crave for now,' she had giggled.

'This is how we are certain we have already been with God in heaven. It is by faith. The truth is the only way you can guarantee that those biscuits are down stairs is through faith and hoping that when you go down there I haven't touched them. In the time it takes you to get down there and find out the truth anything can happen. You can only hope that nothing does until then.'

'Aha but the difference is I know it. I just know because I feel it. I can't explain it but I just know because I was there and I bought them.'

'True my darling. I can't argue with that. But do you remember how our discussion started. I said a prophet had a cross to bear. The difference between a prophet and anyone else is that he knows what would be because he has been there. I'm not saying that you should I am saying that a prophet knows these things and is as certain of them as you are of the biscuit in your cabinet downstairs,' he had replied.

'So you have been there and are certain of what would be?'

'I have.'

'What is it then that you haven't told me?'

'Well the only thing that I may add is that a prophesy is only partially true until the real thing comes to pass. What this means is you can tell me with all the conviction in the world that your biscuits are downstairs but until I go there and see them for myself I just have to take your word for it. This is the same with knowing we have been with God, we have to take his word for it.'

'So then it comes down to trust.'

'That and faith.'

He was so convincing, so assured and without doubt. She had been drawn into his world engulfed by this divine knowledge. She had done her best explaining the details to Hailey. Now she left out the last bit, this she kept to herself it was private, her memories.

Sarai had climbed on Cephas's stomach and put her hands on his neck.

'Do you know that I could suffocate you my darling?' She remembered as her eyes had shone as she spoke. She was looking into his with love and affection and a burning desire to see beyond death as he had said. They had been lying there for what looked an eternity as Cephas had pulled her away from the daily chores of life. He was right in a way. Even the toil of driving to work safely wasn't guaranteed until we were in the office and plodding through work. We knew how to get there, had been there the day before yet there were no guarantees. We just had to go for it and trust in our instincts that we would be intact when we got there the following day.

Sarai had leaned slowly forward as they touched bringing her face close to his.

'So my charming prophet how many children do we have in this place you come from?' she had said allowing her hand to caress his arms.

Cephas smiled.

'Why don't I tell you about the final step of walking on water instead?' he said.

'What comes next then my darling?' she had asked as she kissed him gently.

'The resurrection.'

Chapter Six

Athens.   Rufus arrived just as the meal was being served. The restaurant was empty except for the owners. It was a late dinner, which started just after 10pm but was worth the wait as the fish was fabulous. There was some music and I listened to it, drawn to the picture of a man adorned in ancient Greek attire on the wall, his status complimentary by the petasus on his head. Another time and another place with these same friends I was pushing off the kids that held on to my ankles in the streets of Shenzhen. I hadn't been alone I had worked hand in hand with my spirit, Cephas as we evoked the teachings of God. This was in the past as things were different now. Now Cephas had the reins for were I ended he began. The reality of it all was that it had always been Cephas from the beginning, the spirit that had been known by God before being conceived. However for any journey to have a purpose there had to be an allocation of time, a time to learn and a time to see that which was beyond. Mine had come in waves of an unprecedented voyage and now the man was dead and Cephas reborn. There was plenty of ground to cover. I was no more the active but the dormant being occupying the nocturnal as Cephas took on the diurnal. Our roles had been reversed I became the *sleeper* and Cephas the *narrator*, the link that would put the pieces together. My world became of little importance and it was only that of Cephas, which would be pursued and from it would come all the *answers.* I accepted. I was the weaker being, the darkness that shaded the truth and light. And if I was to find freedom, elevate myself from the dead carcass that came with the responsibility of my world then I had to let Cephas take charge. It was God's way, the Lord's way, the spiritual world guiding the man and not the carnal guiding the spiritual.

'You still up?' I asked as we walked into the John's hotel in Glyfada. The taxicab ride back to our hotel had been uneventful. Still there was life back in our hotel. It looked like the night was still young.

'I am and having a drink,' Charles replied. 'How was your evening with the lovely Erica? Everything you would expect or more?'

'More and more,' Ramon answered.

'Hey, why don't we sit outside and talk, it's a glorious evening and then you could tell me all about it,' Charles suggested.

'Don't we have to be in tomorrow?' I asked.

'We do but we start at nine thirty and it is an easy day, so don't fret. We would still have plenty of sleep, besides we are our own managers or have you forgotten?' he replied chuckling, as he lurched past one of the vases and sank into a chair on the patio.

'You have a point, let's sit outside and enjoy this time. They don't come that often, for once we return to our countries it would be back to working like savages my friend!' Ramon said dragging another cane chair closer to the table.

'At night this place can be anywhere, it is really hot,' Charles commented.

'You miss home?' I asked. I could barely see the main road from where I sat, blocked off by the magnolia tree and other plants in the small orchard before us. I could hear the sea miles away and the cars that sped along the highways. The dim light from the foyer fell across our table making our shadows and those of the trees and plants prominent over the marbled patio. Charles was right we could have been anywhere.

'I miss home. I miss my time with my wife and

daughter and I even miss the time I spent with her family,' he replied.

'So how did you meet?' Ramon asked.

'I was in Asia, I had been sent to start a new branch for our company. They made me the regional manager for Asia Pacific. I was based in Thailand working out of Bangkok were our main office was. I met Mia in the embassy. She was an interpreter. I asked her if she could come and work for me, we offered to pay her well and she accepted.'

'But how did that go I mean going out with her don't they have the Buddha religion over there?' I asked.

'The Buddha religion can be everywhere you know,' Ramon commented.

'I don't mean it in that sense.'

'I know what you mean, I was only joking,' Ramon quibbled.

'It wasn't a problem for us. Mia is very independent in that respect, she had a good education and although she was of the Buddhist faith she still could accept that she could fall in love with someone who wasn't. That, I don't think was the toughest problem. I guess everyone knows Bangkok's reputation, well with Mia I had to get across to her that I wasn't one of those foreign nationals solely looking for one thing only. Before we could even get to second base I had to mention marriage.'

'Did she know that someday you would be moving back to Europe?' I asked. I was tired from the long evening in Athens and had sunk deeper into the cane chair, my arms folded across my chest for some warmth and comfort. We hadn't gone only to the restaurant. Erica had insisted on having us visit the Olympic Stadium, Leofóros Ardhittou; then she had talked animatedly about Greece's unexpected victory at the Euro2004 football finals which had given Ramon all the impetus he needed. They had argued for a while at why Portugal had lost in the finals and before long I was being forced by Rufus and Ramon to try the famous firewater and regretting every sip of it minutes later.

'Well that was after marriage. Frankly I took each step at a time with Mia. I got to know her parents and then learn a bit of the language and the culture. I picked up what I could and before long I wasn't so much of an outsider. I think what helped a lot was her education as I did not appear too strange for her considering that she had worked in the embassy for such a long time and knew most of the foreigners.'

'How long has it been?' Ramon asked.

'Over thirteen years, my daughter would be seven next year but you won't believe how mature she is. I told you of her mother's problem, right? Well you would be amazed what this kid can do,' Charles rambled on hoarsely his eyes relaying a squiffy indication of how much alcohol he had consumed. Perhaps he had taken one too many and as the night wore away he was now losing his voice.

'Kids, that's something I haven't talked about with my girlfriend but Asia and Thailand well now there's a holiday for you. Pucket, those beaches what more could one ask for,' Ramon said.

'A lot more if you spoke the language, there is plenty more of the culture and the people to see as you move inland,' Charles answered. 'Did you try the river ride when you where there?' he asked directing his question at me.

'I did, Chao River I think it was called, right? Well nothing short of a mystery. Even the haggling for the price was something to look forward to at the riverside, and then the shops one passes upstream, all very interesting,' I said.

The brackish water of the Chao Phraya River was located behind the Wat Indravihar pagoda. I had walked down Samsane Road in Bangkok taking pictures before the friend I traveled with had persuaded me to visit the pagoda. I had taken a look at one of the green bells in the courtyard and could not help myself. That had been a mistake. The rattling in my mouth and the sheer pain received in my eardrums was proof that the decision to ring it had been a bad one.

'Do you think you could live back there?' Ramon asked.

'With my wife only, yes. But with my daughter I would say no I want her to learn my culture over here and be educated in this society. Nonetheless we still visit my wife's family now and then and she gets to see the other side of the family. I guess she benefits from both worlds.'

No one spoke for a while as the brisk sea breeze blew in from the gulf. This levanter served a purpose it was a sign. I could hear the voice again. Cephas was present and connecting the dots as was his task; *the man with one eye, the children in the play ground*. The Lord never failed to amaze those that trusted in him. Once more it was his voice directing. Luckily I was now just a bystander and so I could be silent watching from the background as the spirit awakened and unveiled a timeless mystery.

Mougins. Anytime but now, those days that make you lie in bed and feel rustic. Hailey could sense it, that feeling again from the past mounting up and building within her. I thought I had left this behind a while back. I thought giving up Hsu for this new life would change things she thought. I'm in the South of France and away from everything, writing the story I had always dreamed of yet I can't help but feel the long creepy snake of my past follow me forever. Sarai's story had twisted and turned, sloped and taken off to different heights. There was no doubt in her mind that it was spiritual. It delved deeper into the recesses of one's mind than she could have imagined. Yet she was worried. I have to tell her story in the truth by which it portrays but I have to keep my readers on side, she thought.

It hadn't been easy leaving Yong Ding and even getting out of Shenzhen. The first time was late September of 2006. She had been sitting idly at her desk after lunch following the normal protocol of the day in the large campus at Baicaio Gardens. Most of the young graduates slept after lunch. She couldn't. Her mind was elsewhere. I left Yong Ding to see the world and I've been here for over eight months without doing anything worthwhile, she thought. Hailey had been staring blandly at her computer as she struggled with a game of solitaire when her manager had beckoned to her from his office. She had walked towards the door with a lot of reservation. It was probably a filing errand. She was the unfortunate one to be seen awake at her desk so it was going to be photocopying for her for the rest of the afternoon.

'Hailey, something has come up in Europe,' he said to her in Cantonese as soon as she entered his office, indicating for her to close the door.

Hailey was silent allowing herself to get accustomed to the words she had just heard. She thought she heard Europe but it was too early to feel this sense of elation.

'As you are aware my command of the English language is somewhat, how can I put it, lacking. You on the other hand are better than the rest of us. How would you like to go with me to Athens for a week? It could be more, I can't tell yet, we have a conference there and I would need a translator.'

Hailey felt her knees sag beneath her and then water come to her eyes but kept this feeling hidden from the world. A 360 degrees change in an instant that was all it took for one's life to have a purpose, to serve something more than what it stood for.

'I'd do it sir, I'd love to.' She heard herself say.

Within days she was in Greece and then Athens experiencing her first visit abroad and discovering her passion for wanting to write. Athens had pushed home the need to be abroad to fulfill her ambition and passion. However there were the barriers that came with every dream. Hers turned out to be immigration. You couldn't just travel to Europe to live and work. Doing it on company business was okay because they provided the visas that were necessary. Stay was for a short period of time after which you had to return to your homeland. Her visit to Athens only fueled her need to work abroad and the difficulties that came with returning home.

If there was one thing growing in limited conditions gave one, it was the determination not to return to them. She wanted to make it for herself and for those that waited for her back home. Her time alone in Athens when she wasn't needed to interpret documents allowed her to think of her options. She was young and not bad looking for that matter. There were plenty of young Chinese men abroad and maybe even foreigners. Why couldn't she get married? Why couldn't she do what was necessary to keep her dream alive? There had been no guarantees that she would leave Yong Ding for Shenzhen. There was only a need and a deep desire within to become a journalist. She had studied languages and got into one of the best companies in the country. There had been no guarantees that she would leave China yet again her command of languages had made this possible in spite of the odds. Now there was no guarantee that she would find someone that she liked or someone who could be that means for her to live abroad.

Hailey glanced at her watch at the side of the bed. It was almost eleven. Sarai did not have much planned for the day. There was no burden of a time schedule for when they worked. It was like a vacation. They worked when they met whether it was at breakfast or the leisure hours by the pool. All she knew was that she had three weeks to put this story together. That was the time allocated to her. She was nearing the end of her first week and still there were many unanswered questions. She needed to feed her readers as much as she needed to do justice to her host's story. It was easy for Sarai to delve so deep into the spiritual bond that she shared with her husband. She had her own questions. How did Sarai get on with her mother-in-law? There were those things in married life that one could not avoid. Her little experience in getting to where she was in life had taught her that the path in marriage wasn't paved in gold and riches. There was more to it than met the eye. She needed to know about the relationships. Those fragile moments when one was vulnerable as she had been a while back before she got to where she was. Perhaps today would not be so easy for her host. She would ask those awkward questions. She would seek more of her past and relationships. Did Sarai and Cephas ever tell one another about the life they had before they met? Who where the other people in their lives before this, before the south of France? Maybe getting up in the morning and feeling ordinary served a purpose. It made you seek more from life and your expectations. She certainly wanted more from her host.

Today she would throw it out there and see what

happened. Sarai would be obliging, it was her story and she needed to tell the world about it.

Glyfada. I was dead and Cephas alive. The body convulsing, my hands and legs writhing uncontrollably, the words uttered,

'*I love you father, I love you Lord.*'

Cephas was present lying within my dead carcass and I watched, fascinated. This time the journey did not take us out of the room. It looked as though my presence was all that was needed. I just had to be there and be the body for what was to follow. I heard the sounds next as the window opened to this estranged world. The chanting, voices singing so loud it felt as if the roof of the house was going to blow off. They sang like angels if ever I could have heard any and I shook spasmodically, my mouth foaming as I almost choked on my breath. I was bewildered at this next appointment yet assured in the spirit for I had traveled before, been in spirit before. Man dies but spirit does not, I can cope with this will do. I had to stay put, allow the wings of my spirit to remain folded and wait. The chanting continued and I listened to the words from the voices,

'*Amen, Amen.*'
'*We are the righteous, Lord.*'
'*Amen, Amen.*'
'*We are the righteous, Lord.*'

The door began to open in the room but it did not feel like a room, with the sounds, with the singing. It felt more like a church, sacred ground for the gathering of those who believed in God. There was a blinding light and then the bedroom door opened wider and I saw even more brightness as if the incandescent force of the sun was now in the room, the sacred ground. My eyes followed the brightness from the bottom to top and what I saw next was beyond what I could ever have imagined. She was a bride dressed in a snow white dress that shown brighter even than the yellow sunshine that was breathtaking in the background. The voices went up several notches, the singing a rhythmic chant beyond anything I had ever encountered before.

The bride moved to the bed and looked at me. I looked back and listened to myself, listened to the spirit, Cephas say,

'Who are you, tell me your name.'

The bride smiled and looked back at me, shaking her head and said,

'I cannot tell you that, but I can tell you that my God is as powerful as your God.' Then she climbed on the bed and pinned me down. I could sense the wings of the spirit flare opening with the radiance of an eagle about to leap into the sky. There was conception, the dead body, me in another world, allowing the spirit, Cephas to use it for what was to follow. I felt the body release as fluid flowed from Cephas to the bride. They held on, one onto another, with the chanting in the background an endless sound all the time in my head.

'Amen, Amen.'

'We are the righteous, Lord.'

'Amen, Amen.'

'We are the righteous, Lord.'

Time stood still for me as spirit met spirit, a unison beyond comprehension, and then it was over. The bride rose up slowly coming to her feet, her dress still a stainless and glistening snow white as it had been before. She moved slowly, smiling and looking back as she glided in her radiance towards the door. I was speechless, the estranged voice of the spirit that I had heard ask the question before silent, as I watched her still paralyzed by the chanting. Soon she was gone the singing continuing for a while longer as the brightness of the sunlight slowly faded. My body shook uncontrollably as I screamed from beyond in fright, my grizzly cry a lifetime away. Cephas was losing the window it was time to become a thought, the spirit within, as this mission, this timeless mysterious encounter had finally drawn to a close.

I returned, feeling the pounding sensation from my heart like the drums of a rock band. I was scared stiff and touching body parts to see if they were still functional. Next I checked my loins, my garments to see if this fluid was mine, if the flesh had released anything. The stains would be a clue. There was nothing. My pants were as dry as the desert, as for what I had felt, what I had experienced, what had left my loins, was spiritual. The experience in that world wasn't mine but that of Cephas. The pieces were falling together, echoes from another world made sense. The voice and then Cephas, o*pen it, write it down, answers*. I did.

"*Neither shall any priest drink wine, when they enter into the inner court. Neither shall they take for their wives a widow, nor her that is put away: but they shall take maidens of the seed of the house of Israel, or a widow that had a priest before. And they shall teach my people the difference between the holy and profane, and cause them to discern between the unclean and clean. And in controversy they shall stand in judgment; and they shall judge it according to my judgments: and they shall keep my laws and my statues in all mine assemblies; and they shall hallow my Sabbaths. And they shall come at no dead person to defile themselves: but for father, or for mother, or for son, or for daughter, for brother, or for sister that hath no husband, they may defile themselves. And after he is cleansed, they shall reckon unto him seven days. And in the day that he goeth into the sanctuary, unto the inner*

court, to minister in the sanctuary, he shall offer his sin
offering, saith the Lord GOD. And it shall be unto them
for an inheritance: I am their inheritance: and ye shall
give them no possession in Israel: I am their
possession."

They were words from the Bible, a vision from God
to the prophet Ezekiel, I was reminded of my
inheritance. I was reminded of the name given to me
back in China when I had asked my Chinese friend for
a name. The company allocated English names to the
Chinese and so I wanted a Chinese name to make the
opposite true, certify our partnership. He offered me,
Lie Sie Li, meaning a dead *priest.* Then Cephas had
said it was my priesthood, not an elected pontifex but
more, something spiritual. These were directions, clues
and now the *maiden,* a bride of the seed of Israel, one
of God's, Cephas's *bride.* There was the voice and then
Cephas, *answers,* they were coming fast.

Mougins. Sarai could hear the slight rumble in her
stomach. Perhaps it would be a good idea to have
lunch. She had missed out on breakfast as she tried to
look through each of the drawers of the children. Their
clothes were cute, and it gave her a tranquil feeling
each time she folded them and put them into the
drawers. Maids were good for a lot of things but there
was nothing like this time she had, sieving through the
little hands and legs of their little clothes. This she
preferred attending to herself now and again to get
closer to her children. Hailey had put her on the spot
enquiring about the more endearing things of their
relationship. How was her life before Cephas? How
was he's? What was her opinion on the love they
shared with each other? Going back to the past was
almost as complicated as looking into the future.
Although the pieces fell into place easily because one

had been there, yet another time and another place changed one's perspective and how they perceived the past. When Hailey had mentioned love, the first thing that had sprung to mind was their honeymoon and the beautiful beaches of Mauritius.

Cephas had wished for an island, somewhere he hadn't been to before and she had suggested Mauritius. She stopped in mid stride deliberately folding the small skirt before her with exaggerated precision. He had pulled her close in the centre of their hotel room that first night, her hair covering her face as he threw her backwards a slow grin starting at the centre of his face staring down at her startled expression. They were dancing alone in their hotel room. He was humming something and he spun her around slowly.

'Remember when we first met?'

'How can I ever forget?'

'We danced like this slowly, our steps moving together as if we had known each other forever.'

'I was scared of you.'

'Liar.' He said enigmatically. He was so strange as if he was miles away yet she knew he would never let go of her, her heart and her thoughts.

'Why would you say something like that?' she said drawing a face.

'Because you pulled me away from the other lady. Now that takes guts darling not a scared girl.'

'Ah but you didn't know how much courage I had to work up in order to get you from her. I've told you that I'd do anything for what I want.'

'You certainly did then darling. And I'm a lucky man today.' He smiled.

'I love you my darling,' she said looking into his eyes following him wherever he was traveling to.

'And I love you, my darling,' he said with two twirls that pivoted them towards the open patio windows.

She could have sworn at that moment that even the stars were smiling at her. They hadn't seen much of the town, having been immediately whisked away by a cheerful Indian taxi driver to their hotel in Black River. They had both been tired from the fourteen hours flight and had slept most of the way. This had been the first moment on their own since the wedding and it looked like they had found some reserve energy from somewhere to be now covering the wooden floor expertly.

'Where do you go to my darling when I'm in your arms?' she asked quietly.

'What do you mean?' Cephas replied.

'You are here my darling but I know a part of you isn't. I feel it and know it. I want to go where you go to, I want to see it as well.'

'You already do. It's everywhere, it's in you, it's you.'

'How do you mean?'

'Are you in flight at this moment? Do you feel as though we are the only people on this island? Lose your awareness of what surrounds you and concentrate on what you feel from within and you will travel with me.' He replied.

Sarai had taken a deep breath and let her surroundings vanish into thin air.

'That's a part of it my darling, now lose the past, what you know, what you think you know.'

Sarai let that go too. She was falling, her knees sagging as she felt herself lifted off the ground. She had feet but they weren't there. It felt as though she was flying seeing a new place and a new time that did not exist. Very far away she could hear him humming to her as they twirled slowly in the warm weather. The aubade was mesmerizing and she closed her eyes listening to his heartbeat, her chest now close to his and allowing hers' to follow. So this was what it came to, what it felt like to lose ones' self for real, she thought. Tears were coming to her eyes but she couldn't understand why. It was a new sensation as if she was no one and yet she was every bit of herself as she gave up all, to be a thought, a reason and a feeling. She let the tears flow easily and she whispered quietly to him,

'I would spend the rest of my life with you.' Her words were so quiet that she wondered if he had heard her but she couldn't bring herself to open her eyes and let him see the new depths that she had discovered for herself in this world he had opened to her. She wanted him there with her but wanted him to find this place without her guidance. If it was his world, then he would know where to find her. He would have to move mountains if that was what it took. She had lost herself for him. If he wanted her he'd have to look. He'd become the wanderer for it was her turn to enjoy this place. She had shed tears to find it and he'd have to do the same. She had slowly built up the courage within, tightening each eyelid as hard as she could to hide the tears even though she knew he had seen them. I have to look at him she had told herself, I have to see if he knows where I am. I have to see if he has followed me to this place that I have found. Finally she had slowly opened her hers to look at him. Something was different. She was truly flying. She didn't know how he had done it her mind so busy concentrating on leaving behind everything but when she opened her eyes he was carrying her and as he laid her gently on the bed he whispered back,

'This is where I live my darling, now you do too.'

She said nothing. He had found her.

Chapter Seven

Glyfada. We had arranged to meet in the foyer but I knew I had plenty of time to take in an early evening stroll. I needed the fresh air outside and away from my room, as it had now become a cavern intoxicated with vapid thoughts that ran wildly into a scrimmage. It was hard to express the turmoil in one's emotions when you got everything else but victory. You became petulant drowning in your own frustrations as you ran through all the permutations of what could have been had things been different. Next you summoned old losses and became a thrall to your misery constantly dwelling on the 'if only' and querying why victory had departed from your shores. I had not watched Formula One in a while but it was hard not to ask ones' self how a car that had done so well in one season could be so poor in another. Moments like this tested the sane. Why did we care so much if it was just a sport for entertainment? Yes, excuses and more excuses, the dreaded tadpoles that hopped around grinning in your despair and whispering words of insult. They were as faithful as ever and right beside you when you least needed them.

I walked down Pandoras Avenue listening to the insects in the early night as I sought solace from the sounds coming from the gulf on the B' Marina in the west. The night had come early as we moved into autumn and I let my faculties rise above the nagging dilemma of how Ferrari had managed to miss out on a win. I crossed the vast highway of Vas Georgiou Avenue and took a path closer to the shoreline listening to the waves of the Saronic Gulf recede from the beach. It looked like the tide came in at night and dropped off wreckage on this part of the shore allowing daily visitors to witness its dues the day after. Perhaps amongst its rubble were sequin coins because my time in Greece was exposing me to things I could never have dreamed were possible. Who was the woman in the snow white dress that had waltzed into my room and why had she refused to give me her name? I had so many questions and very few places to search for the answers. Was she from my past or in the future and who was I to receive visions of this nature? My previous relationship had propelled my thoughts to new spiritual depths when things eventually did not workout. Like a squib that huffed in the wind before reaching its full level of explosion it had taken control of those internal body parts that mattered leaving me wondering when the pain would end and recovery begin. There was no particular reason why the relationship had ended in the way that it did, still I was grateful that for the purpose it served there were no regrets to look back on. Getting to this place in my life had not been easy but God had answered my prayers.

After graduating at twenty-one I wholeheartedly conscripted to an army of success becoming a human train that rushed from one terminal to the next. I needed to win and our Lord had responded by providing a plenitude of success in my career. Where it was necessary the doors had flown open, as my dreams and aspirations became a reality. I traveled, challenged and overcame. However, even for this human train there was a time to pullover and be refined. Time caught up with me and the lines became blurred as the challenges became infrequent and I cared less about work and more about personal happiness. I wanted someone permanent in my life to share in my woes and joys. There was no harm in this as I was wholly living my time on earth as the world expected me to. No doubt in the spiritual world I was a peddler that had stolen from his master for his own selfish gain.

I hadn't gained so much in a short time through

what I had learnt in education or just by my wisdom. God had always been there for me even as a child. He was my insurance, security through every dreaded escapade. My ranging pole stood firm and not pliable by the many mistakes that were afforded me. As time caught up with me I began to realize the strength of my promise to the Lord. His word to me was truth but so would mine be to him. As a child I had also pledged to serve him truthfully when the time was right. The thing I hadn't factored into this promise was who would decide when it was time to pay my dues. As I receded from the earlier hunger of what the world could offer, so did I respond to what was available in the spirit. The timing of the trials that came with the demise of my relationship was perfect. God called and I answered following his voice on this new path of self-discovery and the spiritual world. My journey began in the New Testament commencing with the name Cephas given to Peter by the Lord when Peter was made a disciple. Its meaning spoke volumes to me and I adopted it as mine giving the goodness and light in me significance. If I could understand this good then I would have answered the voice within me faithfully. One day became two and before long I was counting time served in the wilderness.

It was amazing how easily one could lose touch with what went on in the world. Listening to the sounds of the cars go past me I realized I'd been absent from it all for a while. Glyfada shone beautifully at night as it did during the day. The air smelled fresh and you felt this urge to pick up the yellow dust and let it blow in the wind. The bizarre thing about being away in the spiritual world for some time was that I had lost none of these senses that kept me in touch with nature. In contrast to the past I now breathed it with a wisdom that made me feel alive in everything. The Lord had taught me that the spirit of a man was like the wind that now blew past me. I could listen to it, feel it but have no idea where it was from or headed for. I had spent three years away from the world following the path of the Lord and developing in spirit and faith. I learnt plenty about myself and about God eventually realizing that God hadn't just called for me but had decided to show his world to me as he had done in old times. He was the God of yesterday that had shown those who believed in him miracles and I was a sheep in his herd that would see the same. I allowed Cephas be the witness to this thaumaturge believing that my inferior existence was not worthy of seeing a world enlightened with greatness than I had ever witnessed before. My visions became a reality as the Lord unveiled timeless mysteries before my carnal eyes. Soon it was time to return, walk out of my wilderness and see how the new me would fare amongst the fellow man. I turned up out of nowhere realizing I had lost none of the old me where it concerned my career goals yet the new me now listened to ensure that I never left the voice of my master and creator. I was in the world but no more a part of it. Bread would not suffice for my needs for the word of God was now my life and salvation. I could not depart from his voice or be driven blindly as I had been before. In every situation I listened never departing from that voice that had become my comfort in all those years.

Now it called and whispered a new message, Greece meant more than was apparent to the naked eye. Who was the woman in the snow white dress and who where those children? How where they connected to my other visions? Once again I had to put my hope in my lord and savior, asking God to grant me understanding and interpretation of what I had witnessed.

I walked beneath a lamppost two side roads away

from my hotel and realized how easily time had flown. We had planned to meet at eight thirty and I had ten minutes to retrace my steps. Perhaps there had been no victory to witness in Formula One but I knew I couldn't say the same for the spirit within me. My loss was gain conquering the blaring emotions with peace that absorbed the beautiful night breeze of the Saronic Gulf. Scripture had taught me that faith was the substance of things hoped for and the evidence of things not seen. If I had faith to walk this path then I should have faith to be patient and see it to wherever it took me. One day I would know who the woman was and one day I would understand why she had walked into my vision, my room and my life.

London 2007. The horde of people entering and leaving the station walked briskly to keep up with the busy train schedules on display. The Embankment was a busy place to be in as it linked several tube lines to key office locations. Charing Cross station was a short walk from it and ideal for most people coming in on the National Rail. Sarai walked rapidly as she tried desperately to make it to the Circle line. The meeting was supposed to be somewhere close to Tower Bridge and she knew it wouldn't be an easy ploy at this time of the morning. London took no prisoners in the morning rush hour. You sank or swam in this cauldron practically losing what self-dignity you had in order to keep up with the rat race. It was her fourth year in fulltime employment and she was already gaining the kind of reputation that would propel her to higher ground. She heard the guard's whistle for the platform to be cleared and she ran with a few others. As she stepped unto the train, the guard blew again and the doors shut. The short run from the Bakerloo line had been a good work out. It helped matters that she had chosen the galaxy groove trousers for this particular morning and the black maxter oversize jumper was just what she needed in the early autumn wind.

I'm not helpless she thought as she quickly scanned the carriage for a place to sit. Her destination was six stops away and in that time there was no harm in taking a peek at what was in the papers. There weren't many women working their way up the ladder in the oil industry but those that found themselves in her position had to make it count. The financial market was a loophole with international trade in turmoil by the emergence of so many smaller countries seeking guarantees from the larger ones by joining trade conglomerates globally. Asia was peaking in this conflagration where more familiar markets stumbled and it was the never-ending story of fluctuating markets to meet demand. She didn't know why she had an eye for this but it just seemed as though time had weaved its magic wand and landed her in the oil trade. Two years elapsed by which time she had progressed from a graduate that worked in a supporting role for the director for international duties to having her own account for mainly imports from the Middle East. This was a meeting that she had arranged herself. If all went well then she could be the first female director to take ownership of an account in the Middle East. There were whispers in the right places about her still this did not diminish the hefty task ahead. No one was convinced by enthusiasm. Results paid dividends and she knew that this was what she had to show in order to be given the free hand that she so desperately needed.

A woman was moving, leaving her seat as the train pulled into the Bank and she deftly moved into the empty seat. The tube was an awkward place to be in at times. There were occasions when she'd spend her time watching others and then there were those times that she wanted to be invisible. She opened her paper and briefly paused at the page of the beautiful model that covered the front page of the magazine insert. She could have been eighteen but with an angular face and narrow eyes with a lot of makeup her features placed her somewhere between twenty three and twenty seven. Sarai wasn't looking at the model but at herself. She was edging towards twenty-eight and she knew it won't be long before her parents were on to her. Where was the man in her life, where were their grand children? Pressure found one when they least expected it especially when they were so focused on their career. There was Jonathan, a good friend who now and then she went out with. It was good appearing with him in public, as he had everything a girl could dream of. He made heads turn and was financially astute. They had known each other for four years yet she couldn't bring herself to think of him as the man she would spend the rest of her life with. There was always that resistance in her when things began to get serious. She would pull away, ignore his advances and then when they met up the next time he would reveal to her that he had been dating someone else. There was no harm in this friendship as they both used each other to serve a purpose. He could get what he wanted from the other girls but not from her. Going the distance with a friend that one knew so well could complicate matters.

The girl's grey beautiful eyes held hers for a while. The eyes in a picture had this tendency. They kept you intrigued as if the poser was watching you and conveying a hidden message. Perhaps one could talk to them, tell them truths that they couldn't tell anyone else. I've had someone in my life but that was in the past, a while back. It had been her second year in university. Rick was different, an American student that had decided to pursue his music studies in the UK.

They had met through a mutual friend and before long were inseparable. If there was anyone she would have chosen to spend the rest of her life with it was Rick. They clicked on all levels and for the first time in her life she secretly made plans for the time beyond marriage.

One more stop before Tower Hill and it would be her turn to relinquish the comfort and warmth of her seat to someone else in waiting. She would sneak into the bathroom before the meeting and check her makeup. Her white shirt had no creasing despite the running and with it loose over the black trousers she knew that there was some fashion in her dress sense. If those things were taken care off and her financial merits were unquestionable then it was a case of sealing the deal by astute presentation that allowed her Middle Eastern counterparts the opportunity to choose her firm over their competitors.

Sarai climbed the stairs out of Tower Hill station and made her way to the building with transparent windows that overlooked the Thames. If all went well she would be starting a new life in the Middle East and away from these autumn mornings and beautiful scenery. The days changed in to years so rapidly that looking back now it was hard for her to quite clearly remember what Rick looked like. He was probably a famous composer somewhere exotic leading his life without a single thought of those wonderful moments that they had spent together. She had to leave that past behind her and search for someone else that destiny had awaiting her. She had no regrets and was certain that her success in business, would soon be complemented by the right person to share it with. She passed an elderly gentleman and his wife and the couple smiled at her. There were other looks from men rushing to meet delayed trains and she ignored them concentrating on the task that lay before her.

'If they are looking at me then why should I worry,' she quietly reassured herself. He is out there and could be someone that has seen me from a distance or even one of these men that I avoid making eye contact with. I'd focus on my career for now and leave the rest of my life to fall into place. Rick was gone and it was never going to happen with Jonathan but she was certain that she was meant to be with a man that she would love. It didn't matter that her parents were breathing down her neck, it was their duty to do so. Now and then a little push from them caused no harm and kept her focused on those things in life that mattered more than career success. Things could get even more complicated if she moved to the Middle East but still complication didn't mean impossible. She liked complicated of this kind because it gave her something to work on. One could not expect to play with flower dolls for the rest of their lives, there were times when you made things what they were.

As she pushed open the double doors that led into the reception on the fourth floor her step lightened knowing that she had come prepared. I'm not lost in this financial maze, I'm discovering who I am. I haven't abandoned my life and missed out on the important things I am making my life what I want it to be. Whoever wishes to share it with me would discover this in me and love me for it.

The lady in a black suit behind the desk smiled up at her as she signed in her name. She had been to this office for three months running and had even received a wave from the security guard as she walked to the lift on the ground floor.

'I love autumn, especially early autumn because it is not too hot or too cold and the colours out there are real pretty,' the woman said.

'Are they all in?' Sarai asked returning the smile.

'Yes and waiting for you. Since you are the only woman in the room I suppose it won't matter now would it?' the woman smiled.

'I suppose not, better look my best then, don't you think,' she laughed lightly.

'They're in for a treat,' the older woman smiled encouragingly. She had liked Sarai instantly when she had walked through her doors a few weeks back and liked her even more when she discovered that her beauty did not get in the way of her warmth and friendliness.

'Thank you,' Sarai said and walked towards the wooden door behind her. There was no time to step into the powder room and see if things were all in place. Her mirror was the receptionist. Her smile and warm words had been comforting. Now all she had to do was hold her nerve. She took in a deep breath at the doors and then let it out as she pushed open the door.

Mougins. The bedside lamp was on and her skin glowed in its brightness amidst the white sheets. In the background she could vaguely hear the news from the television set. Such a large house and this is the only sound I can hear. Sarai delicately applied the cream to her hands as she prepared for bed. It wasn't easy going back into her past and visiting that person that was there before who she had now become. Hailey had asked and she had obliged delving as far back as her days working for the investment company in London. No one could determine how things would eventually turn out but now being a mum of three kids made her wonder about her plans back then. It was all about building a name for herself as there was no time to plan for this life she now led. She took a sharp intake of breath as its deafening sound cut through her thoughts.

The telephone rang and she muted the television as she reached for it.

'Are you watching TV again before bed?' were the first words he said to her.

'No it's just on.'

'That would never happen if I was there.'

'How are my children? I miss them,' she ignored his comment as she climbed into bed.

'They miss their Mum too. I have to admit I am worn out from the baby talk but I'm hanging in there for now.'

'Well you asked for it. You can always cut your holiday short and bring them back.'

'Your offer is tempting but I shall try a bit longer. You wanted to do this for a while so I shall let you.'

'Is Rachel sleeping at night? I'm sure she misses her mum.'

'They all do, the boys are no different. Still they sleep.'

'So guess what, I've been busy. I told Hailey about our honeymoon and how you whisked me off my feet, carried me in your arms like a princess.'

'Really? You're exaggerating.'

'You've forgotten. Typical. Then I told her about London, you know the firm and even about Rick and Jonathan.'

'Bet you are having a ball, pulling up the past like that.'

'Then you do not mind. I mean you know I won't do anything to hurt you.'

'You have a carte blanche my darling say what you feel,' Cephas replied.

'I'm trying, it's not easy but I'm getting there. Seriously though do you remember the honeymoon and what you said about being there together?'

She waited but heard nothing. Cephas was silent at

the other end and she allowed him some time to speak and then said,

'I mean do you or don't you?' she asked again.

'We are still there together.'

She grinned like a little girl at his words. She hadn't made anything up. He remembered that night in Black River as clearly as she did.

'How could you be so certain that I would follow you there?' she asked. This was the thing about them. She couldn't remember how many times she had asked him this same question and yet the answer remained the same.

'Faith darling, but you knew that.'

'You always say that, it can be unnerving at times.' If only he knew how much he frightened her sometimes, she thought. She could feel his presence in the room even though he was miles away. It was something she had never understood from the time she had set eyes on him. Sometimes she felt as though they danced in each other's arms for eternity. Before he entered a room she'd feel his presence and Cephas had said the feeling was mutual. It was one of those things in her life that she had never understood.

'Did you have one of them?' She asked.

There was silence from the other end as she waited for him to speak again. Say something dammit! She screamed within herself, I want you to be close to me now and tell me one of those stories, those far away moments of the land that only the two of us share, my darling but why won't you say something when I ask.

'Well?' she persisted.

'I shouldn't tell you darling.'

'Why? I'm your wife I should know.'

'You're my wife and stubborn too.'

'You are laughing at me now. I can feel it, I know it.'

'I'm not. You get this way when I'm not around you, I'm used to it especially now that your kids aren't there.'

'Then you should be more obliging.'

'I'm trying to be.'

'You should have called me earlier so that I could talk to the children.'

'I shall do so tomorrow. I want you to have the time you need.'

'I'm spoilt my darling.'

'We both are. I never stop thanking my Father for you.'

Sarai grinned again. Now she was full, her heart warming to his beautiful words. The house wasn't empty or silent. Cephas called God his father like how others referred to their earthly parents. It came out so naturally each time she heard the words that it had now become such a comfort to her.

'I'm happy.' She said the words as she rested her head back on the pillow and looked up into the white ceiling. Yes I'm happy she whispered quietly to herself because you may be miles away but you are always right beside me. Sarai knew anyone listening to their conversation or reading her thoughts would think they had just met. The truth was it had always been like this with them.

'You got something planned for your guest tomorrow?' Cephas asked.

'Nothing really. I shall see what happens when I wake up.'

'You are a mystery.'

'Yeah, look who's talking,' she giggled.

'I'll tell you about it when I get back.'

'I know you would.'

Glyfada. Horns blared in the night as we threaded a

path through the evening crowd and traffic to the restaurant. Fast cars pulled up side by side and then accelerated leaving behind tread marks from their screeching tires as they posed for the crowds. Four-wheeled merchandise was up for display and the crowd was feeding upon it in a frenzy. I watched like everyone else reminded of my own youth. Once upon a time that had been me, a racer, picaresque, giving in to the glitz and glamour that came with that world. It was my first car and I needed to see what it could do. I left a nightclub one evening with friends and tore off at a blinding speed with my friend's car right beside mine keeping up in the narrow terrain. I don't know how we did it but for whatever reason unbeknown to man we both decided not to lift off the gas pedal. Eventually we had been surrounded by the Police and pulled over for speeding. It had been a moment of madness and we had answered its calling by all the forces of nature available at the time. Youth, arrogance and sheer energy were difficult to avoid. However even in those times wisdom prevailed as we got out of the cars and apologized emphatically. Although the Police were extremely upset with what they had seen, they eventually succumbed to the humility of the drivers.

I watched as a silver Mercedes and blue BMW went at one another on the street believing it was anyone's guess where the drivers would end up that night. The amazing observation to be garnered from what was happening was what God had in store for all of mankind. I had been wild back then living to the whims of a wisdom blinded by arrogance, youth and energy controlled by the forces of the world. Yet God had been present making sure that whatever happened I was destined to be acquitted to fulfill what had been written. The humility shown that late night by my friend and I may have appeared to many as a coincidence, some rare good fortune on our part to escape the restraints of the law. However on reflection I knew that there was no luck where the spiritual world was concerned. God controlled it all making sure that his own were always going to fulfill the journey that had been set before them. It was no coincidence that I wasn't in an accident. It was just the spiritual world doing what it did best and obeying the will of its master.

We filed past the crowd as we peeked into the restaurants to see which would do for that evening. I hoped for something light because it was times like this that I dreaded the opportune of my position. One gained unnecessary pounds trying to keep up with the pressures of a good life.

'I was out of it yesterday,' Charles said beside me.

'I think we all were,' I assured him. These were the after effects of opening your soul out to strangers. You woke up the next day asking yourself why and hoping that you won't see sympathy in other's eyes. I could understand what my friend was feeling and responded accordingly.

'I bet you have a car like those we saw back in London. I think it is all for show. Personally I would prefer a yacht. I'm not begrudging anyone, still it just isn't me,' he said.

'I like cars, I can't hide this even if I wanted to,' I replied. People were different but the truth was I couldn't tell what reaction my friend would have if he were presented with one of the beautiful cars on display. Man made law made us believe that we had to choose our paths in wealth, as some things appeared to be correct before others. I could not read my friends mind still there was no doubting the subtle hints of this judgment in his voice. Unfortunately none of us was free from vanity. We all basked in it whether it was for righteous reasons or otherwise. God did not stop us from being wealthy. He did not say to those that believed in him that they must suffer. However his word guided us to ensure that our souls were not bound by wealth. No one could hide from a craving neither could they use it as an excuse. We just had to live our lives and hope that before our maker we did so correctly.

'So you didn't answer my question, do you have something like this?' Charles asked.

'I do and love it. Got it from Germany too,' I said.

'Well I guess buying from mainland Europe is the best. Did you order it?'

'I did. Took six months too. I enjoyed the waiting as it gave me time to dream of the places that I would visit with it.'

He shook his head and smiled. Maybe I had given my friend back some of the dignity he felt he had lost. I had exposed a lust and in that instant he felt that he was the better man with the right choices.

'Men and their toys, why do we do it?' he said.

'For me I know I love cars. I always have and can't help myself,' I responded. I couldn't hide. I would be deceiving myself and no one else.

'I've got an idea of where we should go to tonight. I discovered it the other day when you guys weren't around. I think the group would like it,' he said changing the subject as we crossed the tramline and moved into the streets that were lined with restaurants. We all moved on eventually. It did not matter how we felt about anything or anyone time defeated us all and overcame our thoughts. My friend was wise to this. Dwelling on the human lust for the simpler things in life was fruitless. Vanity burnt within all veins. He knew this and decided that it was pointless, there were far more important things to think of than this.

'We are losing you my friends, slow down,' Ramon

goaded. He had been talking to others in our group and caught up to Charles and I.

'Charles is choosing for us tonight,' I said.

'Good but be aware that the boys have said they would like to have a three course meal. Most people say they're starving,' he grinned.

'Pity.' There goes my hope of holding back I thought. It looked like I'd have to take on the role of pariah once more. It was almost nine and I could not see myself having three rounds of a hefty meal. I knew most wouldn't agree with my thoughts still they didn't have to lie at night wondering about indigestion.

'You shouldn't look so worried you barely had anything to eat earlier on my friend.' What's with you and food anyway?' Charles added.

'In China it was the same, he would disappear on some days and I'd wonder why he couldn't join us for lunch,' Ramon said as we filed into the Greek restaurant.

The waitress came to my rescue just as I was thinking of something to say. She wanted to know the number of people in our group and Ramon and Charles were distracted. Perhaps they would remember and return to me eventually but for now I felt safe and away from their questions. I don't know how I had survived for so long keeping my eating habits away from them. It hadn't been easy in China as well but I had managed. There were those days when my personal pledge to the Lord came into effect. It was private and a promise that I did not wish to share with others. It wasn't because I did not feel they could understand, I just couldn't think of a reason to explain myself.

As our pretty waitress politely took our orders and distracted my friends I breathed a sigh of relief and let myself enjoy the evening.

Mougins. Rain was the last thing on anyone's mind in this part of the world. Mougins boasted excellent weather most times of the year so it was no doubt a strange sound listening to the raindrops pearl off the large windows in the patio. The women sat in the front room as they talked.

'Why the Middle East and Bahrain of all places?' Hailey asked as she got into her stride.

'Don't knock it my dear, you know their currency is very powerful and besides they host one of the best Formula One tracks.'

'I'm just curious that's all. I mean as far as I'm concerned you were doing well in London, there was no need to move all that way. Besides women don't have it easy in that part of the world,' she continued crossing her legs. Except for today they hadn't missed out on a day by the pool. It rained but temperatures remained high allowing her to wear jeans shorts and a blouse. Her recorder was always on now. Every moment counted as they moved into the second week of Sarai's story.

'I never thought about it, I just wanted to build a name for myself and that was what was on offer,' Sarai said.

'There was nothing else in Europe or anywhere else?'

'There could have been but I'd had these guys as clients for a while it just felt like the natural choice.'

'So what happened there? How did it affect your life?'

'For one thing, the humidity over there surpasses anywhere I'd been to before. But seriously are you sure this is something you need to add to your article, I mean it was all work and no play over there,' Sarai responded.

'Still though it was a different perspective to what

you had known before. I'm not searching for the day to day living but more of what went on in your mind during your time there,' Hailey urged.

Sarai lifted her legs unto the sofa bending them underneath her as her long white summer dress fell over her knees. The ball was in her court. She could say anything that she wanted but it was harder making up something than remembering what had really happened over there. Bahrain had been the nidus for change in her life. One night in particular was harder than the many she had spent over there. It was her birthday and she was lonely. She had lain in the bath for longer than she could imagine eventually falling asleep and waking up in a fright. I want things to be different she had thought. I'm rich but unhappy. It was a new experience turning thirty. It was difficult not being sentimental when every friend you knew was a thousand miles away. She had been very quiet that day in the office. People had asked if she was unwell and she had murmured in return unsure of what she said.

She had climbed into bed after the bath and thrown the covers all the way over her head wishing to hide herself from the world and her woes. I should be with someone she thought. I should be with the man of my dreams and be happy with the wealth from my hard work yet this is what I have. Even the calls she had received earlier on in the day from family and friends could not console her. She needed things to be different to change urgently as she was sinking. These were not the kind of memories that one wished to bring up from the past but she had made a promise to tell her story as it was.

'Where things really that bad, I mean why though? This is the job you wanted?' Hailey asked.

'It was but I wanted someone in my life at that time. I don't know why that particular day was different.'

'Wait a minute I thought you said you met your husband when you were thirty.'

'I did but it was after this incident.'

'So you can say your prayers were answered.'

'You sound like someone I know,' Sarai smiled. 'That's the kind of response I expect from Cephas.'

'Was he in Bahrain?'

'Not while I was there. He had been there earlier on in his career.'

Hailey sat up in her chair now attentive at what her host was saying.

'Are you telling me that your husband also worked in Bahrain at one time in his career?'

'I'm saying that he was in Bahrain a while back before I got there. He worked close by.'

'What a coincidence.' Hailey said and blew a whistle. Sarai had never stopped adding the spiritual element of her marriage to this article. She had never understood why or questioned this spiritual haven that Sarai shared with her husband. Of all the countries in the world for that matter, Bahrain was a rarity. Perhaps she was letting her imagination run wild and adding small numbers to get millions. The warning signs were there. I have to stay focused on what matters to my readers. It's simple and I won't complicate it with the mystery that surrounds this couple.

'Should we do something different, I can turn off the recorder for a while,' Hailey said. It was a good time to change the topic and turn the tables to her favour. The light rain had stopped outside and the refulgent light of the sun was again coming through the windows. The grass would be fresh and easy to walk on. It was therapeutic walking barefooted on it. And therapy was probably what she needed to seek solace from this world she found herself in.

'My husband found his inheritance in Saudi,'

Sarai's next words were so far away she could have been a million miles from the room. 'He knew me at least five years before we met in person, before I ever knew he existed.'

'What? What are you saying? Did he have your photograph? Did he know your parents, a friend, how could he know you?' Hailey asked. I never wanted this she thought. I want her to stop directing my interview in this direction. I want us to talk about the ordinary things, the simple things that sell magazines. Where is this headed for?

'I was my husband's bride in spirit before I was his wife in reality.'

The lounge was sinking before Hailey's eyes as she absorbed the words.

'There are no coincidences in the spiritual world, what is, was meant to be to serve a higher purpose.'

'You really believe this?' she asked astonished.

'I have no choice but to do so, the evidence is overwhelming,' Sarai replied.

'Do I serve a greater purpose?' she asked almost amused at what her host was implying.

'Why did you become a writer Hailey?' Sarai asked. She could see that the girl was fighting her with everything she had.

'Because that is the profession I loved more than all others,' she answered without thought.

'Well many people love many different professions but never fulfill their aspirations. They settle for less or pursue something else eventually in life. How come you stuck to yours?'

'I'd say people are different, when I like something that is what I'm going to do no matter what happens. I'd rather die than give up my dream,' she said.

'Funny you should say that, that's how I was before I got to Bahrain. It felt as though if I never went there

139

then I'd never fulfill my own dreams,' Sarai said.

'Well then I guess we are alike.'

'Which brings me to my next point. What is intriguing is that out of all the writers in your firm it had to be you to write my story,' Sarai said.

'How do you mean?' Hailey said. I don't want her to say it but I'd give her a chance she thought, somewhere along the line she'd see its all a coincidence.

'In life we are all walking towards the purpose we serve some of us would see it in this life others won't,' Sarai replied, standing up and walking towards the patio doors. She pulled aside the blinds and opened the door letting the fresh air from the rain into the room. With the curtains now aside the light from the sun immediately brightened the room.

'My husband saw his long before he met me. He couldn't avoid it. The spiritual world is not fiction; it is real, within us, around us and in what we feel. It can be heavenly if we give our hearts to God and let him control this journey for us. One thing is for certain, we all get there eventually whether we like it or not.'

'I'm trying to understand what you are saying but it just doesn't make any of sense.'

'The spiritual world is not logical. It is not rational bounded by our wisdom and understanding. To get it you must have faith.'

'What if you don't? What if you do not believe? What if you have never had a reason to.'

'Then start by how you feel.'

'I feel okay. How does that change anything? Unless I am ill I feel okay.'

'But you are curious?' Sarai said as she leaned on the headrest of the sofa and looked at Hailey in the other chair.

'Well part of me is puzzled at what you mean and

the other part is saying maybe there is something she is not telling me. In the meantime the rational in me is screaming at me to get back to the story I want to write.'

'Okay let's try something else. Would you have thought you would be here today writing an article all those years ago when you were still in college in China?'

'No,' Hailey paused. 'I could have wished it but never imagined it to be like this.'

'In the spiritual world you don't get to imagine, you get to see it for real.'

'How is that even possible?'

'I return to my earlier question to you, how did you know you would become a writer in spite of the hardship it took to become one from your background. How come you were so certain of this?' Sarai asked.

'I just knew it, felt it, believed it and wanted it more than anything in the world.'

'My dear girl that is what faith is about. We feel it, believe it and want it to be as we desire more than anything in the world. If we have these attributes we can move mountains and see a whole new world. Faith comes from understanding our own world and how we lead our lives. Faith is belief in our dreams and if we see this happen out of nothing then we can understand that God makes the impossible possible. There is no rational in a dream, it just is. However it can serve as a purpose, a desire, a wish and a hope from nothing. Faith in God is belief in what we do not see and agreeing that he made us. It's just what you feel and has no rational. When you get past this stage in your faith then maybe you can start having the other experiences. I would even go as far as to say that some of us have these experiences but tell ourselves they aren't real because we want to stick to the rational and logic of our world. What's foremost on our minds is meeting the task that our world has set out for us. It's a pattern we are very reluctant to break from, a security in a rational that we can all explain. In a sense this rational protects us from the faithful and from what God desires of us.'

Hailey said nothing this time. Her gaze had moved from Sarai to the open doors and then beyond into the garden and further. She was in Yong Ding. She was Hsu again running home from school with her books in the little flowery rucksack on her small back. There was no thought in her mind but the rice dish she expected from her Mum at supper. Then she was on the wooden dining table drawing and making a mess. Soon she was penciling what she thought was her first article. An essay about the elephant she had seen when the travelers had passed her village. She had added parts to that story. After all it was hers she could make it what it was for it was make belief. Yet even at that age she was willing to write something, make a story out of nothing. Was it the village or the simple surroundings that made her so determined to succeed? Why was it so important that she became a writer? No one could tell, there was no rational thought to this just a calling, a wish and desire that she had for the profession. Was Sarai right? Was this what people meant by having faith in a God they had never seen? Did he call to them as her dream had of becoming a writer? Did he give them a purpose and reason to believe in him as her dream had? Did he make them warm and hopeful in a better time to come as her dream had?

'How can you be so certain?' she asked hoarsely. Time had elapsed so rapidly since she heard her own voice that it sounded strange and hollow.

'How can you be so certain?' she asked again regaining some of level of composure as she reached for her glass of water. What was happening to her?

'I'm as certain as you were of becoming a writer.'

'I won't win this argument would I?' Hailey said also getting up from the sofa and walking through the room.

'There is nothing to win or lose. And we are not arguing, I'm just stating an observation.' Sarai replied.

'And I'm left asking myself why my thoughts are suddenly in turmoil and why I have to reflect back to a life in China that feels like a million miles away.'

Sarai said nothing. We coped with our own personal struggles in different ways. A few years ago when she headed out to Bahrain she wasn't as composed as she was now. Maybe in the office environment everyone saw her as this accomplished and successful businesswoman. On the other hand her social life always made her wonder if that success had come at a steep price. The feeling was always there, lurking beneath the surface when she saw a couple in a restaurant or families boarding a flight. She'd been to many places still there was emptiness, a space that needed to be filled. It had always been a tug of war between her career and other aspects in her life.

'I wasn't always this certain. I had my moments,' she encouraged the girl. 'There were times..' That night had been harsh. She had cried alone in the hotel room. She opened a bottle of wine and celebrated with the stars. She even contemplated getting in touch with Jonathan and giving into his demands. Why did she have to be so fussy, after all he had what any girl could have asked for. Yet she just knew that he wasn't whom she wanted. She was free spirited and no one should have to dictate to her how her life would be led. Who she would find would be the man she would spend the rest of her life with. There could be no doubts and whether it took many years or longer she would have to

143

wait.

'I gave up on myself at one time. As successful as I was I was very unhappy,' she said.

'Can one be this way. I mean I think about the poverty in the village I grew up in and believe that if I am successful today then what could make me unhappy,' Hailey said as she stretched her arms and settled back into the sofa. Sarai's revelation had given her back some composure. 'I mean if I am better off than most of those poor people out there why would I be sad?'

'In the past I would have agreed with your logic but when you get to that point in your life it makes so much sense. The prize is not so rewarding as one would expect. The old cliché *it is not money that makes one happy* haunts you.'

'Why though there is so much to do and see in this large world of ours. I mean we would always find someone out there that was meant for us, in the mean time there is no harm enjoying ourselves.'

'That's how we start but then for no reason known to us our world seems a lot smaller when all the materialistic things we desire seem attainable. We want more and we become impatient. We are not so objective.'

'But if you know what you just described in the spiritual world as you call it then you should have known that you'll find that person some day,' Hailey said crossing her legs and looking enquiringly at Sarai.

'That's the thing Hailey. I had to get to this place before I could find this spiritual world. You do not discover this place when your life is full of all those plans and ambitions. You discover it when you have surpassed all those things.'

'So you are saying in order to understand this spiritual world one has to get past their worldly desires.'

'Something like that, well in my case any way. I know if I did not accomplish all that I wanted in life there would always be this feeling within me to do so. When I finally got to Bahrain I discovered how empty my life had become in my ambition.'

'But you are so pretty and accomplished, it's hard to tell that you ever felt this way.'

'Did you know that even the queen of England has to wash her hands after using the toilet?' Sarai smiled. 'In other words what I'm saying is that we all have to abide by the laws of the universe. No one is exempt from learning about those things that matter to us, to our happiness.'

'Would you change anything? I mean if you could do things all over again would you seek your happiness before you sought your career?' Hailey asked.

'Well I won't because I don't think I would be here today with the happiness I have now. Sometimes the hard times we face in life enable us appreciate the good times even more.'

Hailey folded her hands as she listened to Sarai. There were people she admired in her own life whom she would have wanted to be like. Perhaps Sarai was one of those people but she was curious as to how she had embraced this spiritual world as she called it for all the reasons she had just mentioned.

'Why the spiritual world though? What made you want to know God more?'

Sarai did not answer immediately. If Cephas was here she would have let him answer this question for her. He was good at talking about this world better than her. It was easy for people to say one had found religion, the truth was religion did find all of us or those of us that it was meant to. She hadn't gone out of her way in search for the spiritual world, it had gone out of its way to find her. After Bahrain she had returned to London wiser and hopeful for change. Yet in spite of everything she hadn't searched for any one. It had just been a case of being expectant that someone out there was looking for her. She began having this case of déjà vu everywhere she went to. She would be somewhere and believe that she had been there before with someone. The amazing thing was what she was seeing had not happened yet. She just felt it would with the same certainty that her life had succeeded in the business world. Cafes in London began to take a new meaning to her life. Even going to theatre with friends was a different experience to what it had been before. She was glowing most of the time as if someone was watching. People had asked questions wanting to know why the change but she could tell them nothing. She didn't know why she felt this way. It was just there all the time and then the party and then Cephas.

'I wish I could tell you it was one particular thing or incident in my life but it was many things as if they all came together at once.'

Maybe one day she would be able to explain what had happened. You didn't search for the spiritual world, it gave you a yearning and then it was there, suddenly becoming a part of you before you knew what had happened.

Dawn, Glyfada. The pain maudlin, the grip strangling, the cry brazen, the body now moribund; He was here. Putting two and two together in spirit never amounted to anything. Following the path of the Lord meant one had to leave one's plans on the shelf and follow the path laid before you. I felt the summons and obliged. It was Cephas's turn and I watched silently from my world. He had taking over. The body now bespangled and in another world, Cephas emerged slowly. My

146

bleat was a deafening noise very far away in a place called human reality, as places switched, spirit for man. Then the body began to turn, Cephas forcing it to see what he was about to receive.

It was an iridescent glow in the sky. There were a myriad of colours, their radiance almost a breath taking girasol and then I saw them. In the sky were pin-like objects, figurines, very many of them hardly distinguishable in the colours. I watched dazzled by what was before me. And then it happened. A large hand, Cephas's, not mine, for it couldn't have been in this world extracted itself from the body and opened beneath the sky. The first figurine fell into the hand and then there was a second and finally a third and then it was over as if nothing had ever happened, the hand and the figurines disappearing into the spiritual world as if they had never been. The body began to respond as its vital organs took back their place, leaving me in a groggy muddle. The window was shut and Cephas but a thought. It had happened quickly during the early hours of the morning as all of my visions before this. It was another timeless mystery that would require faith in the Lord, the *revealer of secrets* to decipher it. I had to be patient if I was to understand what this meant. It was no more my story it was Cephas's, nescience in human flesh replaced by the purity and majority of the spirit.

Chapter Eight

March, several months earlier, Shenzhen China; It was a hot Wednesday afternoon in the streets of Shenzhen and I could hear my Chinese colleague's thoughts as though they were mine. He was staring at me and shaking his head in disbelief and I could have sworn I heard him utter the word fool. My time in China had let me understand the value of food. Poverty roamed certain parts of the country making a bowl of soup a very important meal to pass by. I was the newcomer that had traveled from England without a respect for this custom. In my colleague's eyes I was no denizen. I lacked what it took to walk the path and withhold the virtues of the company.

There was nothing I could do about this, it was just bad timing. It was unfortunate that of all the days in the week this was the one he had chosen to invite us all to lunch and I was the bad sheep in the fold that had declined.

'What is so important that you have to go back to your room?' Ramon asked as we all walked in the direction of the restaurant.

'I just have to make a phone call. It's the best time at the moment, you know given the time difference,' I replied avoiding any eye contact.

'Well then so be it but today we try the Indian restaurant, your loss my friend,' he said. I could hear the disappointment in his voice and knew I would not live this down in future. I could feel the invisible claws from our group reaching out and strangling my neck but there was nothing I could do.

'You can walk with Abi, I think she is also walking back to the hotel,' he rebuked as I extracted myself from the group and began the long walk back to my room. Abi was only a few yards ahead of me and I caught up to her in no time.

'We are having better weather today,' I made light conversation as I drew closer and walked beside her.

'We are indeed, much better than that over the weekend. Have you recovered?' She asked smiling. She was Syrian and knew very few people in the group but I was one of the few men apart from others from the Middle East that she talked to.

'I have,' I said. 'Not only from the rain but also from the lesson about Chairman Mao.' She referred to the day out we had taken over the weekend. The company had arranged for us to visit one of the famous cultural villages and I had been given a lesson in Chinese history. I visited one of the small stores in the village where the idea was to learn about Chairman Mao and eventually purchase his book. This hadn't gone so well for me until I had been rescued by Abi.

'That woman in the store was driving me insane.'

'She just wanted you to understand their culture, their history,' Abi offered benignly.

'Well I already had a bellyful, luckily you arrived in time.'

We went through the security gates that led out of the main office complex and headed towards the rooms.

'You are walking alone today where is the man I always see you with?' I asked.

'Oh you mean Ameer. He had to change some money so he left with the bus into town,' she replied. 'And you why aren't you at lunch?'

I paused before answering.

'You are fasting right, that is okay. I do too sometimes and I also have the same expression on my face when I am thinking of an answer to give others,' she said.

I was quiet for a while. I had been doing this for so many years and this was the first time that someone had

149

beaten me to an excuse. Only it wasn't an excuse.

'You are right I am fasting. But you caught me unawares usually I don't like to tell anyone because of the ridicule that comes with it. It's not something I like discussing with people especially those that do not understand. They turn to ask a lot of questions and it's not what you need when you are fasting,' I said.

'That is the difference between the West and the Middle East. In Syria you tell someone you are fasting and it is taken as normal. But I know what you are going through. I studied in the University of London and it wasn't easy for me. At first it was easy when I knew no one because people were less comfortable with asking me direct questions but as I began making friends, well, you know the rest. As you are probably aware we have a period in the Islamic calendar when we do fast and believe me during this time it is tough for any of us living in a Western society,' she said.

We then parted ways and I disappeared to my room to burn the lunch hour as I avoided questions from my friends. It was my ritual, my time with the Lord and it was an oath that I hoped would never be broken irrespective of my environment.

Glyfada. As the taxi cut through Nimfon Square and headed for Evagelistrias, I began to feel confident in my growing knowledge of the city. Vouliagmenis Avenue would be next and then the office. I was alone in the cab unworried by the cost. It changed everyday and this did not matter. There were more pressing matters at hand. We sped past the church on Evagelistrias and I looked at the monolith that was a few yards in front of it. I was thankful for the silence. Today was different and I needed my thoughts just to myself. It was the Lords day again in my weekly calendar. It was sacrosanct. It was a dedication, a promise that I had made almost six years earlier. I would fast once, one day in the week for the rest of my life. It was a personal Sabbath to the Lord to thank him for everything, my health, my visions and life. On this day I needed peace, time dedicated to the Lord regardless of what else was happening around me. Through God's strength this promise had been fulfilled and I had managed to keep my vow for six years.

It hadn't been easy. Work had its requirements. There were distractions as I was pulled in different directions. No day was best. No doubt I believed that my colleagues thought I was weird. For several days in the week I would go out with them to lunch, be the social tyrant and then suddenly from nowhere I would have all these excuses why I had missed breakfast or why I wasn't hungry at lunch. I could have told them that I was fasting but then the questions would follow. How could anyone like me fast? I was a regular guy like everyone else, sociable maybe to an extent that it took most by surprise when I stood up for my spiritual beliefs. But what had the Lord said? *How could the spiritual man know of the world unless he had been in the world*? It became even more difficult when clients were concerned. Taking them out to lunch was no small matter. I could hear my pledge - *I would never fail to fast on one day of the week*, it is for the *cleansing of my soul and a dedication to you Father*. It was so little to give back to one so mighty considering everything that I received in return.

The afternoon light filtered though the drapes in the blue walled room. There was silence as all the men in it focused on the screens before them. It was the countdown to the end of the day, the morning and afternoon sessions of our seminar now over. I scanned through the mail in my inbox. There was mail from family and some from friends. They seemed so far away from where I was or the world I inhabited on my Sabbath. God had granted me another vision, the figurine were another mystery to interpret. And I was lost trying to understand what all these visions meant. I quickly responded to some work mail and then glanced at the small digital clock at the base of the screen. It was already five and another prayer was required in his special day of fasting, only this time it would be the last as part of my fasting. I had made it through another successful day. My friends were as puzzled as they had been in China yet I was happy I had kept my promise.

The small tiles on the floor were violet; those on the walls a tad closer to burgundy and I knelt down on the floor of the small bathroom. There were noises outside as people walked in the corridors. I could hear them still I retained only one voice in my head, that of the Lord's. It was the dedication; the gratefulness of one who could not believe the miracles that God had shown him. I said my prayers quietly and stood up feeling my weak body reenergized. Every week I had kept this promise and God had been kind to me, allowing me the strength to go the distance during the day. Today I had been successful in more ways than one and after another long day at work I had managed to evade the direct inquisition of my colleagues. My fasting was private and not hubris to be portrayed before others. It was submission, humility and gratitude before the Lord for all things in my life and those of others close to me.

The dogs barked from the kerbside as we took to the back streets that led to our hotel. The group commented and I was silent.

'In China you would be lunch,' I heard Ramon say to the dog as we went past and everyone laughed. I paid no attention. I was again staring past the gates and the gardens into the mansions, my thoughts a million miles away from my friends. Today I would not be drawn into a fracas. My eyes followed the line of trees at the side of the road, my next point of call would be the local store where I would buy a packet of biscuits and something to drink. I would break this fast quietly in my room and alone with God. Another day had passed and God had again allowed me the strength to reach my goal and beyond.

Sarai walked out of Matalans with the bags hitting her knees as she avoided the flow of people on Oxford Street. The Christmas party loomed in the distance as December descended upon them, it was her first in years. She never attended them but this year was different because she was one of the important guests on the list. People wanted to please her because she owned the largest account in the Middle East. She walked with long strides crossing the busy street and cutting into Bond Street. Soon she was in one of the other fashion houses. I've lost nothing of what I had she told herself. I still know these streets like I've never been away. Soon she was choosing a bag to go with her embroidery. I've got to look my best keep my reputation intact. As her hands caressed the soft fabric of the bags she could see the shop assistant by the counter watching her like a predator to its prey. Soon she was beside her with a jovial smile.

'Some of our best are not even on display yet. Would you like to have a peek before anyone does?' she asked.

Sarai, looked at the girl. She was young but had the wisdom of one that had been in the trade for years. She had priced her out of the other three customers in the shop. She had chosen the right words, making things personal was one way to get your customer to notice. You could not argue with the girl's wisdom and she was curious.

'Why don't I?' she responded.

The girl immediately disappeared like a fleeting shadow in the night to reappear carrying a couple of bags. One was black, medium sized with two buckles in the front. It was of soft leather with the knitting on the handle showing that it had been handcrafted. It was chic in its own way. The other was a lighter colour, a faint purple and smaller purse. It was the kind of bag you carried around if you were going to a ball. She looked at both allowing the pupils of her eyes to grow and dance in the pleasure of holding each by her side.

'I'll take both, give me a good price.'

The girl was delighted. The madam of the store would be pleased. She had worked on her lines well. She had discovered that to close a sale one had to be at the right place at the right time and with some luck it could be your day. Today was hers and she would get the commission.

Five minutes later Sarai was out of the shop and back in the busy street. Shoes and a new coat were the last things remaining on her list. If she carried on this way she won't be able to make it all the way back to where she had parked. However, it was this weekend or never. She was running out of days to allocate for shopping before the party. This was her last. There was no more time left as she was fully booked for the rest of the week and into the next. The party was to be held on the following Wednesday and there just wasn't any more time left. Her hair wasn't a problem, she'd wear it long at its full shoulder length, maybe get it washed and enriched but leave it as it was. There was an expensive necklace she liked in her drawers that would have to do, as she could not spend the rest of the afternoon looking for one. It had a watch and earrings to match that complemented it. It was something that lay on her dressing table, something tried on those boring days when one dreamed of the occasion but never worn. It felt right to do so now.

The vestibule was much quieter than the busy streets outside. It had taken her half an hour to cut through the back streets and head back to her apartment in Marylebone. She couldn't argue the fact that driving had been a bad idea still the car had been parked at her Mums for over two months. She had picked it up and driven from Epsom to Piccadilly. There was no time to park it at her place and then head on down to the tube. Besides she had missed it.

Sarai dropped the bags in the carpeted hallway as she reached into her handbag for the keys to the second entrance. Soon she was opening her front door and walking into the furnished three-bedroom apartment. She took off her coat, climbing out of boots in the process and immediately walked into the bathroom to run a bath. There was nothing better than warm water to soothe the aches from tired legs. She poured herself a glass of water and before long she was lying in the bath with her eyes closed and counting herself lucky for not having to shop daily as she had done that day. She heard the slight rumble from her stomach and realized that she hadn't eaten anything since breakfast. How time flew. If only she could get out of this bath to a warm meal she would have had the perfect day. There was barely anything in the house. She'd have to settle for noodles. There were some in the cupboard somewhere and bread. It would have to be something light because she was tired. If her Mum had her way she would have had her stay at their home. They complained about how long it had been since she was home. They wanted more time with their daughter. She wanted more time with them too but things became a little difficult when their friends popped round. They did not want to hear just about her success they wanted to hear about family, children and all the other things that all parents talked about. She had very little to offer there. She had given up trying to make excuses, now she simple avoided the questions. If only they knew it wasn't by choice but just the way things were. If she was fussy it was because she never wanted to go through a divorce or be unhappily married. Too much time was lost and considered an acceptable loss while people moved from one relationship to the next. It would be different with her. If ever she got divorced it won't be because she never waited for the right person. Things would have to be taken out of her hands.

Another rumbling sound from her stomach was the cue to get out of the bath. She climbed into her bathrobe and stared at her complexion in the mirror. Maybe I've lost a little weight she thought. Still though, I can survive for now without Mum's cooking. Perhaps she would be a mum one day herself and someone would have to look to her cooking. It certainly won't be just noodles, she thought. It would have to be something more. The calamari she had eaten two nights before in the French restaurant in Chelsea had hit the spot. These would be the type of meals she would learn to make in her home. If all failed she could always order Chinese there was no point in worrying about what wasn't there, she grinned and walked into her kitchen.

Mougins. The light calamari in augratin had evoked the past. Her French had improved significantly allowing her to use just the right words, *mot juste* for their order. Now she took in the pargeted walls. They were enshrouded in mosaic stone that hypnotized the customer into ordering blindly. The ardent designer had

156

added simonized alloy wheels buried in the walls to advertise the latest brand of manufacturers. With the music seguing in the background you practically offered your hand to the palmist hoping your good fortune would bring you back to this place time and again. Sarai managed to pull herself back from where ever the walls had taken her to the present.

'It was necessary to hear about London, about the time you returned from Bahrain,' Hailey said from the other side of the table.

Sarai admired the acuity of the girl. She was focused as ever keeping up with a story that traveled through parallels. She had tried to be consistent, build it gradually so that the flow would dictate the sequence of activities until the present. Still it was difficult. Every question seemed to unveil a new emotion and she was left remembering, thinking backwards and forwards in time.

'I made a note to ask you this today, we left one part of your story unfinished. I think you asked Cephas as part of his prophesy how many children did he think you would have. Did he ever answer?' Hailey asked. You acceded to this she thought. Do not blame me for dragging it up.

'He did.'

She was back in the bedroom. His touch gentle as they talked, shared what he knew and what she wanted to know.

'Three,' Cephas said.

'What do you mean three?' Sarai answered.

'In answer to your question of how many children you think we are going to have, my answer is three.'

'And you know this how?'

'You asked and I answered does it matter how I know?' he said, his expression remained the same staring at the blank television screen without once

157

turning to look at her.

'Any specifics prophet while you are at it because I'm lying here perplexed. Do I have a say in the matter?'

'Well it can't happen without you if that is what you are asking and naturally you do have a say in the matter.'

'Thank you because it would be my body and I'd like to think that I can decide too.'

'I'm not talking about that, this is not determined by me. I'm just saying that when the time comes three would be what we would both want and that is what we would get.'

Sarah turned over in bed and lay on her chest, resting her elbow on the bed as she cocked her head to one side in her fisted palm.

'Why do I get the feeling that you are leaving out some details here,' she asked.

'Three isn't enough?' Cephas scoffed. His expression was that of a man experiencing a heart attack as he moved his hand to his chest in bewilderment.

'I don't need your sarcasm, wise guy, just tell me why you are withholding something from me.'

'I like that look on your face when you are angry,' he teased.

'I'm not laughing or finding this remotely funny, I do want to know what you mean,' she said and sighed. Men never seemed to change, she thought. They opened up to you and just when you thought you were getting close to them they showed this insensitive side to them that irritated one.

'Two boys and a girl that's all I know.' Cephas said. Perhaps she was upset with him but sometimes he liked seeing that expression on her face. He just couldn't help himself.

Sarai lay back in bed and played with her thumbs on her chest. He had given her something to think about and she wondered whether what he said would come to pass. Cephas had said many things before but telling her this was like opening a whole new portal into another galaxy.

'I won't ask you any more questions tonight, not that I don't want to but I am afraid of what you would tell me.'

'I have told you before that I have nothing to hide. You are privy to my visions. If anyone must know what goes on then its you.'

'How long have you known this?' she said and bit her bottom lip.

'About seven years.'

She had been scared to say more after this. It was already too much to imagine, to conceive was possible. How could he know so much about something that hadn't happened? The detail was overwhelming.

'Three children, he simply mentioned this casually as you say?' Hailey asked.

'Yes.'

The women were silent for a short while as the wine was opened for them and their waiter poured some into Sarai's glass. She had ordered an aperitif, from Maison Ruinart – a Brut Blanc de Blancs. It was a fine white wine that she knew would certainly hit the right spots with langouste to come. For whatever reason she had chosen Le Suquet as the site to visit and using their time wisely there was no harm in getting some fresh supplies from the popular Marche Ferville. The irony to what was going on was that as she put the pieces together of her isolated past and her time with Cephas she realized for the first time that the French restaurant she had visited so many years before shared the same name as Le Suquet. No doubt Hailey would say it was a coincidence. She couldn't argue with that herself but there were those subtle clues, Cephas had said when you would see them you would know. He said they were like candles in a dark cave. They came alight to pave a path for one to discover new corridors. He said we chose to ignore them because we did not want to believe that in all our wisdom we could be directed by something other than ourselves. There was resistance within her even now as she recognized the name. She couldn't remember exactly why she had been to the French restaurant in London. Perhaps a change of scenery was necessary for her clients from the Middle East. They were taken in by the big spending in football, as wealthy entrepreneurs flocked the market buying large clubs and becoming wealthier by the returns. The men wanted to go by Chelsea driven by money and riches and she had elected to take them to Le Suquet for lunch. She thought of adding this little detail to Hailey and then changed her mind. The girl was already in doubt of her sanity since the morning before. There was no point in making things weird than they already were.

'And that's what you have now?' Hailey asked as the waiter withdrew unobtrusively.

'I do, two boys and a girl,' Sarai said as she seeped some of the wine.

'But how could he know, how is that possible?'

'That's what I've been asking myself all these years. If am being honest I gave up a while back. Now I accept that he knows of those things that I don't and I just have to accept this.'

'You're a strong woman to live with somebody like that.'

'You should tell him this,' Sarai smiled. 'He says that they are visions that he receives from God. There is no predefined time when he is expected to have one and they are not interpreted by him but by God.'

'Is this what he meant by he knew you before you met him?'

'Something like that, he could describe what I would look like what I did. You have to know that it took a while before I could get this out of him. We had known each other for a few months before he told me this.'

'How did this vision happen and how was he able to interpret it?'

'It's not so simple to explain or even to understand. I mean he says a vision is like a dream only you are wide awake knowing that you can come out of it at anytime. He says the things you see and feel are real as if you are really there, present.'

'And the interpretations, how does he know that this is correct?'

'He says a prophesy is only partly true until the real thing happens. He says you are asked to test all things and make sure it isn't by your imagination. If it is by God then it would be impossible to understand or refute. You will accept it because God gives you that understanding and knowledge. He says it is faith and you would have grace.'

'Have you had these visions before?'

'I dream but nothing like this. Perhaps now that I know of them and the ways he has shown me to see the clues in the little things that are around us, I am able to tell that there is a purpose for all things.'

It was Hailey's turn to have a seep of wine as she placed her fork and knife with deliberate care on the table and reached for her napkin. The food was delicious but the conversation kept her away from reality. She had wined and dined in excellent restaurants on 17th Street close to 5th Avenue. She considered herself a connoisseur of fine cuisine. Come to think of it she wasn't a bad chef herself still what Sarai was serving in this article made one stop in mid stride and think.

'But you can still have four children, I mean it is not impossible for you not to?' She asked. One could not refute that possibility, surely?

'It makes a lot of sense until you ask yourself how come I've had two boys and a girl and not three girls or even three boys or any other likely combination different from what he said. The point is I don't want any more kids not because of what he said but just because I don't. I'm content, we are content still why did the three we have turn out as he said.'

'You make a tough case there.'

'I don't its just what it is. I'm the one living the life and I can tell now that it's a whole new world from the one I had before. My past was flaked with this sense of emptiness as if I did things because I was meant to but did not know why. Today it is different as I have a peace that I cannot explain because I just seem to know more.'

'But your work..' Hailey let her words trail off. She wondered why an educated woman who had worked her way to the top of the ladder was held in such mystery behind this man she called her husband. Wasn't OPAEC supposed to be a closed environment a world that very few saw? What was it that made someone change in such a way.

'My work is still my work. The truth is I'm better at it than I've ever been. The life I tell you of is personal, work is kept separate from it but there is no harm in using its wisdom to get me further.'

'You do not feel pressured by it. You do not feel that this spiritual world as you call it takes you away from all that you have known?'

'Well we have been talking for two weeks and

you've learnt of personal and other things in my life which do you think makes me the happiest? I'd say the time after I met my husband does. Everything served its purpose. It looks like even being driven by ambition at an earlier age was necessary for me to understand that not all things revolved around it. If I never pushed myself I would never know this.'

Hailey closed her eyes briefly as she absorbed what Sarai was saying. There was some truth in her words about self-discovery. Being with Sarai had made her visit Yong Ding, maybe not physically but certainly spiritually. Her school days became clearer and for the first time in so many years she thought of her grand mother who had passed away when she was little. The old woman had been the only one that had told her never to stop visiting the village temple. That was a lifetime away yet in this affluent environment where one could be masqueraded away in its glamour and splendour she was enticed by something spiritual. Perhaps it wasn't just Sarai's story she came to write but hers that she came to rediscover. Perhaps it was time she stopped trying to question the spiritual world but instead try to understand it.

'There was something else. There was something else you mentioned a while back during one of your moments with your husband. I'm wondering if he ever told you what it meant?' she asked. There was a weakness in her voice, that of one conceding. 'I want to know what it means, what is the resurrection, I'm curious how did he explain this to you?'

Glyfada. The last supper, our last meal in the Saronic Gulf before we all disappeared to our various countries and carried on with our lives as if it had never been.

'What's going on?' I whispered.

'They just got engaged.' Lung Jun Yuen replied.

We were in a Greek restaurant, in a room that looked from the Achean era as we waited for the orders to come in our last evening in Glyfada. The gloaming light of the evening sun had disappeared just after six and after several painful minutes of discussion in the foyer of the hotel we had walked the short distance to the restaurant at the top of the street. It was a different crowd with different rules. I watched as the toast in Chinese circulated around the room and everyone raised their glasses to the newly engaged.

'It is the first. I don't think we have any other couples working in the company living abroad,' Lung said.

'Have they known each other for a long time?' I asked.

'I think they met in China, I'm not sure of the details but they are both based in Germany.'

I had been invited to join my Chinese colleagues out to dinner and it was a completely different experience to the time I had spent with the westerners. There were fewer jokes, mostly conservative, most people electing to keep matters a tad serious and focus more on their careers and personal lives.

'Maybe we could find you a Chinese wife?' Lung said smiling. 'Take Nazeem over there, he has been with the company even longer than I have and he speaks fluent Cantonese. After his studies he joined the company, been with it for over six years and has now got a wife and family in China.'

'Really?'

'Yep, I have. After my studies I did not see the need to return to Tunisia. I decided to stay in China. I worked in the university first at Shanghai as an English teacher eventually deciding to travel further north,' Nazeem said joining in.

'How much further?' I asked.

'Put it this way Siberia was very close. I lived in Northern China for a year. You won't believe the condition of things over there. But I enjoyed every moment of it. Eventually I joined this company because of the boom in the industry. I haven't looked back since. Now you can say I am like a diplomat traveling the world and taking care of our interests but my home, my family and my wife are in China.'

'Chinese company reward you well if you stay longtime with them,' Lung said.

'Well I guess there are fewer options of companies such as this in China than in Europe,' I offered.

'Maybe, but China not for one person but for us all. You see in Europe the West is divided. Everybody takes care of themselves. In China it is different. We know that we have to work together to make our country better, so we do,' Lung emphasized.

'That's true for now I suppose as China develops. It may change in the future when China surpasses its initial goals.'

'No I do not think so. In China even in the schools we are taught about pride for the country. We are taught about promoting our values to strangers, I don't think this can change.'

'I think I know what he means,' Nazeem said. 'You mean that if there is more influence from other nations, more foreigners working in China then their values may change?'

'True but not necessarily, I also mean the opposite. If more Chinese travel abroad and learn of the western values and customs it would be difficult to return home and abide by the single rule policy,' I said. It wasn't uncommon for paranoia to crawl into these conversations, misguided loyalties based on our inability to accept other cultures hindered progress. China had hidden its true self from the world for so long it had forgotten the art of simply living. I knew that most of my Chinese colleagues would never veto any given law by the company. They were just happy to be a part of it. I wanted to scream at my friend that at times it did not matter whether one lived with success or not. It looked as though the world was now oblivious of this simple fact. The shroud of economic rivalry had taken center stage pushing the simple core values that really mattered out of the equation.

'It take time, maybe a very long time for this to happen. See me I live in Mexico for a very long time and I have been with this company for over three years and yet there is no change,' Lung shrugged. There was a tinge of pride in the grin on his face.

I won't be so proud thinking of myself in this way! I thought shuddering inwardly. Change as a weapon for improvement on its own may be overrated at times in the wrong hands but would be something I hoped Lung should consider in this case.

'You may be only in your thirties but I would already class you as the older generation. I think the next generation is already very westernized. Things like the blogs in circulation and the internet are making it very difficult to retain those values you just mentioned,' I replied.

'Hmmh, you may have a point. When I taught in Shanghai most of the students were curious about the life abroad, all wishing to travel and see the world,' Nazeem added.

'That I accept. Even me I am curious when I am in college to go abroad. However the difference come when you live abroad. Over here, especially for the Chinese they feel lonely. Unless they are born in a foreign country they feel like they have to stick together, to live with one another,' Lung said.

'But that is the same for many cultures in foreign

countries, the Indians, the Arabs and many others. In the UK we have different boroughs that house different communities.'

'Yes we have the same in China, the difference is how the country is developing I say in China the development is more rapid and for this reason they have to stick together to have better growth,' Lung explained.

'You have to admit though that keeping the currency low and undervalued in the international market has helped boost the economy,' Nazeem said.

'Yes, but how I can put it. You say clever, no I think better word for this is prudent. If China challenge at the level of its foreign competition then it would suffer. This is to our benefit, our advantage, especially for Chinese company going out to the west. This way government can sponsor us,' Lung said.

I made my excuses as I stole a moment to visit the toilet. It looked like I was running away because I couldn't hold my side of the conversation. The problem was the bad blood that often came from these discussions when truths were told. I could also have voiced the hardship that emerged with this new race for China's success but then that would be starting a war that was unnecessary. Politics was burdensome, no side worn because each was torn in meeting its personal objectives. I didn't want to become a victim. Peace had to prevail.

I nodded to another colleague as I walked to the small sink in front of the mirror. I was staring at someone different in the mirror. This person was looking back at me and hissing louder than ever.

I am alive in you! *Make no mistake about this*!

But how? When? Should I be asleep or in a trance? Is this during the cross over? Explain!

I just am! *We shall be one soon*!

167

How soon? *Explain*!

It was infuriating not knowing, not understanding trying to put each piece together, as they were copious; the memories, visions, archives with no meaning. I had started building on a few but hadn't succeeded. I watched patiently still nothing. Greece was coming to an end and yet all I had was a voice that insisted it was leading, directing but still no explanations.

I washed my hands and reached for some paper towels. The picture of the dryad caught my eye for a short instance and then I was again averted. In the silence of the bathroom I could hear the cars from the highway and the voices from the tables in the dinning room and the kitchen at the back. I yawned involuntarily wiping of the tears that trickled from my eyes as a result with the back of my hand. The late dinners caught up to one eventually still I had to return to the group and play along with the crowd for as long as the night would keep me sane.

We shall be one soon were the only words Cephas had offered. The only words I could work with. We were in a parallax as I prayed to the Lord for direction from my hemisphere. There was no discernable pattern to those who plied their trade in the spiritual world. The strain of the mystery was unbearable at times but one knew better. I had to avoid this repine thought process as only patience could award the answers; it would forfend doubt and restore calm.

I pushed open the swing doors and walked back to the table to pick up from where I left. I threaded lightly on the flokati in the centre of the room making unimpressionable imprints and hoping that I did the same in our discussion. It was important to avoid any acerbic remarks. The talk about development in China was one that no one could avoid in these forums. I couldn't say for certain whether Gresham's law applied over the currency issue but it was a favourable strategy to reduce poverty and develop the economy in China if that was its aim. And in the long run it did not matter whether this was Machiavellian or not. No one could claim innocence, the hunger for fame and fortune was a cupidity distributed evenly around the globe. It was like living in two worlds switching between societies. Dinner and time out with Ramon and the others had been spent talking about wine, relationships and even holidays. We covered all topics. Dinner out with Lung and my Chinese colleagues was centered mainly on politics and the growth of the Chinese society. It was obvious that because so much had already been accomplished for the modern society in the west, very little time was spent debating about it. On the other hand my colleagues from the east were still just venturing beyond their borders and sought assurances, even some sort of security in knowing that their ploys were world worthy. Every topic generally seemed to end up this way no matter were it started.

I returned to the table and took my seat. I was just in time to see dinner being served.

'Tell me why they serve such huge portions? In China the portions are smaller,' Lung observed as his plate of steak was put before him.

'It is the Greek way,' I smiled. It was amazing how I always found myself in the centre of this divide. With the westerners there was the ridicule of the Chinese to contend with. At times I felt as though the jokes I got into with my friends was belittling. On the other hand when things where reversed the same was true. Both camps lashed out at each other with a desire to prove that they were the better people.

I was grateful for the spiritual world. It was the fulcrum of all things. With God there were no divisions and even those who claimed not to believe in the Lord were given a place, their actions to be recompensed for. This was my salvation, the resort away from a world that was constantly turning upon it self. My fasting the day before had been a success and when breaking it I had found renewed hope in the few words that had stuck out in my mind from the bible.

"I have also spoken by the prophets, and I have multiplied visions, and used similitudes, by the ministry of the prophets."

I found comfort in these words, as God told the prophet Hosea of what he had planned for the Children of Israel. The Lord did not only bring his word through his messengers, the prophets but had revealed what was to pass through their visions. He then gave them clues and explanations by the similarities that they could draw from their own lives. There was hope for the man of faith and if I was patient and had the courage in faith then I too would eventually understand my visions from God.

'How did it go with the Sony Player?' I asked as we began eating dinner. It felt like eons since this happened but a change of topic to something much lighter was required.

'Well I got a report from the police. They say they find nothing but it looks like the company is going to recompense me for what I lost,' Lung replied.

'That's good at least you get your money back.'

Chapter Nine

The taxi cab sped west down the wide street of Vas Georgiou Avenue with no one or traffic to be seen for miles. It was eight am on a Sunday morning and most people were in bed recovering from the night before. I listened to their voices without concern. The driver had explained in broken English that the woman in front of the car was his wife. She would be company in the return direction from the airport as he won't be able to pick up a fare at this time of the morning. I acknowledged that I understood. The driver had then asked if he could smoke opening the front windows in the process. I said nothing. The man smoked while his wife talked, her voice a rising and falling symphony as I watched the deep blue sea that pounded the shores of the Saronic Gulf. Greece was over yet I could feel the slight tension within.

The telic was written in the visions. The man with one eye, the children, the figurine and the bride were memories that would not leave me for a while. Time had defeated me and Greece had passed me by without clues. Still I was a savant to the word of God. His words dictated that man observed days and times, we looked at time for service and for purpose, a failure on our part in the spiritual world. With God there was no time for a vision or a promise to be fulfilled. He was time; he made time. These were my galenic pills. With God's words I knew that my departure from Greece did not mean that these visions were unreal. They would serve in a purpose and time to come and they would be unveiled as those before them had.

The cab entered a tunnel and the man put out his cigarette and shut the window. The couple had lowered their voices now as if they listened. I listened too, the humdrum of the roaming sound within the empty tunnel a distant sonata that seemed to have awoken a voice within. I closed my eyes and was somnolent.

'So you can hear it,' he said.

'Clearly,' I responded. He was there and I could feel him alive within me searing to the top amidst the obfuscations and damning the stygian blackness of doubt.

'Then you are prepared.'

It was not a question but a statement of fact, the cutting edge of each word tearing through me like a warm knife through butter as I absorbed every syllable.

'It is like a tercet,' Cephas said quietly.

'A what?'

'Three paths connected by one.'

Cephas was the soliloquist, spirit awoken and I was the moon, dead unless the brightness of the Lord shone on me. He did through my spirit, through Cephas. In this deontic disposition a world away screamed madness while mine screamed light and my heavenly father, God.

'How?' I asked the question blindly, what did he mean? What were the paths and how could I find them?

'He is the resurrection, the connection. He gets you there, he is the way and the life; you live for him.'

'And the paths? What are they?'

'He would show you them.'

The cab sped through the tunnel but I wasn't there. I was somewhere else, I had passed through it emerging in the sunlight and taking off miles into the distance, into the future and into some place else called spiritual reality. In that instance I could feel and sense the vast vacuum of space believing that my helplessness had to be replaced by patience. My cogent self reminded me that pushing and shoving at the obstacles in my path would only result in them being immediately replaced by others. The tendency was to outthink one's self under these circumstances, placing a hollow net beneath this indecipherable mystery with the expectancy of a good catch. The truth was I was the guest to this party blessed by grace and not carnal wisdom; and if then by grace there was nothing else to do but return to scripture. The Lord had taught me through his word that we would face no burden in life that was beyond our means. It was obvious that my light in this vacuum would be to listen to Cephas's words. They shone through the stars as I heard them echo back to me.

'Then you came prepared.'

He was right for I had indeed come prepared as my time on this earth had taught me a few things that now came in handy. I once set out on a long walk that had lasted almost two hours. In the first part of it, the first hour and the time it had taken me to reach were I would start the return journey I was the ardent traveler. I could feel the energy and excitement of anticipation flowing through my veins taking in everything around me as though I was seeing it for the first time. Still beneath this excitement I could sense the weakness in my legs as they desperately tried to keep up with this enthusiasm. In the second half of my journey, the return path to my home I noticed a change. This time my body felt stronger as if it had acclimated to the conditions that surrounded it. There was a new found strength in my legs and gone was the excitement that was in the outward journey. This time what had taken priority above everything else was seeing the front door of my home. After doing this several times over the years I noticed that this pattern was always maintained. There were notional lines to be considered that opened a leat allowing for a similarity to the natural process of our lives. We often started out in life seeking pastures new with a burning desire that stretched us beyond our limits as our enthusiasm far outweighed what we were capable of. After a certain age we began a return journey. This time there was equanimity, wisdom and knowledge of our environment. We walked this path knowing our limits and tailoring our excitement to keep up with what our body could offer. It had nothing to do with the fitness of our body but rather the knowledge of what we were capable of doing.

It was true that I had come prepared because in this wisdom I would wait patiently. Spirit began this journey before man and it would end the journey for man. It had erected telamones for man to be guided and it was our duty to accept this command as we watched the colure of our spheres. God had a plan in my visions and our Lord and savior, Jesus Christ would be my way, truth and life to unravel them.

Mougins. Twilight and a descending sun into the Riviera just beyond the west of Cagnes Sur Mer could not hide the black cayenne that sped down the A8 towards a rear entrance at the Cote D'Azur International Airport. Sarai could just make out the Falcon amongst the other jets as it taxied slowly to a standstill just before the hangar. Hailey was silent beside her. There were two days still left before she headed back to the US. In that time she would meet Cephas and the children. This was something she was now looking forward to. She had heard so much, listened as this woman told her about a mysterious path that had eventually led her to the man of her dreams and a family that was destined to be. She couldn't say that they were friends for they had to be more. She knew so many things, so many details about the woman's life that she now felt like family. It would be difficult to leave even though Sarai had assured her that she was welcome back at any time. It was not just the sun, the beautiful scenery and a period of serenity from the hustle and bustle in New York that she'd miss. It was also the company and time with her new friend.

Now she watched as the man descended the stairway of the private jet with the little boy that looked asleep in his arms. Next she saw Rachel and Joshua, their names now familiar as if she had known them all for many years. Both children walked on either side of a young woman in smart blue uniform. They looked excited no doubt because they had spotted Sarai waving at them. As the car pulled beside the plane she watched hesitantly, waiting for Sarai to rush to her family. Then her pupils widened, staring blindly past Sarai and the children asking herself if a doctor's prognosis would state that she was now purblind. I know him and I've seen him before, this cannot be real.

I saw them through the window of the Falcon. Naturally it was easier from my confines than from theirs, my window showed me more than theirs did. Sometimes it was the way things were, one window having a clearer view to what surrounded us than another could. I emerged from the jet holding the little boy in my arms.

'Did you have fun?' I heard Sarai ask as the children grabbed on to her.

'Yes.' Joshua answered. His little hands searching for hers as she led them to the car. I put Luke in the child's seat at the back and he opened his little eyes looking up at me dreamily. Before long, Sarai was beside me leaning over and kissing him on the cheek.

'How is my baby?' She asked. The boy giggled as she toyed with his little hand.

'Your baby is tired. He slept all the way here.' I said as I strapped him in and held the door open for his brother and sister to climb in. I shut the door and turned to Sarai. She came into my arms and as we touched I was screaming within, reminding myself that I was now one, Cephas and man experiencing a new world beyond the one I once inhabited as two people.

'How have you been?'

'Good but missing you all, come please I want you to meet someone.' She said guiding me round the car, her arm through mine as we approached the quiet Chinese girl she had come with. I knew who it was instantly. As the girl shook my hand I saw the fear in her eyes. I could have shared in that fear too if I wasn't privy to another world.

'No it can't be,' she grimaced. 'We've met right, I think we have somewhere else.' It looked as if the girl was in a reverie, daydreaming and talking to herself.

'Glyfada.' I said trying to console the ache I knew she was feeling.

'How did you know, how do you remember?' she asked her mouth agape and staring into a past I knew she had long forgotten.

'Then you know each other?' Sarai asked.

'We worked for the same company. I met your friend Hailey briefly several years ago when I worked in Glyfada just outside Athens. We shared a train ride into Athens.' I said climbing into the front passengers seat as Hailey got in with the children. Sarai started the engine and we pulled out of the airport.

'I see you became a writer then, or was it journalism you wanted to do I can't remember which it was back then.'

'It was journalism.' Hailey replied weakly from the back seat.

The worlds had merged, mine and hers stealing away time and doubt for what was destined to happen. I knew she was tapping into all her resource faculties and searching for answers. Where were the connections?

Why had we met on that sunny day in Glyfada and traveled on the same train to Athens? I knew those types of questions and the fright that came with them. Still it was her path and I knew she would have to walk it to understand what had happened. If I were to be of any help then I would do so in good time. On my path was Sarai and the appearance of this girl was taking me back to somewhere else. My beautiful wife hadn't come to be beside me just then but eons earlier.

Glyfada. As we cleared the tunnel at the far end I saw signs that told us the airport was another fifteen miles away. We were now back in the sunlight yet I knew it was no way as bright as the light of the Lord that shone within.

'You have other questions.'

Spirit had elected to take over now, directing the montage and I remained statuesque with never ending questions.

'I guess the most difficult question is how I am able to see a possible future through visions when I am still this person I see everyday?'

'You have to remember,' he replied.

'When and what?' I asked.

'When it began, when you accepted.'

It was 2003 and I studied blindly, page after page of the New Testament and nothing else. I earned my epaulettes then, it had to pay off some time.

'Do you remember the book of St John?'

'I do.'

'Then I shall quote the verses for you:

"Jesus saith unto her, Thy brother shall rise again.

Martha saith unto him, I know that he shall rise again 'in the resurrection at the last day.

Jesus said unto her, I am 'the resurrection, and the 'life: 'he that believeth in me, though he were dead yet shall he live:

And whosoever liveth and believeth in me 'shall never die, Believest thou this?

She saith unto him, Yea, Lord: I believe that 'thou art the Christ, 'the Son of God, 'which should come into the world."

Now do you see how it is possible?' Cephas asked.

'Yes.'

'Then I can tell that your next question would be why you.' Again a statement and not a question, he read my thoughts. He was me, spirit, that which was enshrouded in human, me.

'Yes I feel like this also calls for an explanation.'

'Then there is more. Let's go to the book of Acts, what did Paul say to Ananias and Felix the noble:

"But this I confess unto thee, that after 'the way which they call heresy, so 'worship I the God of my fathers, believing all things which are written in 'the law and in the prophets: And have 'hope to ward God, which they themselves also allow, that there shall be a resurrection of the dead, 'both of the just and unjust."'

'The resurrection is for everyone regardless of who they are. However there is the resurrection into life and this comes when you have accepted Christ. To be chosen as one of the Lord's and in the likeness of him, you must also be buried with him by baptism unto death. You must give up the oldman and be reborn,' Cephas added.

'Then this is my resurrection?' I asked.

'This is you accepting spirit to lead and guide you wholly and truthfully in this life time.'

'I thought I did I thought this meant accepting the Lord in one's heart.'

'That is a part of it. In the book of Romans, Paul said: *"For 'if we have been planted together in the likeness of his death, we shall also be in the likeness of*

178

his resurrection: Knowing this, that 'our old man is crucified with him, that 'the body of sin might be destroyed, that henceforth we should not serve sin. For 'he that is dead is 'freed from sin." It is easy to say you accept the Lord wholly and truly it is harder to walk the path he sets before you to die and be resurrected as he was in this life.' Cephas said.

The sounds of the planes landing and taking off from the international Airport in Athens were an indication of the journey that had been laid out before me. It was easy stating our claim to a righteous resurrection it was a completely different story walking the righteous path to it. God had granted me the visions and the tutoring. He had allowed me to venture into his world as spirit and see beyond a lifetime into another world that many could only dream of. Perhaps I could still not interpret the visions but it was evident that fulfilling them meant I had to walk a new path, one that left behind the past to understand what I was to become. Greece had served its purpose I had been resurrected into spirit to see beyond the present now it was time to see this world in mine and be resurrected into life for spirit and man to exist as one.

Mougins. Hailey watched the little girl playing with her watch before the bedside table. Children were fearless creatures that had no boundaries, they descended upon you determined to fulfill their wishes and driven by a determination that was worthy of the success they gained from eventually getting their way. Rachel played with the watch, mesmerized in her little world without even acknowledging the presence of Hailey in the room. She had turned up out of nowhere like a stray puppy giggling and once invited into the room was practically taking over it.

Hailey folded her things neatly placing them in the

travel bag as she prepared for the nine hours flight back to New York. Her trip to Mougins in the South of France may have come to an end but seemed to have opened doors to a new story. The fact was she knew Cephas. They had worked in the same company several years before, during her first visit to Europe. He had been there in Athens. He was one of the managers from Europe called like hers had been to the summit. Now it was evident that whatever had made their paths cross before felt it was necessary for them to meet again. The whole thing was bizarre and had kept her awake at night believing that maybe this article wasn't simply about Sarai, it could have been about Sarai and Cephas. Would she be able to? What would Susan say? The difficulty was justifying her lengthy stay over in the South of France. She could hardly return to the office and start relating this twist of events. It hadn't happened in the simple fashion by which anyone could imagine. There had been a build up to it. Sarai hadn't known of Hailey. She had told her story including the mysterious husband she was married to and that had already taken Hailey to new depths. The spirituality that surrounded the couple was a mystery that she was now trying to incorporate into the article. Discovering who Cephas was had added a twist to things. It wasn't just about them it was about her. There was a purpose, a reason and she was serving it.

As she reached for her swimsuit she caught the eye of the little girl watching her curiously.

'You okay there?' Hailey asked.

'Yes.' The child answered and continued staring.

'You are staring, that's not good. Why are you?'

'I don't know.' The girl said bringing the expression of defiance to her face.

'Won't your Mum be looking for you?'

'No, she knows I am here.'

'I see.'

'How old are you?'

'I am four years old.' Rachel replied proudly.

'So are you going to stare all day or help me pack?' Hailey asked as she walked to the closet. She had made room for her shoes and even extra room for another pair that she had picked up in Nice.

The little girl watched her walk back to the bag without saying anything. She looked indecisive as if she wasn't sure about committing herself to this new task.

'I promise it would be fun,' Hailey said, stopping to give the child her devoted attention. 'I would tell your mummy that you were very helpful.' She said placing her hand on her chest.

The child moved slowly towards her. Her tentative steps that of a person unsure of what lay ahead. Hailey reached out and offered a hand and the child put her little hand in it. Hailey lifted her unto the bed and offered her some of the small face towels she had purchased.

'You fold this for me while I pack my computer,' she said, 'you can even put them in my suitcase for me.'

As the child settled to the task at hand Hailey looked around for her laptop bag. It was time to put aside the tools of her trade. Her recorder had several bytes of data from Sarai's article and she was proud to say that included in those bytes was the answer to her question about the resurrection. However getting the complete answer out of Sarai had not been simple. Instead of a simple explanation for the article Sarai had attempted to show her how to discover for herself what the resurrection was.

'If you ask me if my faith is strong enough that I would do those things that I won't normally do, follow

181

my heart to those places that I won't normally go. Then I would say to an extent,' Sarai had said, 'put it this way, if I can walk on water to the point at which Christ is and take his hand then I am fully resurrected. If I can't then I've got some way to go yet.'

'But how do you know you can do this, how do you know that when you face this test you will perform as asked of you?' Hailey had asked.

'How do I know that my children are going to be okay when I am not around? How do I know that the next morning I will rise again and be healthy? How do any of us know anything? The fact of the matter is we don't but we hope for things through faith. It is this same faith that makes us walk on water to Christ. It is this faith that teaches us that drowning is not the end, that death as we have come to know it does not kill us. If by this faith we can walk to Christ then we have been resurrected to life with him.'

Sarai had gone on to explain to her that it wasn't so important that we were resurrected. The importance lay in whether we were resurrected on to life or to death. Life it self was a process; we lived it and eventually died going to heaven or hell dependent on whichever the Lord decided. If this was the case then understanding the resurrection was more valuable when we understood it as a resurrection onto Christ and to heaven. Having this knowledge while we breathed in the life we had on earth served us for the life to come. Walking to Christ without doubt and overcoming our fears meant that we had accepted him as the resurrection on to life and were free from a second death. No one could tell another whether they had been resurrected onto life or death as the process was incomprehensible. It was an individual journey of self discovery based on our faith.

Hailey placed her toilet bag into the suitcase along

with the towels that the little girl had managed to make a mess with. She lifted the child in her arms and smiled. These were the true people of the resurrection on to life. They had no fear or reservation. They did what they had to do trusting in the powers be to take care of them and most times they got their way. Perhaps this is what she needed to become to have her resurrection on to life. It was a thought well worth processing and she would have a lot of thinking to do when she got back to New York.

Glyfada. I stared at the entrance to the airport insipidly. I had been to many, traveling from one destination to the next as I sought pastures new. Those peripatetic escapades were endless, as they took you on an insatiable odyssey because they never delivered as promised. The path of the spirit was edulcorate. Going to the Lord was a destination that offered the ultimate fulfillment and mine was calling, whispering from the shadows beyond and I was responding.

I strode into the airport watching the heavyset man and his wife galumph across my path. This was the real world. In this insatiable odyssey you carried baggage, a heaped Pelion strapped across your shoulders amidst every other thing that the world claimed you couldn't survive without. Its perfidy was subtle and hidden from your eyes as you breathed it, believing it was the only thing that made any sense. In the spiritual world you flew freely piloting without burden and trusting in a supreme being.

'There is one more verse that would put things into perspective.'

'I need to hear it,' I said, my flight was in the next hour and the check in desk was quiet. Cephas hadn't resided and I had the feeling he wouldn't for a while.

'This is from the book of Philippians and it reads,

183

"That I may know him, and 'the power of his resurrection, and 'the fellowship of his sufferings, being made conformable unto his death; If by any means I might attain unto the resurrection of the dead." We are to share in the fellowship of his sufferings to understand his resurrection, to understand my existence, for us to be one.'

'When does this happen?' I asked, not that it mattered because it was inevitable. One life must be left behind for another to succeed it. The voyager was present and so were the means, now time was the only thing left to put the summons in effect.

'Soon,' he said, quietly disappearing into the background and watching as I did for what would happen next.

I took a seat by the window and waited to be called for boarding. At one time in our lives we were all called to take our seats at different terminals to be called. The Children of Israel were no different when they waited through the woes for the journey to the Promised Land. Now it was my turn.

Part II

Exodus

Chapter Ten

Riyadh, July 2007 two years later; 'I have a package for you, it would be to your advantage to come into the office as soon as you can to collect it,' he said.

'What did you say your name was again?' I asked.

'Ali Rezan.'

Cephas was searing. Finally it had begun!

I entered the coolness of the Abrawj tower and followed the stairway to the elevators. I had tried desperately to forge a path through the thicket of the man's abruptness but had made no headway. Mr Ali Rezan had almost turned peevish as I pushed further. I had to be calm. Why had I received this package? Had I missed something? I couldn't remember any phone calls from any one about this.

'It won't be long now.'

The whisper was soft and kindred. A trade mark of what we shared and an identity that was destined to be one when the time was right.

There were more people than I expected in the recreation room that was an extended part of the kitchen. Everyone was engaged in conversation along with the plasma television set in the background blaring out the news from CNN. Financial figures from Bloomberg streamed through on a red ribbon with most of their arrows inverted in red. Two men occupied the pool table in the centre of the room while two others talked beside the coffee table. My appointment was easy to spot. He sat close to the entrance holding some documents and looking expectantly for my arrival. I sat before the Arab and looked straight into his eyes. He was a heavy smoker with the symptoms of the dreary look and the blackness of his fingertips. In his eyes was the look of betrayal. He had been chosen specifically for this job, not to show any form of emotion or expect any in return but to deliver one for the team. The man's eyes were shifting wearily, his smile pretentious, his words meaningless as he handed the white envelop over to me.

'Your contract has been terminated and as of today we no longer require your services. You are allowed to work through to the end of the month and then leave. Thank you.'

I knew the man was watching me closely, waiting to see the change, the reaction he had been paid to anticipate in order that he might give a good account to his superiors. None was forthcoming. I had been taught well by my master and heavenly father. Had the Lord not said to the people committed to crucify him that they couldn't do this unless his father granted them the power to? Even if this was a ruse, even if none of my good work for the company had been taken into account, one thing was a certainty I would not afford them the weakness they wished for. It was no more my time, no more my place to relate events as they unfolded through the human eye. It was Cephas's turn to bare witness.

'This is the package?'

'Yes. You will have to sign this form indicating that you have received it.'

I said nothing and signed the white sheet of paper.

'Who do I talk to before I leave?' I asked looking up from the paper my eyes unyielding, wearing the calm mask of impenetrable peace and tranquility.

'Me.'

A *stranger*, this was who they had sent; the rest hiding behind in cowardice, their rebuff a clear indication of what I meant to them and the company. Perhaps if I was some one else I would rant, cause a scene and make them pay for the humiliation. I wasn't. There were standards to uphold for the Lord and a New

Testament that had been scrolled in my heart and soul. *Turn the other cheek.* Everything served a purpose and nothing happened without reason. I stood up and extended my hand.

'Thanks for the letter.'

'You are welcome.

Glyfada was two years in the past yet I had known of this day and I had been warned that it had already been written. Time had made no difference for the inevitable. I had lost touch with my friends moving into a foreign land that was worlds apart from theirs. Our parting of ways had not been easy but it was necessary. The last time I had spoken to Ramon things had been terse. A year had elapsed after Athens when I had called with the news.

'I leave in three weeks for the Middle East,' I said.

'You cannot be serious my friend. That place is hell, you would have no life and you would be demoted to the bottom of the food chain,' Ramon had replied.

'But I have to go. I have been waiting for this opportunity for quite some time. I would like to work somewhere different.'

'Choose anywhere else but Riyadh. I am told that there is no life there for westerners. The place is a desert there is nothing for you there. My friend I always thought we would work together for years build upon what we have here. You would miss our trips to China, to Greece.'

'I know and I have given this careful thought but it is something I must do,' I said. Ramon wasn't the only one that felt I was insane. I was under pressure even back in London as Lung had also felt that I was betraying his trust and leaving what we had built together. Still there was no escaping. I had to make this journey to where ever it would lead me.

'Well don't call me and complain when things go

bad for you, when the sun burns your brains out!'

I said farewells to my friends and before long eighteen months had passed by. My epaulettes in the spiritual world increased significantly as the Lord granted me a new livelihood in Riyadh. Now it seemed that this life too was about to end for the one that had been decided before it. Greece was no holiday and what had taken place needed to see it's light of day. There had been a resurrection still it was incomplete without spirit and man becoming one. It was evident that my break away for two years was in preparation for this. I was being tutored for a path to be fulfilled. If this was happening now then this was what the Lord wanted. The pieces of the puzzle were being fitted together in a fashion that could only be explained by God.

My eyes shown like crystals in the dark behind the sunshades but no one was to know how I felt. I descended the stairs of the huge building and walked beneath the palm trees past the HSBC bank. The water traps had opened and the plants were receiving their daily nutrient. It was any ordinary day for most but not for me. I had been humiliated to the core. A stranger had been sent to do the dirty work, no warning, no messages, no phone calls from any one in management. People I had shared dinner with, laughs and tears as we fought relentlessly to build an organisation in the Middle East. There had been no consideration, the execution thorough. Anything else would be *child's play* before me.

I reached the parked hired Honda and got in. It was like stepping into a furnace but I was past caring, I needed the silence and waited. Cephas took over. God had said this day would come. I wasn't aware of this but Cephas knew the truth. No one could accept God in the way I did and not expect to be chastised. It was a cleansing, chiseling the chaff to get to the real substance within. What mankind considered longsuffering, characterized by humiliation and the dregs of despair were in reality direction and strength that weaved a faith that was second to none. Cephas was proud of his universe. I had not faltered. I maintained the teachings, we were in synchrony, the ballad had begun and there would be more to follow. If I had overreacted and succumbed to the misery of the first steps into my indoctrination then there would be cause for concern of how I would cope through the darkest of times that were to follow. Now I had hope for the reunion and the time when I would be one with spirit and serve the Lord.

Mougins Present Day; I looked up as Sarai entered the room. She wore a pair of faded blue jeans with a white turtleneck. Her black hair was loose on her shoulders, her brown boots just about showing beneath the jeans. I'm a lucky man, for who wouldn't want this woman by his side. God had been good to me.

'We are going out, would you like to come, it's a walk by the pond.'

'I don't know, I just got into this…' I replied my eyes straying back to the black laptop open on the desk. I had been searching for the words for days. It was difficult getting the story and now that I was in rhythm I did not want to leave.

'Mummy, I'm waiting.'

Sarai and I looked at the little head that had popped round the door. Rachel was staring at us and demanding an answer. Her little face flushed with excitement and before either of us could answer the door was thrown open and Joshua strode in past his sister.

'Mummy can I take my bike? I want to,' he said

walking straight to his mum.

'You didn't knock!' His sister shouted behind him without entering the room. Her face had changed to one of the instructor scolding. The boy looked at her and then immediately returned his gaze back to his mum enquiringly.

'I thought I told you guys to wait for me in the hall way,' Sarai said looking down at them. She then turned her gaze to me expectantly.

'It would be fun besides we haven't all been out in a while,' She said charmingly, her eyes hosting a raffish glow that made me wonder if I could resist. She then tilted her head allowing her hair fall to the side as she reached down and picked up the boy.

'Take your sister out and wait for me in the hallway. I'll be there shortly,' she said and kissed him on his forehead. She put him down and the boy ran to his sister and soon they had disappeared slamming the door in their wake. I shuddered throwing both hands to my head as I curtailed the hemorrhage that came with this level of responsibility and sought solace from yonder.

'Sorry darling but we want you with us. I want you with us,' Sarai said smiling.

My life Lord, this is what you told me it would be like. Those times that had gone before I became me would be forgotten. Ahead of me lay a new path, a journey that I would walk with my own people, those that you had given me charge over. They would want me, need me and love me. The difference is my past would be forgotten but I would remember you always father for this gift and love that you have bestowed upon me. I thank you father.

'You're children are waiting don't disappoint them and most importantly I am waiting,' Sarai said.

'Give me a couple of minutes.'

Sarai beamed. Mission accomplished and she

would get her way this time. I granted her that besides I knew she wouldn't ask just for the sake of it. She was aware of the difficulty it took for me to settle down and find the right words to write. I had to respect this. She had hoped I would be available and I was. Maybe a walk in the park with her and the kids could be what I needed.

'Okay I would get their bikes while you wrap up here. See you outside,' she said.

My life, my God, my hope and my dream that descended upon me without my knowledge, I give thee thanks. Where was the time, where was the place, where was the past emptiness, the loss and humiliation that took everything away from one leaving you shattered and searching, never knowing just believing that someday it would all be better. The spiritual world could reveal many mysterious things to one but time brought them physically before us. We were a people that did not understand where we originated from but if there was anything that could give us comfort it was where we were headed. If we stuck to the path we would see the wonders that God had reserved for us.

'Daddy, mummy said we are outside and waiting,' Joshua said throwing the door open and staring at me. He now had his helmet on raring for take off.

'Then we better not keep her waiting, little man.' I said as I came round the desk and reached for his hand. I shut the door to the office and then grabbed the boy lifting him high above my head and the child screamed in delight.

I smiled up at him. God did not show us everything we wished to know at the beginning. We weren't born ready. We had to learn to find a place called faith, a place called patience, a place called perseverance and many others. However through all this there was a place called dreams, what we desired in life, what we wanted for ourselves and what we hoped would become. This, God showed us when we were ready.

Riyadh. When the children of Israel entered the wilderness of Sin they murmured against Moses and Aaron complaining about hunger and wishing for the life they had back in Egypt. God heard their cries and provided manna from heaven. He told them that they would collect for six days before holding a Sabbath unto him. He told them that on the sixth day they would collect twice as much because on the seventh they would rest and hold the Sabbath to his name. God had a plan. Our Lord had given us for the day that there won't be any manna. He had prepared us for this day. In the New Testament our Lord and savior confirmed these same words by saying, "*To him that overcometh will I give to eat of a hidden manna, and will give him a white stone, and in the stone a new name written, which no man knoweth saving he that receiveth it.*" Nothing happened to those who believed in God without him preparing us for it. We had the manna and it would help us in our day of need.

I gasped at the sight of the dent on the hired car. It was a hideous gash with scratches as metal ripped into metal on the back door of the car. There was no note, nothing to indicate that the culprit had a conscience and was mindful of the horror to be experienced by the owner. Why had I chosen to park in that spot today of all days? Wasn't the termination of my contract enough for me to deal with in one day? Now *this.* I had returned to the client's office like a being defoliated of its natural external resources that now breathed solely on the resources of those within. Although traffic had been hell on four lanes of the Jiddah Road that headed in the direction of Dammam, I had managed to remain equanimous as I kept my thoughts isolated from my surroundings. Things didn't end there. I arrived at the client's office only to realize that there was nowhere to park. It was an hour after midday and a bad time to find parking space, especially when most people would have returned from lunch. After driving around the block into the side streets with unfruitful results, I had returned to the front and spotted this space as another car pulled out. It was an event so rare in the type of day I was having that I began to believe my fortunes were changing for the better. It was now apparent that they weren't. I put my bag in the boot of the car and got in. There was little point dwelling on what had happened. This was another characteristic of the world one lived in. Accidents like this happened all the time and people vanished without a trace if they could. In Riyadh it was something the hire companies were accustomed to. I had to move on. Time was on my side as it was only six in the evening and if I rushed I would just be in time to get to the store before the next prayer hour begun. Some refreshments and a good meal was what one needed to ride the testing times I was facing.

I heard him and knew he watched quietly in silence. We shared this time, he was my new name and manna afforded me for times like this. He was Cephas and spirit and I was man. I wasn't sliding backwards, I hadn't bailed out. I was holding my head up as events unfolded, one after the other. It was the path, the parable of a camel threading the eye of the needle to achieve the ultimate goal.

The mall was vacant when I got there. During the summer months most families elected to shop late and avoid the heat. It wasn't surprising to find people holding picnics late into the evening and beyond midnight. The rules in this part of the world were shaped around the sphere of the country's religion and the weather. It worked in my favour. The *screaming* in my head had stopped and my nerves quieted down still I had no desire to face an unruly public.

I walked into the shop spotting items I would never have taken notice of. I was throwing in extras into my shopping trolley for reasons unknown. I walked past the pastry section and reached for croissants. I rarely had these but today was different, they would be a welcome distraction. Events had happened so quickly it was hard to tell which way I was headed. A month ago I had wished for something like this to happen. I had preempted the thought by setting my sights on another role, another position back in Europe believing that I had out run my quest for adventure and already achieved my goal in the Middle East. I had begun searching for alternatives. I believed I needed to settle down and curtail ambition in order to find a base, my nidus on which I could set my sights for a family. It would not be easy given my natural instinct prone to adventure but I would start looking and there was no place better to start this search than in Europe. I'd lived there for most of my life and it was like none other when you knew your way around. If I moved before the summer then all things considered I had plenty to look forward to. I had done my time in the Middle East and knew it would serve me in good stead. My next move would be the last in a long time and I would rein in my chariot and settle down. My plans but not God's as I was just beginning to understand.

Mougins. 'You were there,' Sarai said as we walked. She pushed the pram with Luke in it, while Rachel and Joshua rode their bikes ahead. 'I saw it in your eyes, you were there again.'

'Where?' I teased as I walked beside her.

'Don't be clever,' Sarai said.

'You read me so easily darling.'

She had come willingly. I had led and she had followed me into this strange world, this new world that I had come to accept as mine a while back. Having a companion in it made all the difference. It was good to share what God provided for one. It was even better when more people danced in the radiance of the spiritual world.

Rachel and Joshua had stopped ahead waiting for us to catch up.

'I want to throw pebbles on the pond Mummy,' she said.

'Go ahead darling.' Sarai said. The children jumped off their bikes and rushed to the side of the pond. I gathered the bicycles moving them on each side of me as we joined the kids.

'You know I live there with all of you.' I said.

'I know, I know,' Sarai said as she reached into the pram and lifted Luke. He giggled in his Mum's arms. 'Do you ever let go of it?'

'I don't know how to, it's like letting go of you guys which is virtually impossible,' Someone had asked me once upon a time ago to let go and I had tried only to discover that I had traveled further within than I thought was possible. I became the child succumbing to the father and listening to a voice that guided me through the hollowness. I found that we couldn't let go of God even if we tried. He had chosen us to be with him for eternity and our feeble minds were incapable of understanding this.

'The weather is changing we may have to go back,' Sarai said as she placed the little boy back in his pram.

'Did your article get published yet?' I asked as I reached for the other two terriers and got them back on their bicycles.

'Not yet, I spoke to Hailey three days ago and she says things have changed. They now want an additional piece about us and not just about me. They would like to hear about you too.'

'What do you think?' I asked. She was centre stage on this and I didn't think I had more to offer.

'Well I told her I would ask you. I know you don't like talking about yourself unless you need to. I said it could be difficult but I'd try.'

'What can I tell her that you already haven't? Your words are mine.'

'Thank you darling but I guess it adds more drama to the article if we both have a say,' she said.

I said nothing this time as we climbed the small hill.

'I told her a thing or two, a bit about Black River.' Sarai said as we reached the top of the hill. 'I told her about your charming method of seduction. How you moved me into another world on our honeymoon night.'

'Details my darling I guess that's what she wanted,' I smiled.

'Then you don't mind? At the time I thought maybe this was too much.'

'How can it be it's your article right, something you wanted to do?'

'I think she wonders about our sanity,' she said offering me a benign smile while touching me lightly on the shoulder.

'Most people would,' I returned. It was the way of the spirit one lived in the world but was not of it.

We walked past a couple of trees and spotted the house in the distance. The children did not need an invitation. It looked like they had rehearsed for this moment because they jumped off their bikes in unison and took off leaving me wondering whether they were being chased. No doubt they had left their appointed servant to push their bikes home.

'Don't fall!' Sarai shouted after them, 'I don't know

why I bother as if they listen.'

'I guess they've left their bikes for me then. I can't wait for the day when they shall ride them all the way home,' I said.

Rachel and Joshua were sitting at the door when we got there with their little cheeks all flushed from the run. They got up and ran into the house as soon as I opened the door shouting at one another querying the winner of the race. Next they were before their Mum asking her to decide who had won. Sarai told them that they both won but this only opened room for more debate as they sought a winner to the contest. I shook my head in resignation acknowledging my shortcomings in understanding how their little brains functioned. Perhaps their competitive spirit would help them in life but as far as I was concerned they had a plan to make my grey hairs fall off and leave me bald.

I slumped into the sofa giving rest to my weary thoughts. Sarai joined me with the same intentions no doubt after putting Luke on the carpeted floor as we watched the children play before us.

'I thought this would make them tired. Now I am wondering,' she confided.

'I've given up. They are putting me to sleep,' I offered.

'Well what is your answer then? What do you want me to tell Hailey about your participation in our insane family?' Sarai asked turning to look at me.

'Do you want me to do this? I have to admit there is very little I can add.'

'Yes. Never mind about the details we would do it together,' Sarai said comfortingly as she put her arm in mine. 'Don't you always say our life is a testimony for others to see and hopefully grow in their faith. I think we should tell the world about this life of ours and what it means. I for one can't wait to see what she would write.'

'Sure darling, why not.' I said now turning to lie back into the corner of the sofa. It was hard work writing all day. I was working on a book and the effort going into it was already exhausting enough since I had spent most of the night awake. Sarai followed suite lying on my chest as we watched the activity before us.

Chapter Eleven

Dublin, September 2007; My birth means his death, my strength his weakness. A mere thought but a candid one and Cephas was obliging.

'There won't be any other new contracts coming your way because you have already signed that which matters,' Cephas added.

Maybe I had high hopes for myself but so did Cephas. We had both been growing in different ways. I was strengthened with experience living in different countries, working with many different people and surviving the numerous woes and throes that man could throw at me. Cephas had his own experiences to account for. He had the visions, the miracles as he had grown with the Lord using the same body, me, as the host with the same eyes to see as God took us through unprecedented territory. It had now become apparent that spirit and man had to be one to serve God completely and truthfully. I could not serve man and then wish to accept God. It won't work - not after the miracles and especially not after the visions. Cephas knew he had won, knew that the truth was sealed in spirit; the question that remained unanswered was time. How long would it take for me to understand that my wishes and desires as man were now wasted on deaf ears?

The girl stood before me with the tray of food and I looked at her already relating to how different things were. There was no female service in Riyadh. It wasn't allowed for women and men to share in dialogue unless they also shared in matrimony or another relationship.

'Here we are sir, enjoy your meal,' she said and offered a smile.

'Thanks.'

Some customers would have said more but I didn't.

Instead I turned my attention to the pasta. Dublin was turning out to be a let down. I had been looking forward to the new start telling myself that there won't be any of the old judgment calls, those instincts that had been built over time and dwelt on first impressions. They had served me well in the past but that was then, now things would be different. Dublin couldn't be that bad, there had to be more to it than the way I felt. Besides it was practically living in Europe, it was a cultural city with more than enough distractions. I had tried to look for those distractions from the tinted windows of the coach from the airport but had been disappointed. Why did I feel so empty, so lost? Had I not made up my mind in Riyadh to settle down, that if a good opportunity came along I won't judge it on instinct? So why was I reverting to type and already dismissing all positive aspects of the place?

'It's not enough, you seek *more*!' It was a scream, a yell from Cephas.

'Yes I do,' I replied under my breath but where? The job had taken it's time to come along since Riyadh but I had been patient, waiting. Now it was here and I was doing everything in my power to fail. None of this made any sense.

I pushed the plate aside and looked around the empty restaurant. The last customers for the night had just walked off and I was left to rue the thought of having to spend the next few years in this city establishing new roots.

'But it would just be for a start, nothing permanent, just something to get me going,' I thought.

'You have had many of those and how did they end up?' Cephas responded.

'And then there is the prestige to consider. I would be working for one of the best companies in the world, keeping in synch to what I have always done, winning big.'

'Yes but you have done this too in the past. Who are you trying to impress?'

'No *one*! I said this was for me, a chance to settle, take a break from searching the world.' I was the petulant infant holding my corner in the only way I knew.

'Who are you kidding, wandering is who you are until you make the choice.'

'Let's think of the alternatives, I would soon be in debt or put it this way I already am. I cannot live this life where I waltz in and out of debt every time, it's driving me insane,' I confided.

'You chose insanity when you decided that you could serve man.'

'Now what's that supposed to mean? Are you saying that having a decent job and settling down means I cannot serve God?'

'Interpret my words as you wish, the fact is you know what *I mean*!'

'But you have seen my situation in the last few months I have slowly slipped back into the red and guess what, the next few months don't look rosy either.' Losing my job in Riyadh hadn't helped. I was now in debt moving in the opposite direction to my plans.

'Tell me something I don't know. Haven't we been here several times before and you made it. What makes this time so special?'

'Well because... you know.'

'No I don't know you must say it!'

'I guess I am getting old,' I said. Age had never been an issue in my life because I had always lived the life of a man without a care in the world. I went about my business refusing to be held by the restraints of the world. For whatever reason unbeknown to me as the world shrunk before my eyes and I explored those places that I had always dreamed of, I suddenly felt older. It was as if it wasn't enough for me alone to see the places, I needed to share it with someone else, with family.

'You are not getting old; you are old. You are old because your world wishes you to be old because like all humans you adhere to the conditions of observing days, months and years but does this matter in the spiritual world?' Cephas said, his kind words a hard slap back to reality, our spiritual reality.

'Okay granted it isn't about falling back every so often into debt. Still I feel insane and unable to relate to anything.'

'It is crazy, the spiritual world is meant to be illogical and not open for interpretation by man. What about the words that are written in the bible, in the book of Proverbs? *"For a just man falleth seven times and riseth up again: but the wicked shall fall in to mischief."* Do you seriously think that this verse would make business sense to man? Where is the success in this?'

'Touché. But I thought this was what you wanted; I thought my pursuit of adventure around the globe was crazy, that settling down was what was right.'

'Perhaps. But it is right for those who it belongs to and not right for those that it does not belong to.'

'A *conundrum.*'

'Your words not mine. I would say that all lives have to follow a path and not all paths are as we wish them to be. The wisdom of man is foolishness before God and vice versa,' Cephas said. 'How do you explain your visions to other people?' he asked.

'I can't, not to everyone. Most people think it's a dream or some kind of hallucination, very few accept what it is.'

'But you are willing to believe that they happen for real.'

'They do happen for real. I have seen them come to pass. You are present!'

'Then if they do not believe you for something that is so real that you are so convinced has come to pass what makes you think they would believe you for something that you don't even believe in, that you are so unsure it is what you really want to happen?'

'I told you that I was getting old,' I replied weakly knowing my excuse was shared by many under a mobocracy that mankind could hide behind. The fact remained that I was in a quandary unable to move forwards or backwards and lost in the present.

'You are old, it would be wise for you to remember that pleasing mankind other than God never rewarded you with anything else but problems!' Cephas winced.

It was two years ago in this same city on assignment that I had decided to go to Riyadh to start a new life. I shifted uncomfortably in the black turtleneck I was wearing, my eyes following the rows of booths in the Hilton dining room to the large windows and beyond. Darkness had descended through the city along with a large moon and stars. It had rained earlier on and now it was the turn of the wind as it lashed out repeatedly at the thick glass, its whirring sound a slight cause for concern as the trees outside wavered beneath its fury.

That decision had worked in my favour. I had discovered a patrimony. An inheritance from the Lord to be kindled by traveling the surfaces on which the ancients who had believed in him had also walked. I had my own experiences and in a vicarious presence I could also relate to those of the ancients. I could not regret Riyadh as I had liked the rugged nature of the land and even the mistreatment in the end emphasized why I went there. Now I was stalked by something new. It wasn't boredom or an aching for adventure it was a calling, persistent and determined.

Time was ticking away and it had just gone past ten. It was late yet I felt the night had barely begun for my thoughts to wander.

'Sir would you like anything else?'

The waiter's question cut through to me and I shook my head. The man placed a small bowl of pastilles before me and walked off. I yawned, I was exhausted and needed sleep or I would appear heavy eyed for the interview in the morning. Cephas was right again! Who was I kidding? It would be like old times the need to win making me rise to the challenge but would it mean anything? This wasn't the *calling* that stalked me. There had to be more, something else.

Mougins; I woke up to the grey darkness of a breaking dawn and lay motionless on my back with my eyes closed for a short while, afraid to open them in case it was too soon. There was something about jumping out of bed quickly that disoriented one throwing your brain into confusion. It was better to stay still for a while, get your bearings right before making any abrupt movements. I couldn't tell what the time was but it felt early. I climbed out of bed slowly and quietly to avoid disturbing Sarai. Soon I was on my knees bowing my head and saying my prayers. It was a practiced custom something I had done for as long as I could remember. Then I was moving, walking with light footfalls to the bathroom and quietly shutting the door behind me. I had added two new routines to this ritual that had taken a lifetime to perfect. Now I had responsibilities, there were other people to take care of, other people to bring along with me. For now they were incapable of understanding anything, they just lived their lives.

I left the bathroom and walked silently to the

children's room. Sarai had said because they were still so young it was best if they all slept in the same room. The room next to ours was large enough to accommodate three medium sized beds and the preferred choice so I had a short walk ahead of me to my next point of call in the large house. I pushed the door ajar slowly and as expected Joshua and Rachel were still sound asleep. The surprise was Luke. He too slept but I knew this would not be for long. He would be the first to wake up. What followed next was anyone's guess unless Sarai or me were prompt in getting to him first. If things went according to plan then a chaotic morning could be avoided, else the rest of the household was in for a treat. Today was different for it looked as though the Lord had spared me from my parental obligations. I walked back to the room and climbed silently back into bed. Sarai hadn't moved. I listened to her silent breathing, her head barely visible beneath the covers. My duties were complete for now and perhaps there was still a little sleep left in me. Things were so different now from what they used to be. In another time and place I would lie down to be transported to be the other person the other body that walked in a world, a different world far from the reality of one's imagination. I was glad God had showed me this world. I was glad that God had given me the grace and courage to accept it. Then I had been two people, the man, a human being that led one life, one in which he faced obligations of the world and its desires. My spirit was considered a separate entity altogether by choice as I watched it lead me through valley and doorways that would eventually make us into one.

It is a life that let's us see the world for what it is, I thought, as I listened to the quiet breathing of my wife beside me. It is a life that let's us fulfill dreams beyond understanding. It is a life that let's us cherish nature and our blessings. It is a life of poverty hope and understanding. It is a life where riches make men hate one another. It is a life where there is less of us and more of them. It is a life where a few encounters mean more than many. Hand in hand spirit and man walk, spirit guiding man away from his past in order to have a complete future. So much had been lost back then that it was hard to fathom what would be gained. And gain it had been because what God had given back to me made what I had lost a figment of my imagination. I had to learn to live without in order to appreciate how to live with. I had to push away everything and everyone, alienate what was familiar, to find what was true and real. In this I discovered the true light and love that God provided. If the man fully loved God without then he would love God in truth and in spirit within. It was an exodus, leaving behind a past life of slavery to what man was, in search of what spirit was to man. If one fully appreciated and understood this then they could gain a better resurrection with Christ. The words were easier said than done as it took almost a lifetime to leave the past behind. If that wasn't too much of a burden to carry, understanding the spirit certainly put things into perspective. This was another world, a new universe of numerous possibilities yet one truth, one way and one life. Only one person could merge the two together and that was Christ. When this was complete the man would be anointed with the name of the spirit as he had been reborn into the new being. I passed this test. It wasn't because I was good at what I did or I was wise enough to understand the teachings. I had passed because God had granted me the grace to. I had passed because I knew that the lesson was never over until I met my maker. It was visceral and the spiritual world, no one knew where it started or ended they accepted the alpha and omega, the beginning and the end as God because there could be nothing before him or after him.

'You will have to warm Luke's milk.' Sarai said sleepily as she rolled over throwing her hand over my chest. She said nothing after that and continued sleeping on my chest as if she was speaking in her sleep. I did not answer rubbing her arm gently as I let my mind visit those places that it so desired. Spirit and human had traveled together searching to become one. Finally they had done it, united in one but it hadn't been easy.

London2008; The squirrel hopped unto the fence navigating its way along the narrow beam until it reached the wall. Two more leaps of faith and it was there. The window ledge had safer bearings than the fence. It looked beyond the window ledge for any signs of life within but there was none, none anyway at this time of the morning. It was safe to go further. It climbed the short distance up the wall and then it was in the roof. Soon it was in the confines of the loft away from any prowling eyes. It began its next task of shifting the scrap of cardboard. It would attempt to make its home here and no one would be able to get at it from inside. It was safe here.

I heard the noise and shook my head in dismay. If it wasn't the rats then it was the cats and now I had a new adversary in a squirrel. The trials were endless it was one animal after the other making my life a misery. London was throwing everything it had at me and it was working. I had lost count of how many rats I had maimed. The house was wired with traps but the things just kept coming and when I thought I had finally finished them off I discovered that a squirrel had moved into the loft.

There was no need reliving Dublin as it had been far from a refreshing experience. I had lost that opportunity on sheer boredom, the humdrum of the process painstakingly overwhelming. Bodies had come into the room and left, their gait and mood a practiced routine to subdue the candidate and shock them into believing that they were getting more than they had bargained for; the idea an entryism into a modern world that most would hope for. It was inept even previsional to say the least. I had done the same to others in the past and was no charlatan. Break them; take control. A clever strategy that - works if you were planning to use it on someone that knew nothing about it! Surely this wasn't the future I had in mind? More importantly I was now certain that the calling was there, the answer even more prominent. And it had been present on that day - this is not what you're looking for. Then there were my new surroundings to consider. The colourful rooms were more like a children's playground even though I was certain the idea was to put back enthusiasm into the work environment. We are modern, hold no restrictions and boundaries, accept all through our doors. The place was farcical and obvious! Show me a knife and I would show you a fork! Give me something to wake up for! You're annoying! The ghosts were back! Vipers in a dead alleyway! How would I cope? I had no motivation for the job. I had become the victim of my success. Nothing appeared to be new in the business. The jittering I was feeling came from the early years of attaining too much in such a short time. Was I *losing* it? Impossible, surely I am much better than *this*! I was a dreadnought in this business and had a reputation to maintain. I had taught many and would teach me if needed!

Two months after Dublin I took on the task of rejuvenating the old enthusiasm. I had done this many times over before. I was sanguine, had worked for many companies and believed I had the experience and depth to bring my old ambition in from the cold.

I was wrong.

Every new paper I opened, every new advert I read or applied to felt like a long walk into hell. They were all the same. The money wasn't the problem the issue was I knew what lay ahead. I had seen it all before! I had walked the paths before and no amount of money or position would make a difference. Even the pressures that life was throwing at me couldn't instigate a comeback. *Something else* matters! *Something else* needs my attention! *Something else* is my *de jure*! Settling into the normal rhythm of society that had been established by many was not my desire. I needed more; I had been shown a world beyond the confines of the universe. The real question was what I was willing to forgo in order to seek this.

Poverty and tribulation loomed in the distance.

I was now financially downtrodden. I could barely pick up the phone or open another white envelop. Some of the credit card banks had resorted to a more colourful approach. Hide and we would find you! You would have to try harder than this! They disguised their letters by placing them in coloured envelops as opposed to white, adding their personal touch by addressing it to the recipient handwritten. It was a clever idea to deceive the recipient into opening the letter believing that it was personal. In my case it did not work. The threats paid no dividends; I had already declared my possessions *bona vacantia*, if they wanted them they could take them. All doors had been shut to the outside world as I sought guidance from within. It looked like my plans to seek normality had vanished because I was incapable of living this way. If I could not follow the path that I had deliberately returned from Riyadh for, then what else was there for me? To be more precise where else was there?

I lay in bed with my arms crossed at the back of my head, my clavicle resting on the pillow and stared vacuously at the ceiling. My situation was now exigent; *use thy davit to lower the lifeboat*! It was warranted. I had nothing left, no money in the banks or on my credit cards but I needed to live, to exist. The difficulty was how easily my mind cried out while my body did nothing to support it. I was in free fall and telling myself to survive by the day for that is all that was needed. *Madness*! There was a growling sound from my stomach and I knew that I had to move. I knew that somewhere in the house I had some money. I had a lot of foreign currency from my travels, if I could change this it could get me to the end of the week and then it was anyone's guess what happened beyond that. It was the only way forward, one day at a time.

'I oppose this line of thinking,' Cephas was distraught.

'Do I have a choice?' I scorned.

'If thou faint in the face of adversity then thy strength is small.'

Another slap in the face! The kind of words you wish you never knew especially when you were in hell.

'We want the same thing albeit one of us knows exactly what this is and the other doesn't. To reap the rewards of the spiritual you have to undergo the tribulation of this world. We have to make the final *leap*! We have come too far to fail,' Cephas said.

'Perhaps I need something to get me started because I am stranded,' I replied. It was the voice of a junky, one that had fallen to the street crawling on his knees helplessly.

'God gave us plenty, we saw so much, we had so much, do not forget.'

'I haven't.'

'Yet I can hear the murmuring, have you forgotten

who murmured in this manner before? Have you forgotten the hidden manna in reserve for these times?'

It was my turn to be silent. I was shutting out sound and the dreaded ghost voices subduing the termagant and its league of crones. As peace descended to my wounded mind I turned to God. I had to find the Lord and he would show me the way.

The movie had now been on for over an hour as the children sat before the television with their round eyes glued to the screen, their every thought going into whether the man would be given some kind of signal that the villain he pursued with such tenacity was his brother. The men had been separated at birth and brought up as orphans in different homes and now their upbringing had set them against one another. No one spoke in the room. It was on rare occasions that they could watch a movie without the electricity shutting down on them. Besides there was a deadline to meet, the movie was borrowed. They had promised to return it the next day, this way they could get another. It was an insatiable appetite, it was the holidays and this time was what they craved for all year round.

In the kitchen the sparks had begun to flare. The iron on the shirt had now burnt through to the wood and this had slowly ignited. Its cord had caught fire and was now burning its way through to the plug.

'What's that sound?' one of the children asked.

'What sound?' his sister replied without taking her eyes of the screen.

'I thought I heard something.'

'You did its coming from the movie.'

'Don't you smell something?'

'Oh no I forgot the iron....' Their housekeeper said and ran into the kitchen. She was too late, the flames had gathered momentum and taken to the kitchen which was nearest; the cupboards acting as accelerants. The place was on fire. The girl screamed in fright and all the children ran into the kitchen.

'*Get out*!' she shouted even louder. 'Can't you see that the place is on fire?'

They all ran out frightened at what they had seen, what they had done. Someone had to do something soon, real soon.

'We should cry fire and get help!' one of the older children said to the younger ones as he looked around for something, anything to put out the fire.

It was West Africa 1983, there were no fire trucks or any emergency services. The children made do with what they had. In the field at the front of the house some of the younger ones screamed at the top of their voices for help whilst the older ones rushed back and forth to the pile of sand at the back of the house returning with buckets and throwing as much as they could at the fire. Soon the children's cries were heard. Their neighbours had entered into the battle and they all fought the fire relentlessly. Eventually the fire was subdued as the tired hands and legs worked at the remaining flames. They had won and the fire had claimed no lives but burnt the kitchen outright. The children stared at it in dismay. This was a nightmare! No food for that evening, no kitchen, no movie for that matter and worst of all what would they tell their mum when she returned. They had been careless! It was rare but they had almost succeeded in burning down the house. No one spoke as they stared blindly at the kitchen.

They all heard her before anyone could see her.

'Are they okay? I mean I hope they are alright. I don't want to lose my children.'

Their Mum spoke to one of the neighbours who related the events of the evening. None of the children moved. They sat outside with their hands on their heads.

'Now wake up and remember!' A croon. It was soft yet audible and just enough to get me moving.

I practically jumped off the bed. I had dozed off lightly. That annoying squirrel had finally disappeared allowing me some time for an early nap. Now it was as if someone else was in my head shouting.

'Remember what?' I heard myself cry out aloud.

'The conversation with your mum, she said all she could think of then were her children, nothing else mattered at the time, not the kitchen, nothing else.'

'So?' I replied puzzled. There had to be a clue somewhere, Cephas was prone to these riddles still I had never known him to give a wrong clue especially in times like this.

'Was it the fire, did it have anything to do with my past?' I asked foolishly.

'Not the *past*! The *present*! *Children*!'

Cephas was practically screaming at me now. I lay in bed puzzled, why *children*, what did this have to do with anything. Why had Cephas taken me back to this time and this image of the burning flames? What had my mum said then? It had been years since we had held this discussion but there was something she had said, something Cephas wanted me to see. My mum had said it was very difficult to lose a child, my mum had said you carried them around for nine months in your stomach and during that time you got to understand that they were a part of you, that they belonged to you.

'Snap out of it!' Cephas muttered.

'I am trying my best here. I have very little to go on.'

'Nine months!' Cephas hissed and then he was gone as if he had never been there.

215

I snapped to attention and sat up in bed. I swung my legs of the bed, my hands already searching, something had just happened. I had to find out, make certain. I rushed for my diary.

'It *can't* be. No, this isn't *possible*!' I almost shouted alone. They *were* children but no they *weren't*? How many had fallen into *my palm*? *Three*! That was the number. Yes, three figurine had fallen into the palm of my hand. The *vision*. The pain had been excruciating to start with. My back had hurt like hell but Cephas had been present, opening the spirit palm in the spiritual world and the three pin like objects, *figurine* had fallen into his hand, my hand. But this weren't three little men or children for that matter. The clue was in the *nine months*. And the pain it took for the pregnancy. *Children in a woman's stomach* is equivalent to *it*; the *pain*! They were identical, maybe not a perfect match! But identical nonetheless! I knew that I had seen something like it somewhere else. I just needed to be patient and search for the right verse. Yes! I have *found* it! I turned to the book of Revelation and read,

"And I went unto the angel, and said unto him, Give me the little book. And he said unto me, Take it, and 'eat it up; and it shall make thy belly bitter, but it shall be in they mouth sweet as honey.

And I took the little book out of the angel's hand and ate it up; and it was in my mouth sweet as honey: and as soon as I had eaten it, my belly was bitter.

And he said to me, Thou must prophesy again before many peoples, and nations, and tongues, and kings."

These three men were the *trilogy*. They were *three books* that I must write. They were the interpretation of the *vision*, they were the terms of *my scroll* and there was no running away from this. Cephas had opened the spirit palm to receive the figurine and now it was my turn to bring them to life. I had to recount events from my life as instructed by the Lord; they were my testimony of faith and a message from God.

I lay back in bed and allowed my heart beat to settle down to a calm rhythm. I had done two and there was still one more to go. It won't be easy but I would ask the Lord for help.

Cephas was silent this time. It had been two years since Glyfada and finally I understood one of the visions, the figurine. It won't be easy but at least I had taken the first step in the right direction. If I could forget the woes and throes of my environment then I would make it through the difficult journey that lay before me.

When God chose Jonah to cry against the city of Nineveh his first instinct was to flee the scene. He ended up aboard a ship to Tarshish thinking that he had escaped his mission. However, his efforts were rewarded by spending three days and three nights in the belly of a fish. His last words of prayer to the Lord before he was vomited upon dry land where, '*I will sacrifice unto thee with the voice of thanksgiving; I will pay that that I have vowed.' Salvation is of the Lord.*' And in that instant Jonah was reinstated to carry out his mission.

I knew this story all too well. I knew I could not deviate from the mission at hand. Spirit knew this and spirit had awoken a past for me to understand the present. I had to let go, leave behind this quest for a family for now and my financial woes and focus on the task at hand. My mission was to complete the books as the vision instructed me to. The timing was perfect. I was stranded between worlds and unable to return to that which I knew because I was bored stiff having been in it for so many years and accustomed to all comforts it provided. Seeking pastures new was one thing but doing so without guidance made one's steps a little tentative. The Lord had come to my rescue. He had provided the spirit to allow me see the past, live the vision and interpret its purpose. Now I had to fulfill it.

Chapter Twelve

Mougins. Is time a true reference point for what we are about to experience? When does the old die for the new to start living? Fingers, creepy extensions now on my face that crawl like spiders on the wall. Has fear become a companion or is this new friend a foe? Doubt died many light years ago. Where do I dance in this magic? My heart beat, a pounding sound, loud drumming of rain on a windshield. Change will come, will find me, find you, who hides from this truth? Banished, abandoned, escape, run, sprint, change velocity, no, fly!

'Cephas!'

'Cephas, darling!' Sarai called to me again.

'You're back,' I said shutting off the traveler and returning to my present reality.

'Yes and terribly exhausted,' Sarai said throwing her bag on the sofa and slumping into the cushion beside me. 'Darling give me the green light and I shall leave work immediately.'

'You know you can quit anytime you want. You prefer to work.'

'A girl's got to do something with her spare time.'

'I'm not the one complaining.'

'You strange man, very strange man,' Sarai said rolling her eyes at me. 'Did you get any work done today. I know I left you in it.'

'I did. Although I have to say I played with the kids for a majority of the day.'

'Then I take it my babies are all fast asleep?' Sarai said slinging my arm over her shoulders.

'Your babies couldn't stay up for you,' I replied. 'They gave it their best shot but as usual were defeated by droopy eyes.'

'Zurich was damp and I have to say I almost cut my

day in half. It made me wish I was back here in the sun with you guys. It is always difficult getting back into things after a lengthy vacation.'

'You could be on vacation all year round.'

'I know, I know. It's hard to leave after building so much over the years. However I have to say that the past few days have made me begin to reconsider.'

'My last days of a normal job as people would say were difficult. I left Saudi sooner than I expected and then it felt as though nothing was good enough until this.'

'My problem is I haven't given much thought as to what I would do if I leave. Zurich made me feel I could be a consultant, work for myself and take on international projects. I'd feel bad leaving the team though. But I could be here for my babies always and spend more time with you without these trips.'

'You do work from home though. They see you all the time.'

'The operative word there is work. I work from home,' Sarai said, I could read the frustration in her eyes. Why did men have to be so rational? Why couldn't I just tell her to stay at home? Instruct her to quit? The real question though was would she listen? I'd be chasing shadows trying to read what was going on in her mind and it was advisable to seek a different course of action.

I pulled her closer to me kissing her lightly on the forehead and allowing her to bury her head in my chest.

'Have you eaten?' I asked.

'No but it's too late. I shall just have some soup and bread. I called Elodie this evening and told her to leave something for me. I just need to heat it.'

'Would you like me to do this for you while you get changed?'

'Will you? Thank you, darling. I would take a

shower and check on my babies, so don't rush to it. You can have some with me. I know you waited. I made sure there was enough for two.'

I tightened my grip on her and then got up from the sofa to pull her up to her feet. 'Always the clever one aren't you? Why wouldn't I have eaten, it's almost ten.'

'Yes but you always wait for me. I know you better than you know yourself,' Sarai said with her back to me as she walked towards the stairs. Even if I had eaten there'd still be some room left somewhere for her, she did the same for me when I was away. This way we shared a meal together. We had done this even before we got married. She was right, she knew me better than I knew myself.

"*Ye gather money with holes in your pocket.*" That's how I left darling. When she had talked about leaving her job this was what I had wanted to say but held back. I was a different person back then with an insatiable appetite that haunted me. I wanted some then more and then everything, nothing was ever enough. I wanted to be the best, knew I could be but also knew with this came the burden of an entrapment. I had to run, escape from myself, sprint, change velocity, no fly! I had to leave to be with you, to find you to find the future and leave the past behind.

'Things are different now my darling,' I thought. I'm here, I'm now, I'm me and I'm real.

In October 1992, on the High Road at its axis with Lordship Lane in North London, the intense rivalry between shopkeepers had lifted business on the high street. It was almost lunchtime and the small Jewish bakery was already crowded as orders were shouted to the back of the bakery for different types of bagels. They were famous and unlike most of the other high street shops their nearest rivals were located moving

221

central, closer to Stoke Newington past Stamford Hill. This wasn't common knowledge, even for those who had lived in the area for years but it was to me. There were very few places in the area that could do a warm bagel with tuna as these two.

However today was different for me. It wasn't that I did not fancy one of my favourite pastimes it was the fact that I couldn't afford such pleasantries as I was on a very tight budget. I headed for the government office located midway down the High Road my thoughts focused on the interview and what I was going to say. They would ask me if I had been trying to get a job, to which I had proof. There were a hundred or so rejection letters from the companies I had applied to. They would then ask me to walk across the road to another of their buildings to pick out employment adverts off their advertisement walls. I would yet wonder whether any of this would make a difference. I won't argue. It was their way, the government's way in believing that they had a program to get those less fortunate as I was into work.

I took the twirling stairs two at a time until I came to the reception area. There was a long queue as expected and I stood in line to be called forward. The faces beside me bore the expressions of the forgotten, the depressed and the downtrodden. Society had found a way to cater for us, a modern day *chautauqua* and I was sampling one of those outlets.

'Sir what are you capable of doing? What work can you do apart from those you have applied to?' the lady asked me. She was probably reading these questions off some sort of government pamphlet. No doubt their experts had taken the time out to train the staff accordingly. I almost shouted at the woman. *Nuts*! If I couldn't think of those questions myself what was the point of my education. Why did these people make one feel less than one already was? My expression must have said it all for her next question was,

'Sir I am only doing my job and trying to help. How long did you say you had been out of work for again?' she asked, this time her eyes revealing compassion. I did not know which was worse, her empathy or the contempt I had felt with her previous words. Either way it was a no win situation for the poor lady. Someone had to deal with the menagerie and it was her job to sort out the misfits. I hadn't a choice. This was what I knew. This was the service my government had told me that I was entitled to. This was the guidance I had received after all the prayers and tears. The compensation was little but it was what was available to get me through the tough times. It was my first exposure to the real world and these were the only tools available.

Cephas's time would come.

When John the Baptist baptized the Pharisees and Sadducees his words were:

"I indeed baptize you with water unto repentance: 'but he that cometh after me is mightier than I, whose shoes I am not worthy to bear: he shall 'baptize you with the Holy Ghost and with 'fire:

Whose fan is in his hand, and he will through purge 'his floor, and 'gather his wheat into the garner; but he will 'burn up the chaff with' unquenchable fire.'

After this it is written in the Bible of the coming of Christ and of his baptism with the Holy Ghost.

There was a process in place. There had to be, for the scripture to be fulfilled. Paul seconded John the Baptist words with more teachings in the book of Hebrews. He taught of the faults with the old covenant that God had made with the people:

"For if the first covenant had been faultless, then should no place have been sought for the second." Paul

then went further to describe the holiest of places that had been created by Moses and the anointed priest Aaron to make sacrifices to God for a remembrance of sins. He said that this changed with the coming of Christ, the Lord himself being the main sacrifice by his own blood allowing for the coming of the Holy Ghost to man.

London, March 2008. Cephas could also hear the sound and assumed that even the birds in the trees could hear it. They fluttered time and again as if being driven away by something mysterious. They were sounds he was all too familiar with and they were coming from his entity, his being, me.

I shuffled over to the fridge and looked inside. There was only water and my heart sank. My stomach had been growling all night. I had fished through the cabinets the night before and come up with flour and salt. I had mixed the dough and come up with dumplings; it was giving myself credit for calling them dumplings considering that they had no real nutritious content still they had appeased my hunger. Now I stared at the empty fridge. In the bible the children of Israel had asked God why he had taken them out of Egypt hoping for a Promised Land only for them to suffer in the wilderness. I was at the point of my life when I was feeling almost in a position to ask the same questions and be justified by them. It was not as if I wanted anything else, not a new house, not a new car, not a new wife or even a dog, just something to eat and appease the noise that was now deafening.

However I knew there was no going back to the man of old I had to rely on something new and different this time. Even if it killed me I won't be returning to the government for support. The *past*! That outlet had served its purpose during the dark days of 1992. It had been the manna from heaven to feed the hungry during their cries in the wilderness. Now I was different I knew someone else. I was no shavetail, I had been there and received the medals of a man that was prepared to face all kinds of havoc that would be thrown at him. Besides I wasn't alone. We were two, where I failed Cephas took over and more so he was my spiritual avenue to the Lord and to salvation. I couldn't falter so easily, I would have to dig deep. There had to be a way.

If thou faint in the face of adversity then thy strength is small. We have to share in the fellowship of his longsuffering for us to be one.

I began a dreaded search for all the pennies in my flat. I had exchanged all the foreign currency the week before and survived. It wasn't so important planning for the future because the Lord had said only God knew what the future entailed. It was important to keep my head steady and focus on the day. Those pennies I threw around the house would come in handy someday. Today was that day.

Mougins. Sarai put down the phone and picked up her spoon sipping some of the soup that was left in her bowl.

'That was Hailey,' She said looking across the table at me. 'Looks like we are on, her boss has agreed for her to do a story on both of us.'

'I still can't think of what I have to add to what you already told her,' I said looking quizzically at Sarai.

'Oh you have plenty to say. What about what you write, there's more to you than meets the eye,' Sarai chided.

'It's so different though. Is that what her readers would want?'

'You won't get out of this one darling. You will do it for me. I don't care what her readers want, I care that we both do it together, besides if they don't like it then tough.'

'You're a tough cookie woman, determined too.'

'That's why you love me, besides what's wrong with people knowing about God and the spiritual world? It won't harm them. It might even be enlightening. Look at me, look at us. Aren't we okay?'

'I'm left speechless with that argument sweet heart,' I replied. If only she knew how happy I felt at her words. God is my life and my salvation my darling, I would want nothing better for the world to hear about him, hear about what he has done for me and how he still makes my life so different each day.

'And so you should be. You should know I would stop at nothing to get my way, our way.'

I reached across the table and opened my hand. Sarai put hers in mine and I squeezed lightly.

'Do you feel it? Feel my heart my darling, I'm singing and dancing. There are no words to this music but who needs them to a song that is sung beyond the stars. Your beauty is not just in your looks but in the warmth from your heart. I am humbled when I meet a fellow traveler that isn't afraid to talk of the Lord.'

As the words escaped my lips I felt the warmth come through Sarai's hand. She said nothing. I could feel the quake so strong within her that my hand jerked as she shivered. I knew what came with that feeling. It was spirit and you felt rain and warmth, then the rainbow. If you were at one end then spirit was at the other. The bridge between worlds was our Lord. My words weren't mine but his and Sarai was moving across this rainbow now following these words and letting the Lord in.

'My beautiful mysterious man, why won't anyone wish to know about you?' she asked.

'That's the thing my darling it isn't about me they would be hearing about. It would be about the father. I am but the tool, a mere extension.'

'You are the tool I love and I thank the father for bringing you to me. Let them hear about the father.'

'And here is me thinking I was a faithful servant. Once more I am humbled by such courage,' I said. Inwardly tears of joy flowed, overpowering the damp as spirit and man cried out in unison. Look Father! Look! Am I thy servant that never screams in vain! You brought her to me and she commands the seas and the mountains to be moved and they move by your grace. Dare I quote my Lord, such faith have I not seen. Ah but I am the fool dear father for not understanding that you won't send any less to walk alongside me on this great voyage. I'm singing father and dancing in your light. Let your name be glorified.

'Giving up everything for what we believe in is a pill all of us need to take sometime in our lives. We took it right, darling? We did at some point in our lives, you more than others so why shouldn't the world hear about it. I did and never ran away instead I ran towards you. We'll give them a story, we'll tell them about this world that God gives us,' Sarai said as she moved both hands to squeeze mine. Her long black hair had fallen over the bathrobe. Her beautiful face was arched forward intent on making me happy. It was her duty. This was why we always had to eat together when we were home. Neither of us wanted to miss these moments for anything in the world. We were locked in a place far from anywhere else and even when the silence descended our hearts whispered. It was the nature of this world. It was what you gained from leaving the past behind. It was what you gained from sacrificing in abundance.

I nodded and knew she understood why.

London. The small Asian man behind the counter in

Sainsbury looked at me in dismay. I could tell he was asking questions, something personal. Had I just wasted his time and those of all the other people in the queue by allowing him to tally up all my shopping without any real money?

'Sir you cannot use those here. You have to exchange them at customer service. Do that and you can pay for your goods, I will put them aside until you return.' He said politely and looked to the next customer.

'Thanks,' I said and walked off. I smiled to myself as I walked out of the shop. I would change the vouchers for cash elsewhere. They won't know me there and I won't be nervous as I packaged my goods. I would choose correctly and take my time with a list. Many people lived like this, I hadn't over the years because the Lord had given me more. Now the Lord demanded something else of me and I would stand up and be counted. The cashier may have thought nothing of it but unlike before, unlike *1992* on the High Road were I was annoyed and humiliated before the employment benefit's employee this time I was proud to be taking one on the chin for my faith. I had seen the world, I had been to new cities, to ancient cities, I had been rich and I had been poor, now I was immune to either. There was no humiliation in what I was doing, just faith and determination to make the journey as I had set my mind to. I wasn't complaining I had been thinking of going to the other shop in any case. It wasn't that far off and more importantly they stocked my favourite biscuits.

It was getting late and Cephas was lingering. I had succeeded through the day. I had changed vouchers for bank notes and bought food. I had made do with what I had and survived through the day. I could now fully comprehend the words:

"Man cannot live by bread alone but by every word that proceedeth from the mouth of God." I was months into my odyssey to be one with spirit and our Lord and savior. Hunger had not taken away my faith it had strengthened it. With the growling sound from my stomach gone there was peace and as a new dawn descended upon me I felt the calling and a new vision. I was again spirit and Cephas was present.

It was a wide hallway. The walls were covered in plain white but shown as yellow from the reflection of the sunlight. Cephas followed the path past the shut doors until he got to the end of the hallway. He flew to the centre of the room. There were showers everywhere. I watched from beyond, from my world, earth. He *wouldn't* do it I thought. *No*! He couldn't I feared. I needn't have worried. I wasn't Cephas; not yet anyway. Cephas flew to the shower drainage. No one could be seen or heard, not that it mattered for he was invisible, he was spirit and could hardly be discerned by anyone. Soon he was diving through the drainage and then the pipes making his way to the other end of the building.

He emerged just outside the building at his desired target. The man was built like a small brick hut. Cephas approached him and offered his hand. I watched, this was my hand, the hand of spirit offered. Why? The man declined or rather from what I could discern made no effort to take it. I knew that he was the intended target and so the Lord had allowed the man to see the spirit yet the sailor was unwilling. In his all whites he stood before the building not bulging and believing in the strength of his well built physic. His years of training in the navy were good enough for him. He didn't need anyone or anything to save him. The navy was his home. He needed no one; it *wasn't his choice*, spirit was present, I was for a reason. I had been doing this for a while now and I knew that when God revealed these visions to me they weren't by my choice or those of whom it was intended for. These missions served a greater purpose than those at the end of it. Spirit went at the sailor in blistering speed lifting him from his current position and throwing him several metres away from where he had been standing. I watched stupefied and perplexed at Cephas's actions. Why this sailor and why not anyone else? And why had he thrown the man so far away? I didn't have to wait too long for the answer. The explosion that followed shortly was shocking even for a witness from a world, miles away from that of the spiritual. The building went up suddenly and the sailor was left staring in shock at what had just happened.

I was stirring, as I felt the refluence of spirit return to man. This vision was another mystery and another intriguing event that would take the Lord's grace to understand. I just had to wait and see.

Chapter Thirteen

New York. Hailey watched as the siren went screaming past her on 6th Avenue. It was just a normal day in the busy streets of New York, before long it would be forgotten for something else to take its place. She watched the pedestrian lights as the taxis wrestled for positions in front of her. Soon she was walking across the road and branching off into 17th street. It would take her to Union Square quicker, she had been to restaurants on these streets numerous times so it won't be difficult finding Susan's loft. Before long she was at the intercom waiting to be buzzed in.

'You found it then,' Susan said as she let her into the flat.

'Yes. I've been down here a few times.'

'I use this place sometimes to entertain. It's spacious and has good lighting, also one can do plenty with the huge windows and high ceilings,' Susan explained. The convenience of the location served its purpose for some clients.

'I can see how it would work with an artist or even a fashion shoot, it's ideal,' Hailey replied.

'Well come, come, let's use the facilities while we are here. I have a kitchen and I am brewing some coffee, I would pour you some.'

Hailey watched Susan at work in the wooden floored kitchen. The cabinets had been picked out from an IKEA catalogue. It was basic furnishing, one could tell that no one spent anymore time than was necessary in the apartment. If she changed a few things and made it a little cozy, it could be transformed to the ideal home and with its prime location she would be eating part of her hand to have a place such as this.

'It could be expensive, for something like this,' she said casually as she picked up the cup Susan had poured for her. There was no obligation for her boss to tell her the rent but one never got anywhere in life without asking.

'Well let's see I think this is about 2500square feet so it works out to about $5000 per month.'

Hailey blew her cheeks, whistling softly. I couldn't afford this even if I tried. Still one never knew whether they could hit the big time anytime soon. It was a pleasant dream to have, perhaps not one to relish yet.

'Do you know when I started building Rezance, I would have been shouting something insane if anyone had told me I would be paying for a place like this and using it for just entertainment. However it's what the clients want right? They want to be in the centre of everything. We are not doing so badly so we can afford places like this.'

'True. I was thinking the same thing just now. I like the location especially with all those restaurants.'

'Speaking of good food and good weather, you have been having a lot of that these days haven't you?' Susan said as she led them back into the centre of the room where there was some contemporary red furniture on a snowy white rug.

'I've been and may get some more thanks to you.'

'So who are these people and do you think we would be able to make something from this?' Susan asked. She had been in this business for as long as she could remember. There were all sorts of causes that people wanted her to write about but the readers demanded something in particular. They paid her wages and those of her staff for that matter. She was astute about chasing lost causes. One couldn't get ahead in the business without having an eye for what brought in the big bucks and what didn't.

'You know you've already signed my ticket to return so whatever I tell you now shouldn't make that much of a difference since I fly this Sunday.'

'That's why I called you here, I want to make sure I made the right decision. Tell me more about them.'

'Well the woman as you know is Sarai, she is a successful financial director for a firm based in London. She works in several countries in Europe but decides to be based in Nice, Mougins to be exact. I think most times she works from home. She has also worked in the Middle East.'

'Doesn't sound like one of our type then?' Susan quizzed. She was used to rich and bored house wives willing to tell their story. Most of them had gained their wealth through inheritance by family or marriage. They had been beautiful and glamorous at one time in their lives and now wanted to make the world understand that they still existed.

'I know what you're thinking. I was thinking the same too before I left here the first time. I still do even now but she certainly scores for the beauty and glamour part of our business. I mean we write stories on artists, even musicians at times.'

'We do.'

'I would say that we even stretch it to politicians when it benefits us.'

'No one said our public was subject to grimalkins. We bring a sense of alacrity to their lives. The news is not what one would want to hear these days so you have us balancing what is acute with what is glamour. A difficult place to be in still if tuned just right gives us the audience we require.'

'My point exactly, Sarai is one of those ladies that is beautiful, mysterious and yet there is a seriousness to her that makes other women want to be like her.'

'Well if you have her story why do you need to go back there?' Susan asked as she cradled her cup of coffee. It was good having something warm in her.

Perhaps the room needed more furniture. The emptiness made it feel colder.

'That's the thing I don't think I have. Well let's say I do and don't because I need some more especially about her husband.'

'You do know that our audience is primarily women. You do know what they are looking for. I mean this is what we breath into you day in day out.'

'I do, Sarai's husband is an author and they have three children. My article is still about her but there is something I can't explain or tell you right away which makes me feel I need to hear about him for her story to be complete.'

'How's that? I read what you have so far, it contains mystery, romance and something spiritual. Well I admit that it is a little different from what we usually have still you have kept it within the confines of what our readers want. Why do you really need to go back there? Do you wish to change your story?' Susan asked. She had ten writers including Hailey covering the main stories in the magazine. They had been carefully selected, interviewed by her with careful scrutiny on their backgrounds. She didn't employ marionettes still one couldn't run a successful business without acuity. She worked with the motto that efficiency in quality was better than quantity. If this girl wanted to keep progressing within her firm she would have to do better than this. She needed to convince her and so far she wasn't hearing anything different to what other writers said when they wanted to get their stories out.

'I don't know whether you got to read my complete submission but there are some specifics which are certainly different from anything that I have seen or written before. I mean Sarai's husband knew her before they met? How could he know how she would look like or what she did? Let me rephrase, what she would be doing long before he met her?' Hailey said.

'My dear girl it is not only women that fantasize about who they will meet and share the rest of their lives with. Men do too.' Susan offered benignly.

'The three children, two boys and a girl how did he know this?' Hailey asked. It was hard to believe that her role had now changed from one of doubt to that of the protector of faith. Why was she arguing Sarai's story? Hadn't she called it a coincidence when she had first heard about the children? Something was different.

'Okay say I was willing to say that all this was true and this man is some sort of prophet, a vatic for that matter how would this change what you have already written?'

'I know him, knew him before I got there, to Mougins I mean.'

'You knew him? You met him before? How when?' Susan asked. Perhaps Hailey was hiding something from her.

'We met once, very briefly I had just turned twenty-three and was working outside Athens in a town called Glyfada. We were all there for a conference. It was my first time in Europe and I was having a tough time believing in my dream of becoming a journalist. I met this stranger once at a bus stop who was kind to me. He told me that whatever I dreamed of becoming would happen if I believed in it. Except for my mum I never met anyone who believed in what I could become before then. Cephas was different. He spoke so convincingly to me about it and that day even I knew it was real, that one day I would become this person. Before I left Mougins Sarai and I went to pick up Cephas and the children from the airport. He remembered me immediately. Like you I had doubts about this man being a prophet until I met him again. It was then I realized why I must write Sarai's story.'

Susan was silent for a while. Her gaze had moved from Hailey's face to the large window behind her and beyond. Was our world this complicated or rather this small? It was one thing for this girl to desire a story but another for all these coincidences to be so cleverly shaped.

'What would you do differently this time around? What would you ask that would change what you already have?' She quizzed.

'That's the thing I don't think I am going there to ask about them but rather to confirm that this is the story to write. I think when I get there the pieces would fall into place. It's one of those things that I am certain I won't regret and it would do a lot for our magazine.'

'I have to admit your part in the story adds a twist to it that even I find difficult to ignore. I am curious now as to what you would find,' Susan said puzzled at her own words.

Hailey grinned. She wasn't alone. Sarai had said this spiritual world of hers brought something different to everyone. You could be anything or any person in the world until it descended upon you, leaving you marveled at its brilliance. She was seeing it first hand as it affected this powerful businesswoman.

'You said you leave on Sunday.' It was not a question but a statement.

'I leave on Sunday,' Hailey replied. One hurdle over there were others waiting, soon Nice and then who knew what lay beyond. Perhaps the future looked blurry from where she stood but she couldn't help but feel that this was her own chance to learn to walk on water, learn to drown and then be reborn.

London. The man rang the bell twice, then thrice. He could hear the bell chimes ring out inside the house but no one came to the door. He dialed their number.

'I can see a car at the front of the house, maybe it is his. I have rung the bell and I can hear it within but there is no answer. There is no one in there.'

'Well I think we should try again and if he doesn't respond then we would have no choice.'

'I shall leave him a note just in case he is out maybe he shall call then.'

'Maybe,' the woman answered her voice pessimistic. She had been dealing with clients of this nature all her life. They often vanished into thin air as if they had never existed. Left to her she would start with the courts. It would save the heartache and the process of hiring a consultant. However it wasn't her choice as before the law the lenders had to be seen to be doing all they could to help their clients. It had been the company's decision to hire out consultants. They said the clients would respond to a sympathetic and friendly face before them than a voice over the phone. So far according to her records, using this method had resulted in a less than five percent success rate but still it was the law.

The man slid the note into the letterbox and climbed into his car. He hoped the client would call. It would be a pity if the matter had to go to court. Then there would be nothing he could do to help.

'*Wake up!*' It was a hiss so sharp that I almost jumped out of bed. I was suddenly wide awake and staring blankly at the ceiling, then nothing, no response.

'What is the point? Why are you bothering me? I have no one or time to answer to or anything planned for that matter so why the fuss. Let me sleep some more,' I replied. '*Wrong!*'

'Wrong? Why what has changed?'

'I shall quote the verse for you:

"*And though the Lord give you the bread of adversity, and the water of affliction, yet shall not thy*

237

teachers be removed into the corner anymore, but thine eyes shall see thy teachers.

And thine ears shall hear a word behind thee, saying this is the way walk ye in it, when ye turn to the right hand and when ye turn to the left."'

'I know these words but how do they relate to me?'

'The *contract*, the *man with one eye*, you *know him* you've met him. He *is real*,' Cephas said.

'Are you saying what I think you mean?' I sat up in bed. My eyes were now wide open and almost bolting out of my head.

'*Yes*!' the hiss now harsh and excited. 'What is your agent's name?'

'Jewel.'

'He is the man with *one eye*. He is the *vision*,' Cephas said.

I was dumbstruck. *Glyfada*! *Athens*! *Greece means something remember Thessalonians!* Cephas was watching. Spirit had waited on the Lord for this moment. It was only now that Spirit had been given permission to tell me of the contract, of the *man with one eye*, the *man in the park*. God had sent spirit there on purpose, to sign the contract. Make it real in his world before it descended into mine. This man was the link. In the vision God had shown the man in the park to have only one eye. It was the name of the man, *jewel*. The jewel represented the single eye in the man's forehead it was the sign that God had given.

'I *can't* believe it.'

'*Believe it*!'

'But I am nobody. I mean before God I am no one. How do I qualify to receive such a contract from the Lord, what have I done to deserve this gift?'

'It is not by works. Although works are important but the Lord has granted you this contract that is why everything else has failed. There won't be any other jobs. In order for this to happen you had to agree to *the resurrection* now there is no turning back it is only this way forward.'

'I work for God? God pays my wages, directly? And through a vision, he explains that he has signed a contract with me through an agent for books that I saw through a vision? Am I hearing this correctly?'

'*Yes.*'

'I am lost for words.'

'How do you feel?'

'Scared, excited, overwhelmed whatever else is beyond that, I feel it!' I screamed alone in the room. Who where my heroes? The prophets, the men chosen by God, inspired by their faith to preach his word, write his word. Now Cephas was telling me that I could be the same person, one of so few individuals blessed with gifts that were beyond this world and able to see into a future of what was to be. When the vision had happened I had thought nothing of it. It was one of those complicated visions that no matter how hard I tried I could never understand what it meant. Several months down the road I was calling to family and friends telling them that I had finally signed a contract with an agent who would market my books for life. This had been very difficult to come about and it had taken a long time but it had happened. *I can do my day job now in peace and not worry about the books, it makes sense it is the wise thing to do.*

However since penning my signature on paper all else had failed. There had been no work available no matter what I did. And worse of all I could barely motivate myself to do anything about my career. The only thought in my mind was my dream of becoming a writer. I never knew that this had already been certified by higher powers. It was a vision beyond this world. God had truly selected me amongst many to bring his word to the masses. First Cephas had told me of the *figurine*, the books and how they were related and now this - the *contract*, the *man with one eye*, my *agent*!

I heard this as my cue to get out of bed. I heard the sound. I often heard them circulating the area, the park. Perhaps they were called into the area for emergencies or it was just a routine sweep. However I did not have double-glazing to block out the droning rotors or make them less intrusive. The helicopter was almost above me now but today it meant nothing. I had more pressing matters to hand. I had been chosen by powers beyond this world *for real* to do *a job*. First I would call my mum and deliver the good news. She was the only person I had told of the vision. It was important that someone was privy to what happened, she was my witness, had been for some time now and she would be as excited as I was to see how this mystery unfolded.

I was in front of the mirror brushing rapidly and spitting out. How would I start? I would ask my Mum first if she remembered the agent's name. She would, she always remembered those little details then I would tell her just what Cephas had said, she would go beserk just as I had. It would make her day.

'*Look*!' the hiss was sharp and to the bone.

'What?' I replied my mouth agape, my toothbrush still in it and held by my hand, a statuesque figure.

'*Look*!' Cephas said the second time. '*Look at the picture*!'

'No!'

'*Yes*!'

'No it can't be. I am seeing things! *Madness*!'

'But *real*, He hasn't forgotten, never does and is faithful to those who love him. Look I say,' Cephas said.

I looked at the picture of my t-shirt. They were in it! Two boys, a girl and a woman, *no man*!

'It can't be,' I said aloud. 'It just can't be. No this is impossible! I am not looking.' Cephas was grinning. Spirit laughing at man and his frailties. He had waited for many years to tell me this. It was now taking just moments to reveal. God was the *revealer of secrets*.

I retraced my steps, there had been another vision I had been to a schoolyard and I had met a girl and boy and then I had flown to meet their younger brother. At the time I had wondered about this vision but now it was revealed. They *are my children*! It made sense that the spirit was first to have knowledge of this before me. Like the contract I was not only going to work for God but the Lord had given me a family, I would have two boys and a girl.

'Read the words.'

I did.

"*Your blood could be my blood.*" And beneath the picture it said,

"*Share your heritage… donate blood.*"

'Are you for real? It doesn't make any sense? I am imagining this, it is a coincidence,' I said.

'Call it what you will but you could not explain the man with one eye now you know who he is. Well this too is something that God has given you, given us. They are *yours*, *ours* if we see it to the end,' Cephas said.

I was perplexed. The pieces were fitting into place. It was like a gigantic puzzle. I had to be in place, had to serve time for the whole to be complete. If I had never chosen to write and to write spiritually I would never have received the contract. If I had taken the job in Ireland pursued an existence that looked normal in the eyes of man I would have missed this moment. If I hadn't been brave to see the vision then I could not have been here to receive its meaning. If I hadn't lost so much to keep me alone and isolated, away from the world, from the door and bell chimes I would not have seen this. The list went on forever. It was as if my life had been mapped out in one great puzzle with the Lord connecting all the dots in it for everything to work out the way it had. Everything and everyone served a purpose. There were landmarks, clues and counter clues to show me that everything was related. It just so happened that I had been to New York the year before and had collected the t-shirts from my brother and since then my brother had changed jobs. It just so happened that I had worked in Saudi Arabia walked the earth were many others had and faced my own trials and tribulations to grow in faith for this moment. It just so happened that after my contract was terminated I had returned to England and signed with a book agent, throwing away my past and seeking something different in pursuit of a dream. And then Greece, the visions, *do not quench prophesy* - everything had happened as in the visions. They had served their purpose. They had been explained. I had always wondered whether I would have a family of my own and now this.

'You aren't imagining this. It is for real.'

I tried to finish brushing my teeth with a determined level of calmness. The events of the morning had crammed my livelihood into one day and a lot of information to assimilate all at once. Cephas may have been taking this in his stride but for me there were levels of proportions to contemplate beyond reason. *Why me?* I wasn't such a good person, wouldn't put myself before the likes of those who sat in church and worshipped the Lord endlessly. However God had looked upon me with kindness and love to grant me visions that were beyond this world. It was impossible to think them up or plan them they just happened the way they did and I was there to observe, assimilate and be grateful. A contract, a wife and three children, two boys and a girl, all in one morning, it was out of this world.

I slipped into Nike trainers as I prepared to leave the house. I needed to go out into the fresh air and breath the essence that the Lord had provided. I went on my knees clasping my hands before me, it was a practiced routine only this time there was more than enough to be thankful for. After my prayers I trotted down the stairs, stepping on the note that had been dropped by the stranger earlier on in the day. I didn't look at it. I was destined for greater things. I would have to call my Mum. The earlier the better, there was too much to discuss, too much at stake to fail in this mission. Telling her was the half of it. This was only the beginning, the implications were far more important than anyone could imagine. I could lose everything, would lose everything as no time could be placed on God's promises. If my memory served me correctly then for the scripture to be fulfilled as in parts of the bible there were no deadlines set. *Do not observe, days, months, years and time*! The birth of Isaac as promised to Abraham hadn't happened immediately. The crossing of the wilderness by the children of Israel to the Promised Land hadn't happened overnight. Many prophets had voiced God's promise to the people of the coming of Christ, yet time had not been a factor for when this would eventually take place. When God promised it was guaranteed that he would deliver but who could tell when and what happened in between. If I had any questions such as how I would survive in the society of today with these visions, no money and no time for when they would be fulfilled, then the answer was there, *thy faith is sufficient for thee*.

The noise from the helicopter had vanished when I hit the streets.

'There is proof, *evidence*,' Cephas said.

'Will you stop sneaking up on me like that? You almost gave me a heart attack.'

'If they don't believe you then believe the word of God, you have proof.'

'I have faith and that is enough.'

'I know it is but God gives his own proof. *Remember Jonathan, before he went into the camp of the Philistines?* God proved his words to the prophets of old he will do the same with you,' Cephas said. 'You have always followed the paths of the prophets and believed that God spoke to them for real. If that is the case seek those words of old and you will find that this contract, the man with one eye is for real. His words of yesterday are the same today. Remember the terset, our resurrection, the connection, *all one.*'

'Which words should I be looking for and where?'

'The first book to start with is Exodus:

"Moreover he said, 'I am the God of thy father, the God of Abraham, the God of Isaac, and the God of Jacob. And Moses hid his face; 'for he was afraid to look upon God.

And the LORD said, 'I have surely seen the affliction of my people which are in Egypt, and have heard their 'cry by reason of their taskmasters; for I know their sorrows;

And I am come down to 'deliver them out of the hands of the Egyptians, and to bring them up out of that land 'unto a good land and a large, unto a land 'flowing with milk and honey; unto the place of the Canaanites, and the Hittites, and the Amorites and the Perizzites, and the Hivites, and the Jebusites."'

'I remember these words.'

'Then note that this is *your exodus*, you are being delivered from the old to live spiritually with God as he did for the children of Israel. However that is not all,

God also gave Moses a contract for the work he had to do.'

I was silent and listening. Cephas's words were like the chiming of the pendulum on an old clock, each sentence evoking a different tone.

'You asked the right questions earlier on.'

I said nothing. These moments were crucial it was better to listen, it was rewarding.

'Your words were: *Why me*? Remember? In the bathroom as you brushed your teeth.'

I remembered. I still had no answers to this. Why me, I was no one.

'Now hear Moses words and God's response to them:

"And Moses said unto God, 'Who am I, that I should go unto Pharoah, and that I should bring forth the children of Israel out of Egypt?

And he said, 'Certainly I will be with thee; and this shall be a token unto thee, that I have sent thee: When thou has brought forth the people out of Egypt, 'ye shall serve God upon this mountain.'"

Cephas didn't need to explain. The coin given to Cephas in the garden near the fountain in the park from *the man with one eye* was the token for the resurrection, the freedom from the past.

'That is not all. I told you that God's words of old are still those of today. There is one more verse that proves that God is with us on this mission.'

Silence was the key here and I was breathing. I had to listen to these words as carefully as I could. I was grateful that the helicopter had now left, that sound had been deafening. It was important to listen to all the evidence that supported my contract. When I stood before others they would be the ammunition that I needed.

'Let us go to the book of Malachi:

"Then they that feared the Lord 'spake often one to another: and the LORD hearkened, and heard it, and a book of remembrance was written before him for them that feared the LORD, and that thought upon his name.

And they shall be mine, saith the LORD of hosts, in that day when I make up my 'jewels; and 'I will spare them, 'as a man spareth his own son 'that serveth him."
And further on God said:

"Remember ye 'the law of Moses my servant, which I commanded unto him 'in Horeb for all Israel, with the statutes and judgments." These words are related with another wise saying from the book of Proverbs:

"There is gold, and a multitude of rubies: but the lips of knowledge are a precious jewel."'

Cephas said nothing after this allowing his words to sink in, allowing the words of the Lord to reach me. The man with one eye had delivered the token, God had said when he makes up his jewels he will spare those who trusted in him. Even if I searched through the archives of historical proof I couldn't find a better explanation for this vision. People would call it a coincidence, some a mere paraphrase. They would say they could draw conclusions through their lives of similar situations that linked them with words and phrases within the bible. It did not matter. *Faith needs no reason to be.* They could call it whatever they chose to but it would not eradicate the evidence. It was written in stone within me for me to see and abide by. God had made up his jewels and I had been spared. Faith was the measure of all things hoped for and my life was now one complete mystery that only the Lord could explain.

I took huge strides, my gait swifter as I hit the street. It was sunny outside as the summer months were near. However none of this made a difference. Life was brighter within me for nothing in the universe shown brighter than the wisdom and mystery that God had revealed to me. There was no time in my agenda that morning for returning calls to consultants from mortgage lenders. They were doing their job as I was doing mine. God had spoken to the prophet Haggai saying,

"Ye have sown much, and bring in little; ye eat, but ye have not enough; ye drink, but ye are not filled with drink; ye clothe you but there is none warm; and 'he that earneth wages earneth wages to put it into bags 'with holes."

If the house had to go then so be it, it would be sacrificed for something greater. In the Bible Job had lost his and gained more. It wasn't something that anyone planned for or wanted to happen to them but who could tell what God had planned for mankind. My visions were God's promise to me and they were all I had to go by. Everyone else and anyone else would have to wait.

Chapter Fourteen

New York. The high ceiling of the Cathedral traced contours that joined the main support pillars of the building. One could only but imagine what delicacy had gone into the design by the architect. Settling into one of the pews in the Lady Chapel just behind the Crypt was what she wanted. Hailey had stayed back from the tour group asking discreetly if she could have this short time alone within the chapel. No one could tell why she would be in a Cathedral at this time of the night except no one could also tell why she was experiencing the kind of changes that she was going through at this point in her life.

Her little discussion with Susan had elated her spirits as she triumphed against one of the toughest ladies in the business. Victory over the business mind to see that there was more to it than met the eye to this story, was already an indication of why her own involvement was meant to be. Susan was not the type of lady to cower to the visceral she protected her resplendent image in a shroud that was virtually impenetrable at the best of times. Still she had won and it was one step closer towards completing the tasks she had set for herself before heading out to Mougins. Now it was time to turn her attention fully to the perspicuous nature of the spiritual world. I know very little of what I am getting myself into but I have time. It was this time that she now relied upon to understand the mysteries that were suddenly carving out her existence. She had stolen a little bit of time to herself away from the busy streets in the ten minutes cab ride from Union Square to 51st. This had helped put some perspective to her plans. I can't go there empty handed. I have to learn how these people feel. I have to understand the tranquil that befalls one delving in to those places that seem unreachable. She knew it wasn't something that she could achieve in a day but she didn't plan on doing so. She just wanted to feel different and give herself the opportunity to do so within the confines of somewhere spiritual before her flight on Sunday.

The light falling into this part of the Cathedral was not like in the main sanctuary. It seemed darker isolated and away from everything and everyone. What were the rules in these confines? Was it customary to say a prayer? Where would she start? Do I listen from within, is it I searching or is there something within me, that would talk to me? Perhaps a day in a Sunday service would offer her more. However that would be praise and worship. She wanted it to come from within. I have to learn to feel, to know. Where do I start? Why do people say they know God, they feel God? Where did faith come from? There was so much history to the church, to religion, as people flocked to places of holiness seeking and searching for the spiritual person within them for enlightenment. How could one truly search for this without having to do anything? Sarai had literally told her that she reached this place just by giving up the past and allowing herself to believe through the words of Cephas. She said you were called by God and then granted the grace to seek him. It sounded like a plenary meeting that one acceded to without any knowledge of what the outcome would be. Who was the guide on this acclivity? Was this situation like before when she had a dream and a purpose and walked towards it with ardency that no one could dispute?

Once upon a time I was Hsu of Yong Ding. Once upon a time I was in another world were people could barely get clean water to bath with. Dreams were limited, reduced to old posters on one's bedroom wall with the knowledge that all one could accomplish was a good marriage and a kind husband. For most people that was enough but for me I wanted something else I wanted to search the world, report and write about it. China itself had so much history that if it was history she desired then that was the place to start. The difficulty was how the world measured things. It all came down to fame, a group of nations holding a franchise that made everyone else feel that without this they weren't successful. Still it was arduous to feel this way unless one believed it, or bought into it. So it wasn't down to this group of countries but the individuals that believed in them. She hadn't gone to Europe or to the US to seek success in becoming a journalist. She had gone to Europe and the US to seek approval from these nations that she was capable of doing those things like anyone else within them. If that was the case it wasn't their fault but hers. If she wrote an article for what was considered the acclaimed to read and approve then she was a great writer. The question one had to ask was whether the approval and enjoyment of others made the story any less appealing. Could music not be enjoyed by anyone regardless of background or origin? So how could this be any different?

It was already getting late. She had been staring blindly at the chapel looking at her past and the person she was then. She had to leave, have something to eat and get her things packed. Leaving the past behind wasn't leaving the place she had once lived in. Leaving the past wasn't about leaving Yong Ding or the name Hsu. She had strived ambitiously inspired for the trade that she loved. No one could begrudge her this, people did this everyday of their lives changing their circumstances for the better. Who could say that her ambition whether for the wrong or right reasons hadn't helped others. The real question was whether this ambition had deceived her, fooled her into believing that it had made her who she was and without it there was nothing else. It looked like reliving her past in the tranquil confines of the Chapel had shed some light within. It was the blind ambition of the path she had trekked that had to be examined and not Yong Ding.

Hailey walked out of the huge steel doors of the Cathedral and joined the horde of people in the street. There were all ages in the crowd; there were all races with many individual journeys. We constantly changed different things in our lives for different reasons but whom we were within stayed the same. If I hadn't been ambitious I would never have driven myself to come to Europe or the US. If I hadn't gone to Europe I would never have met this man Cephas. If I hadn't come to the US as a journalist, I would never have had this story that brings me on this roundtrip to meet the wife of Cephas. Each thing served a purpose, each pattern a time and place for what it achieved. The ambition had antecedently preceded this moment. It was obvious that any angst she may have felt digging up the past and Yong Ding could now be forgotten. It wasn't a past ambition to run from but one to understand. It looked like her first unguided tour in this unknown spiritual world had revealed something new. There was more around us than could be seen unless we searched for it. Sarai had talked about the spiritual world that she shared with her husband, perhaps she had meant the real world but with a better knowledge of what was around us. Maybe God wasn't someone you went to look for in a Chapel, he was someone you looked for when you searched for yourself. There were so many things to learn, so many different things to see. She had just started but she knew that she had given herself a chance before she met Cephas. At least she would have the right questions, have a feel for this place he called the spiritual world before she met him.

London June 2008. It was hard to tell what I was watching but I knew that I was in spirit. They came up as circles, the numbers barely visible. It was a count down from four and at one the movie started. This was even more difficult to follow. The man in it may have been arguing with the woman and then some children appeared from nowhere. Everything was happening at an incredible pace as it would in this type of movie. It was a black and white film, incredibly old and without sound. To understand the movie one had to watch the gestures as the people moved in the white empty space. Their lips worked a storm but there was no speech forthcoming and then the man was lying on the ground passed out and the woman standing over him as if she had been the cause of it. It was extremely confusing as I tried to see more. However it was the best I could make out of everything. Presumably there had been some kind of an argument and then events had taken a turn for the worse, the wife succeeding in overpowering the husband.

It was the passage, how it had manifested itself in that way was beyond my understanding but spirit was out. Cephas flew to a height close to the ceiling and then he was somewhere else, another time and another place. The woman was in her garden but she had seen me, I was sure she had. I recognized her as my mum. And then I was flying further past the garage and heading towards the neighbour's garden and then it was over as if it had never happened. Cephas was back in his entity, in me and his short voyage was another mystery that had been a welcome break.

I woke up. It had been confirmed. The day was my birthday. It was any ordinary day but I had asked quietly. I had needed confirmation for my actions.

Perhaps the events that had unfolded in the past few months had been a cause for concern of my sanity. Some of my friends had come to the conclusion that I was in a state of depression that the pressures of life had gotten to me and so I had decided to quit. They were wrong.

It was now several weeks since Cephas had confirmed who the man with one eye was. And as he had predicted things hadn't gotten any easier; my financial status had declined rapidly. There were no breaks, no outlets. I was waking up in the morning and going back to bed at night with only one thought, when would the Lord grant me the freedom from my cell? The days seemed longer and the nights, my only respite from the fear of a knock on the door from one of the debt collectors had become extremely short. Yet even then I was unwilling to budge. I could not go back on my word; my oath and the contract I had signed were inviolable. However the numerous obstacles that lay in my path had made me ask the Lord for further confirmation. I had gone on my knees the night before my birthday and spoken honestly to the Lord.

'I am not crazy father, I know that I hear your voice but let it not be my imagination that is making up these visions and their interpretations. Let it be you. Father I need a sign. Tomorrow is my birthday. I have never celebrated it, never wished for anything on it. I have no need for it and feel nothing on this day but I wish for one thing, a sign, a vision. This would be a present beyond the realms of this world that would erase any doubt that it is you that has decided for me to walk this path.' I had said these words and then gone to sleep. In the morning Cephas had been in his element and the vision had happened. *God was with us*. It wasn't my imagination it was the Lord confirming in his own way that I wasn't crazy or in a state of depression I was working hand in hand with the Lord to fulfill the promise and I had received my annuity in the token, in the coin placed in my palm.

Mougins. Sarai closed the door behind her gently as she tiptoed out of the room. Her babies were asleep and at last she too could get some. Luke hadn't slept easily for the last couple of nights. The boy had a cold, which made things difficult for his mum settling him. She had brought him into her room for the past couple of nights so that he did not disturb the other children when he woke up. Having separate rooms for the children was still out of the question, as she needed them all to be together. They were just still so little to be far apart. Besides it was nice seeing them all together, a little cozy but at least they kept each other company.

She could hear some music down the hallway as she walked towards the stairs. She was lucky it was rather soothing than loud. She couldn't take the risk of anything disturbing Luke at this hour.

'He's asleep at last,' she said as she came into the lounge.

'Thank God.' I said shaking my head as I searched through my library of books.

'What are you looking for?'

'Nothing in particular, I'm hoping that I would see what I want when I find it. It's a scene I am working on but I need some pictures. I think I have a book somewhere with just what I need.'

'Are you going to work now? It's almost eleven.'

'Well to be honest this is one of the best times to do so especially when everyone else is sleeping and the house is silent.'

'I know darling but this is the time I have with you,' Sarai called out as she walked to the kitchen.

'You have all day with me. I'm always here,' I said

when she came back into the room carrying a small bowl with ice cream.

'I had to try this. Elodie said she gave some to the kids after dinner and they loved it. It's my turn now to be spoiled.'

'Thanks but no thanks.'

'Did I offer you any? I know unless I force you, you won't have any so I won't,' she replied taking a sit on the sofa and looking at me as I searched the stack of books. 'I wish you would stop doing that and just sit with me. I like this song what is it?'

'It is called Sentossa. I have to check who the artist is, I think it is part of another album.'

'I don't know where you find this music. I love it though.'

'I can see that you love something else too.' I said with my back to her as I pulled out another book that wasn't the book I was looking for. I had been at it for half an hour and this had prompted me to put on the music. I hoped it would help the painful process and distract me from the search. Nothing changed.

'Don't laugh at a girl enjoying her delicacies. Besides you are very stubborn, you should come and sit with your wife.'

I rubbed my face with both hands and took up a position in the sofa opposite hers. Perhaps she had a point for all the wrong reasons, as my search was now a frustrating one. Sometimes it didn't matter how one searched, things just seemed to disappear. I was sure I had seen that book in the shelf a few days earlier.

'There isn't that better. I think you were getting nowhere fast,' Sarai said and giggled. I could tell that she was having fun seeing the expression of disappointment on my face. She had me where she wanted. I would have to listen to her. It looked like her success in finally putting Luke to sleep had brought out this new joy in her. The boy had suffered for two days and she needed to celebrate with someone. I would have to join her in whatever capacity whether I liked it or not.

'I mean I can't understand, I saw this book right there the other day.'

'Poor baby, perhaps you don't need it. I can be inspiring if you try me.'

'I know you can,' I shrugged leaning back in the sofa resigned and depleted of all hope in finding the book. 'I like the way you are caressing that ice cream. You don't want it to finish do you?'

'I don't. Children know what is good,' Sarai said as she dipped her spoon once more into the bowl. 'Perhaps we should go out somewhere soon. It has been a while, the kids would love it.'

'What of your parents, they'd love to see the children.'

'That's for vacation. I'm thinking of something short or rather for a couple of days, like a long weekend or something.'

'We could do that.'

'I'd like to bring our guest along too. She arrives tomorrow,' Sarai said as she finished the last of the ice cream and put the bowl down.

'Where would you like to go?' I knew that this was a set up. When Sarai started a conversation she usually knew exactly how it would turn out.

'Italy, we could drive, it isn't far,' she said bending her head to one side raffishly and willing me to say yes.'

'Now I know where those children get the habit from.'

'Yeah! Then it's on. I'll have something to look forward to next weekend.'

'I'm surprised Hailey's magazine let her come back.

What story do they expect to get?' I asked puzzled.

'Ours, but I think Hailey misses us too,' she replied getting up and walking over to me.

'Come let's get an early night, writing can wait for another day. I need my husband,' she said as she opened both hands for mine.

I pulled myself out of the sofa to my feet with her help. I hope it's our story together my darling, I thought, because just mine by itself would make her readers run and hide.

Outskirts of London Reading M4, November 2004. 'There, there's a gas station,' she said, her index finger almost touching the windshield. 'There, the one on your left, careful don't miss the turning,' she said with some urgency.

'You always say that yet I never do. We have been married for over twenty years and you still have to remind me every time I pull into a station,' he replied scornfully.

'You don't need to bite my head off dear, I was only trying to help.'

'We did say that we would stop at the next gas station and have breakfast didn't we? So why do you always have to remind me of what we have discussed. It is annoying.'

She said nothing. It was a pleasant morning and they still had quite a way to go. If she irritated him then it would be a very long and tiresome ride. They did not need this. She was too old to go through this. Peace was more important than making her point.

'Help me look will you. I don't know why the car park would be full at this time of the morning.'

'*There*! Dear, over in the corner not far from the entrance. There, there's one.'

'Thanks,' her husband said as he covered his mouth

with his gnarled palm to cough. He hadn't wanted to go out but he needed to. I am sick to death of that damned garden and its gazebo! He needed the break and his wife's suggestion for them to visit Bath was just what they needed. He turned the steering wheel to the right as he tried to navigate his way into the parking spot. The space was tight but he was sure it would fit.

'Oh, careful dear you are too close to that car.'

'You worry too much, how can I hit a car that I can see right before me? Don't be ridiculous,' he replied, his face a pale glowering mask in the sunlight. There were dark rims around his eyes from exhaustion.

He spoke too soon.

I sat with my eyes closed in the car. I needed a rest, time to put my mind in gear after the early morning start that avoided the traffic heading out of London. Soon I would be on my way and in another hour or so talking my way through the interview. It wasn't the company I had hoped for but it was what I needed, to get out of the house. At least one interview after the other would get my mind functioning again and then who knew what could happen then.

The sound almost knocked me unconscious. I shook my head and cursed beneath my breath. I don't need this Lord, not now! I looked in my side mirror and saw the old couple trying to pull into the space beside me. They argued and I imagined their story. If I went out there all guns blazing then I'd be the fool before them. I have to be calm when I get out of this car! I could not lose my temper; I had an interview in the next hour. I got out of the car and came round to the back. I was lucky it was just a scratch things weren't as bad as the jerk had felt. The woman spoke as she came out of their car.

'Oh sorry dear. We would pay for it just give us your insurance details.'

'I am terribly sorry. I thought I had made it but it looks like I hadn't,' the man apologized.

'It is nothing, forget it,' I said.

'Really? Do you mean that? I mean we are terribly sorry and we would pay for the damage. Please, it is our fault,' the woman said.

'It is a mere scratch no harm done please forget it,' I waved.

'Well then we are terribly sorry but if you say so then we shall leave it,' the man said and got back into the car. I got back into the front seat of my car and watched the couple manage to pull in carefully into the space beside me. Soon they were out of the vehicle and walking towards the shops. It must already be an eventful morning for these old folks, I thought, for me that would be the understatement of the year. I had been having eventful mornings for the past three years. If the truth ever came out then I was the lucky one to make it through the incident unscathed with just the scratch on my car. The fact of the matter was that I had no insurance, had driven without any for over a year. I had been living dangerously for so long relying solely on prayer and the Lord that it never occurred to me what I would do if an incident of this nature occurred. However it only confirmed one thing that God hadn't given up on me. Maybe I was wrong in the eyes of the law to do what I did but the challenges I faced were far greater than worrying at what the law would do to me. If I could not drive then how would I get to the interview and to the job? I couldn't afford the public transport to the place. The petrol in the car would last much longer even after the interview. The decision was simple – *take the risk and hope the Lord comes to your rescue.*

He had.

London 2008. Nothing much seemed to have

changed since 2004. It was four years later as my thoughts raced back my present situation. It was autumn *2008* and the siren could be heard for miles as the police patrol car swerved between two vehicles behind us and then changed lanes. I looked in my rear view mirror.

It *can't be me.*

I was angry, then frustrated. I indicated to go left moving to the middle lane as the road signs for Tottenham exit appeared on the gantry above. The patrol car gunned past us, its blue lights disappearing into the darkness of the underpass at Edmonton. It *is not for me*!

'They said they would take it away from you. You have to be careful.'

I said nothing.

'If you need some help in legalizing your documents you just need to ask and I would help you. You don't want to lose your car, not now.'

Still no *words!* My silence I hoped was a clear indication of how I felt; if only my friend knew how self aggrandizing he sounded he could have taken the hint. *They cannot take my car away unless the Lord wants them to nor can they do anything for that matter that he has not given them permission to*!

My friend's lanky frame twisted in the seat next to mine.

'Take the next left you come to,' he said. 'It would allow us to park closer.'

Two months before then my friend had elected to borrow my car and had been stopped by the police. They had asked him to produce his license and a permit for driving the vehicle and then he had discovered that I had no insurance. Since then he had taken it upon himself to ensure that I was legal. I appreciated the advice but pondered about it. I was no fool and I knew that what I did was illegal. However so was my existence if all things were put into perspective including my past. There was no point in having a heart attack about the police seizing the car. There were more pressing matters to consider such as what I had planned for supper. It was too late to start being scared of life considering the experiences I had been through.

My silence wasn't a rebuff, I had *proof.*

A week earlier I had adhered to my friend's advice. I had taken the car for its service. From there I had spent all morning trying to get the vehicles particulars through the system. Nothing had gone my way. The post office had requested paper work, which I couldn't find when I was so certain that I had examined the documents in detail only the night before. After this I had elected to travel by train because I wanted to avoid driving the car illegally. It had been a no win situation on my behalf. Everything that could go wrong had. I was late for appointments and held up in unforeseen delays. My legs could barely carry me by the time I had navigated my way through most of the day.

I came to a conclusion. It was impossible to stem the flow of our lives living to the rules we had created. I had to make a decision then and did. I took the car. Everything began working in synchrony from then on. My chores were completed within a couple of hours and then I discovered that the car documents I had spent all morning searching for were beneath the same papers I had carefully looked through that morning.

'You cannot serve God and man,' Cephas whispered.

'I know and that is what I have been trying to tell people about my actions but it doesn't seem to work.'

'Then do it your own way until God gives you the penny for the law.'

'I have no arguments with you there. I guess one

must be prepared to lose high in order to live spiritually.'

'You won't lose, you are not abusing the law. What you are going through is not by your will.'

'I know but how do I explain this.'

'You don't have to explain yourself, they would not understand. You wanted confirmation and you received it.'

'Yes. That was something. To ask the Lord to prove that he is talking to you and then he does is out of this world.'

'Then you should have no qualms about what to do.'

I said nothing I was prepared to go through the lecture that my friend had in store for me. There was nothing I could do about this but I knew that time would tell whether my actions at this point in time were for personal gain.

I parked a short walk from the football grounds.

'I don't like to see my friends suffer or lose things so please if you need my help I am here for you,' my friend said as we got out of the car.

I nodded. There was still a light burning in this disparaging darkness. Cephas was in the ascendancy. My friend wasn't at the Reading station when the couple hit me, God was. My friend wasn't in the desert in Saudi Arabia when my car broke down and there was no help for miles, God was. When I decided that I could use some help from my friend then I would do so accordingly but when it was God's will that I faced tribulation for the cause, for *the resurrection*, *the contract* then I won't. I did not break the law on purpose. I was in no desperate need to drive the car illegally. I was in pursuit of a greater cause that was constantly reminding me of which path to follow. If I deviated because I was scared or had lost faith that the Lord would come to my rescue then even this car that I was so scared of losing would be gone. God had shown me the vision, the three children. No man could do this. No law could give me this guarantee. Yet now I had a purpose in life and a job to complete. If man wanted to take from me what I owned then let it be so. There was no shape or pattern to the spiritual world. I was prepared to give to the world what belonged to the world but I could only do that by the means by which I had been provided with.

'I know a place where we can get some hot soup in you to cut off this cold weather,' my friend said.

The hazy twilight had quickly vanished into the horizon. The streetlights now shown brightly on the road surface, with the dew from the mist clearly visible. Above this was a star strewn sky that reminded those beneath it that there was more to its universe than met the eye. People walked in different directions, their lives tuned to the demands of society. I found myself digging into my pockets to check for my keys and then taking a glance back at the car. The lights were on.

'The car must still be open,' I said.

I turned and walked the few metres that had elapsed back to the car. The door to the passenger's side wasn't locked properly. I had suspected nothing. It was instinct to reach for my keys, instinct to turn and look back. Perhaps there was a law that surrounded this instinct. I knew it couldn't be human.

'Evening,' the man grunted as he walked by, his voice a guttural sound behind me.

'Evening,' I replied as I shut the door and punched the key alarm for the second time. We would never be equipollent with our creator, I thought. We weren't meant to be. One did not have an ambivalent attraction to the spiritual world. You accepted it and listened to the guidance from within or you didn't. There was no time or space in its vocabulary to question God. I wasn't in the running for setting a precedence of breaking the laws of society but I was in the running for fulfilling a journey that had been set before me. I knew that not everything I would do or say in life would be law abiding but there was some consolation to this. Not everything the law said and did, abided by the Lord. The law was man's way, I would do my best to work with it but not live by it.

My friend could be forgiven for not knowing the truth behind my actions but I did not need a regular doom crier, certainly not in the past or especially now. It was the wrong medication when one was hanging off a precipice and staring face downward into the maw of a kraken. I was in no mood to don the armour of despair, mine would be that of belligerence.

I caught up to my friend as we exited the side roads and joined the manic crowd that had thickened further moving east on the high street. They were dressed in banners made from hats, gloves, scarves and even jerseys representing the teams, their intense and animated chatter carried highly through the night as they discussed team strategies and players.

'Man this atmosphere is more serious than I anticipated,' I said allowing a benign smile to escape through. The zeal exhibited by the shoal of people that went past me was bouncing off the shop fronts, cafes and bars next to us.

'Out here it is a religion. These guys eat, live and breath football. Wait till you get inside and hear the chanting, it's something else.'

'You have been to several games like this?'

'Every other week, I told you I was a seasoned ticket holder. You are lucky this is a quiet night.'

'I don't think I could handle this madness on a regular basis. I hope this game is as good as you say it would be, it is a welcome distraction. Thanks for the treat.'

'Well I won't say anything to that let's just see how you feel after the match.'

Chapter Fifteen

Mougins; I stood alone on the patio watching dusk settle in Mougins. The colour of the sea had already changed from a bright blue in the morning to shades of black as the sky slowly hid the sun from the beach. Autumn had moved quickly over the horizon making the nights much cooler.

'What are you thinking of?'

I felt her warmth and her breath on my neck even before her arms went around my waist.

'Nothing.'

'Your hands are cold, you should come in,' Sarai said as I grabbed her arms pulling them to me.

'I like the feel of yours, they are warm.'

'Would we always be like this?' Sarai asked as she buried her head in the hollowness of my back.

'Like what?'

'Dreamlike, so far away, I seem to forget everything and everyone when we are like this.'

I gripped her hands a little tighter. There were no answers to her question. She knew the answer, knew we had found each other because it was meant to happen that way. I had spent years alone lost in a world of hope, prayers and dreams. She was one of those dreams unimaginable to fathom at the time. Yet it had happened as I had seen in the visions. The script was written before we walked the earth we just fulfilled it. Time was relative, a thousand days as one and one as a thousand. Promises exceeding our expectations and realized before we knew they were happening to us. No, I had no answers for her. I would hold her and speak to her from my heart and she would realize that there would be no place else she would wish to be on earth but where we were at that moment.

'I came to tell you that our guest awaits, darling.'

'How is she?' I asked looking at the darkness that had settled through the hillsides. A few lamps were already on in the narrow streets. Soon the nightlife would take over most of the city that led into Cannes.

'She is probably rested after her hot bath. I had Elodie prepare something for her. We can join her.'

'How about the little people?'

'They are still up in their room. I should think they are waiting for you. Did you make any promises?'

'Yes we have been reading a story together. Let's hope I'm not the one falling asleep.'

'Let's go in darling, I'm getting cold.'

I took one deep breath of the fresh air and then followed Sarai into our bedroom, drawing the curtains and shutting the double doors to the patio.

'You will have to go ahead without me. Remember I have an appointment with the kids.' I walked towards my closet to grab a shirt. I had been standing outside in a T-shirt. The shower earlier on had been refreshing. Suddenly there was this urge to be on the patio and catch the evening sunset. Things were different now, as Sarai had confirmed. It was getting a bit chilly and I needed more clothes.

Twenty minutes later I was walking down the stairs and into the living room.

'Out as a light,' I nodded towards Sarai as I took the chair next to hers. Sarai had already poured me a glass of wine and seemed deep in conversation with Hailey.

'I was asking Hailey here how she managed to convince her boss to send her to us for a second time?'

'And I'm trying to explain to Sarai that I did very little. Her story speaks for itself.'

'It certainly does,' I said sipping the moscato with one hand and reaching for Sarai's with the other, 'and doesn't she tell it beautifully too.'

'I have to admit I did some work of my own before

getting on the plane.'

'You did?' Sarai quizzed. No one could tell what the payoffs were from what they had sown in the spiritual world unless revealed to them. Perhaps Hailey was evidence that Sarai had made an impression. I knew she had gotten to me when I succumbed to the gynarchy that made women's magazines so popular. When Sarai had asked to get her story published I had told her she had my full support. Now it appeared she was bringing a sheep to the fold. Still it was too early to jump the gun, the world was plagued by profit margins and a business sense that generally overrode most things.

'I tried to look back into the past I had before now, before this to see what I had left behind, I wanted to fully understand my reasons for doing so,' Hailey said. We watched curiously and in silence. It had taken this girl courage to come this far. I could not forget the time in Glyfada and the sadness that she had beheld on that hot afternoon as she wondered about her dream.

'Okay I know I am delving into new found territory but I just needed to know for myself what you meant by leaving the past behind and following something else, a new path like you put it,' she said hesitantly.

'A sort of self discovery?' Sarai asked looking at the girl. She was already warming to Hailey and knew I was too even though I said nothing.

'At first I thought I would find fault in leaving my past behind, I mean forgetting China and the things I grew up with as a child. I thought my pursuit of a dream, desire and ambition had made me leave other valued treasures,' Hailey said.

They were there, the questions, doubt and insecurity that one first experienced when you traversed unknown territory. Her discoveries made her want to share and who better than those that had pointed her in this direction. 'The funny thing is where I thought I would find blame, I found reason. Where I thought I would find blindness and selfishness I found purpose. It was as if without being the person I was then I won't fully understand the person I had become.'

'You mean one served another's fulfillment, purpose,' Sarai said.

'That's it. The first person, the person I used to be in China was driven towards becoming a journalist. She was ambitious to a fault without necessarily having a solid reason for this desire. The world gave her the desire by showing her what she could gain if she succeeded and what she would miss out on if she gave up on her dream. I couldn't think of anything else back then except what I had to have, what I needed for me to be counted a success. When I first looked back on this person I thought she was selfish. Now I feel she brought me here.'

'That's a good place to start, no regrets,' I said. I had been listening to Hailey quietly with Sarai's hand in mine. I had done this a million times over yet I had the humility ingrained in me to know that listening to Hailey would serve me in good stead. If one had no regrets on what had gone before then they carried no baggage into the future. They lived freely knowing that someone greater controlled the outcome of things. Had the Lord not said leave the past where it is and follow him? The past was not only made up of physical things. They could be psychological, regrets, shortcomings, one had to let go of this believing that someone greater was now in charge.

'I have to admit I felt stronger. If one has no regrets they are free to do as they wish, they leave the worrying to someone else. It's a little nerve racking though,' Hailey said.

'How much work did you do?' Sarai asked her face was now resting on the palm of her hand as she listened. Their talk had not been in vain. If only one person got something from it then it had been worth it. Hailey seemed to have grasped so much in such a short time.

'Talking to you now it feels like a lot. The truth is it is something that I am always aware of now since my last visit. You can say I am always working or rather thinking about what you said.'

Sarai leaned back in her seat and looked at me.

'I'm truly amazed,' She said. 'I just never thought...' She said allowing the words to fail her. The connection we made in life was spiritual, it was difficult to see how it worked but it certainly had done in this case. If the spirit wished for something it made it possible through that connection. Our job was to act when we felt the instinct and not to deliberate the outcome. The outcome of all things belonged to God.

London, Summer 2009.
TWO FLIGHTS AND A BITE

The words were printed in blue ink in my notebook although the handwriting was crooked since I had been lying in bed whilst writing in the book. It was a custom I had adopted ever since the visions started occurring more frequently. My shared existence had been split evenly between spirit and man. The visions had never happened so frequently before in my life. And now it seemed as though every two days there was something new to feel and to understand. This new experience left me even more puzzled than those of the past. However I had begun giving them brief titles to help jog my memory whenever the meaning was revealed. Cephas hadn't been kidding about the *resurrection.* It was now happening for real as I could sense the change within me and my surroundings. There was no more fear or sorrow of the past. There was now a future to look forward to. The ties of old had been severed and I was a free man with a willingness to live solely within the realms of my *contract*.

I lay back in bed to contemplate my most recent expedition into the spiritual world. It would do no harm to understand it a little, at least this way when the meaning came up I would remember.

Cephas was rested. The Lord had not taken spirit from the body for this mission but had shown me something else. This was certainly a new mystery. I was right to scribble in the pad – *two flights and a bite*. I had felt as though I was on a plane. It had flown one way and then another and soon I was back were I had started and then I felt it, first the heat of its breath on my palm. I did not pull my hand away; perhaps because in this domain I knew Cephas led and if that was the case then I was in the spirit and nothing could harm me. Then I felt its tongue, warm but wide almost like that of a dog and then it bit me. It was not a vicious bite; a voracious appetite being appeased by a predator on its prey, this was different. It felt like the type one got when you placed your hand in a dogs mouth that wanted friendship. I could feel its canines but that was all. The jaws were large probably of a creature much larger than a dog. I thought I knew what it was but was careful in my assessment. It was best that the Lord did the interpretation. It would be presumptuous sin on my part to make any suggestions.

My analogy had been accurate. This scribbling would pay dividends. The bite had come after the flights but this was enough to work with. The creature had then pulled its mouth away and the vision was over as if it had never happened and spirit returned to its host while I tried to make sense of what had taken place.

It was another morning gone and I turned over in bed. I had lost count of the days and the weeks, even months. Nothing had changed. Nothing was changing, I would get up every morning and straddle through the day until night came and the next day the whole activity would begin again. It was a painful slough. There was nothing I did not know about my house, about my surroundings and about London. I was stuck in a doldrums with only my visions to go on. I had lost count of the times when I was happy or sad. I had lost count of the times when I could motivate myself to feel something, anything. One day could seem like heaven when I had a revelation and the next would feel like hell if I had none. It was as if being Cephas was all I had to live for. My person in the flesh was dead to the world and only in the spirit did life make any sense. However there were no regrets, there was no wish to go back to the life I had lived in the past, but there was a relentless aching for what awaited me in the future and I knew that one day too this would come to pass.

I rolled over to turn on the side lamp as I had done so many times before this, before I read the bible. It was my only companion in this solitary confinement. It kept me sane and was always a good place to start the mornings with. At least this routine meant that I had my wits about me.

The lamp was dead.

'*It's time.*'

So it had happened. My electricity had finally been cut off. The letters had been ignored like all the other amenities and in the end the threat had been applied and the power cut off.

'It's time.'

I got out of bed and said my prayers as I often did. I managed to read a psalm pulling the blinds aside to allow the sunlight through. I was lucky that it wasn't winter and I did not need to have the central heating working. Things could have been far worse. Cephas was right. This was the sign I had been waiting for. In the bible it was written that when the children of Israel left Egypt and traveled through the day they had been guided by a pillar of cloud and at night by a pillar of light and when either wasn't available they kept camp. I had been keeping camp for some time and now there was a pillar of cloud in the day, which could only mean one thing I had to get out.

Mougins. Water gushed out of the fountain in the centre of the field, its droplets flying high and clear in the bright sunlight. The other sprinklers opened in unison as the garden took a deserved shower. The little boy and his sister were running wildly one after the other. They raced away from the water as it sprayed the grass shouting hysterically with laughter, their freedom a plight any keen observer would envy. Hailey had been drawn to the noise throwing open the bedroom windows and watching as the kids played in the sun. She had worked all morning until the noise had distracted her just after noon. They were at school in the morning and had just returned. It looked as if they had gone straight into the garden drawn by the spray of water that showered the grass and the flowers. This was a much needed distraction for her. It looked as if she would have to seek her host. She couldn't lose valuable time isolated and buried in her notes. She would have to interact and get more out of Cephas and Sarai. What was puzzling about everything was that most of the time she did all the talking and mainly about herself. It was almost scary as if understanding herself would better understand them. Things had gotten a little awkward when she realized that it was just herself and Sarai doing all the talking. She had attempted to invite

Cephas into the discussion by asking him a direct question. She wanted to know how his relationship with God had started. In her experience, people often sought a higher understanding for particular reasons, personal reasons that turned to shape their lives. She was sure she could get him to talk then.

'I don't know if there was a time that I never believed or knew God. I was born into a family of faith,' Cephas had said.

'I mean knowing him in the way you do now, this evolved person that seems to be in touch with every emotion and every thought that is spiritual,' She had persisted. He wasn't telling her something and she needed to know, confront the truth, perhaps not even for the story but for herself.

'You make it sound as if I taught myself what I know of God. On the contrary God teaches us what we know about him. I barely do anything by myself. What I have done I think is learn to trust in him, I mean give up what we consider control to him more than most people would. This makes me see more of his work in certain places that other people wouldn't.'

'I mean how did you know it would be Sarai, how were you so sure that you would have three children, two boys and a girl?' It was her voice she had heard asking those questions. In her element she was a journalist, ready to delve deeper and seek answers that would keep her readers guessing. She had heard Sarai's version of events now she wanted to hear Cephas's.

'In our worldly wisdom we always say the proof is in the pudding.' He had said looking to his wife beside him. 'God tells us what to do, shows us what would happen sometimes through dreams or visions. However all things must be proven. My own wisdom or knowledge does not perform the act. I follow instructions without doubt then I see what happens.

Sometimes nothing does happen. But when it does as in this case it confirms everything and God's name is glorified.'

'The children and I are his proof.' Sarai had said and smiled at Cephas.

Hailey watched as Elodie managed to grab the little girl and boy on both sides of her and walk back into the house. She could sense their desire to stay longer on the grass and knew the feeling. Their effusive laughter had now been reduced to mumbling. They were kids and they wanted to play still we were all responsible for something in spite of our age. It was her cue to return to work. Perhaps another time other than the present would be more suitable to seek her host. If the children were going indoors to have something to eat then it would be difficult to work. She would leave things until the evening. Besides she couldn't expect too much until later. Sarai had mentioned at breakfast that her office had called very early and she won't be available until late afternoon. She hadn't seen Cephas at breakfast, Sarai had said he would appear when he was free. She wasn't bothered. He had accepted to do the article, support Sarai in what she wanted the magazine to write. He hadn't refused to answer her questions instead his answers had kept her awake wondering. Did this man's faith make him believe he could see God? He said he followed every word without a shadow of doubt. When she had asked whether it was possible for anyone to get to that level of faith and certainty that God spoke to them, he had said it was listening and obeying the little things. He said if one obeyed the simple things then they would do the same for those that seemed complex. We had the power to make those things that seemed impossible possible if we truly believed.

London. The room was now in darkness with the

fading light a distant past from several days ago when I had electricity. This is my resurrection, Cephas's resurrection for the Lord had said a man could be resurrected even in life as long as he believed. The decision had been taken from my hands.

After first discovering that I had no electricity I had put my mind into gear asking for guidance from the Lord. My pillar of cloud was present but my final destination still loomed away in the distance. It didn't take long to get the answer. I had family in the US and it had been a while since I had seen them. It was time to leave the wilderness of longsuffering to survey the land without it. I had been gradually guided into the wilderness now it looked like I would receive the same guidance out of it. Since Riyadh I had lived alone and isolated from the world for almost two years. The only voice I knew or recognized in that time was that of the Lord. When I spoke spirit responded. When I laughed spirit laughed with me; and when the darkness came spirit brought through the light. My confines had now become uninhabitable by purpose, it was time to survey pastures out of my wilderness. Yet, I couldn't rush to the dreams I desired, as I needed tentative steps to get there. The children of Israel had not immediately moved to the Promised Land, taking residence and dividing it amongst them. God had said this would take some time, there had to be a survey and then slow migration in order that the wild animals did not return and take the land away from them. I needed a slow migration back into society; I needed to learn again how to interact with other people before I could also receive the promise that would be mine. My family was a good place to start.

It was time to put these plans into motion. I said my prayers and set about the task of reaching others. I did not need my bills paid or sympathy, my circumstances were my inheritance, the cup placed before me by my heavenly father to drink from. God wanted this perpetuity in spirit for me and anyone that tried to make my journey any easier was only placing obstacles in my path for the resurrection. It wasn't a case of will power and strength it was just what it had to be.

I walked to a payphone and placed the call. My family was delighted; they wanted to see me, would be glad to have me with them. Next I called a friend for the ticket. I did not expect anything in return only reminding myself that if all worked out as I had planned then it was God's will that I would travel to the US. He responded positively. He wanted to do this for me. The proof was there to be seen my cloud pointed me to the US for the time being. Spirit was right; it was time.

I left the living room and walked into the kitchen. The evening was closing in fast and I had to have my wits about me. I had several candles in the house from a while back when I had been romantic. *That is in your past*! The circumstances then were different, those ties now severed. However I would use those candles for now. That was the darkness taken care of. *Water, bathing*! Another pertinent time on the agenda, at least I could boil the water on the gas stove. This too would allow me to cook dinner. So food and bathing were not a problem. *Clothes*! Washing my clothes wasn't a problem either, I had clean clothes packed in the drawers, they would last me for the next four days until my departure to the US. On my return I would attend to the electricity, there would be a way and a means by then, the Lord would come to my rescue. This wasn't something I would have to live with for the rest of my life. It was just for now, for the impetus; to carry me through, to seek and search for where my future lay. It looked like I had been planning for this moment all my life even though this morning as I lay in bed everything had appeared bleak. I was confident that like the children of Israel the Lord had provided me with a pillar of light that would support me through the journey at night. I was sure my friend would come through with the money for the ticket.

The question that remained was the phone. *Communications*!

The modern society demanded a means of contact for me to keep all these plans alive. None of these plans would work if I had to tell my friends of the power cut. They would immediately come to my rescue and take away the spiritual element of the moment. But what could be done about the phone? I walked back into the living room and placed one of the candles on the centre table. I placed three others adjacent to it and the room suddenly shown like a temple in the dark. The candles glowed in the dark and I felt the fear and excitement at the same time as all the shadows in the room came into play. I would be alone with God during this period and no one else; no television, no computer, nothing until I was free to seek new pastures and understand what lay ahead. There was no doubt now in my mind that I was making the right decision.

Still pending, the phone! My friend would call to confirm about the ticket, how would he reach me? I had a mobile but with a flat battery the thing was useless. I needed to find power. I needed to charge the phone so that I could receive calls. I couldn't run back and forth to the phone booth, it wasn't close by.

'If it is not by my strength that all of this has happened then God would give me a means of communication in order that this path to the resurrection be fulfilled,' I thought.

'*Check the drawers.*'

I did.

I walked into the second bedroom and opened the drawers. I stared at the gadget dumfounded. When I was offered it I had almost refused telling myself it would just add extra luggage to my things. However it was my last day at work in Riyadh and one of my friends had insisted. He had said I should take it as a present to remember him by. He said I had to keep it and I would always remember our time in Riyadh. Today was that day. I pulled it out from amongst the other things that I had received. It was a small device with all the adaptors you could find in the world. My friend had said all it needed to work was batteries. That was simple enough now that there was no electricity I did not need the remote controls for the television. I could use those batteries for this. I walked back into the living room and transferred the batteries from the television controls to the gadget. I tried out several of the adaptors until there was a perfect match with my Nokia. A red light glimmered on the device and the phone beeped into live with the message – battery charging. I punched the sky in victory! *God wants this time with me, God wants this to work*! It was God's will that this gadget had been made available to me. It was another sign that I wasn't self-sustained, that it wasn't by my powers that this would work. I had never touched this gadget. Never once examined what my friend had put in his magic bag as he had called it at the time. Now *this*!

There was a reason for all things and God was true to his!

Cephas grinned in the distance. *We are close! Soon we would be one*!

Mougins. 'I can only feel what I am meant to feel. It is by God's grace that I feel this sense within me. I wish I could show you, show the world but it is not I that

279

controls it. At one time I am full with riches and at others I am empty to be replenished. Our journeys are cyclic. We are looking for a better understanding of the things we already know. More light is shed upon them and unto what they mean each time we apply them differently. Eventually our fears become less and we are willing to let go.'

'That's the journey but why one person as opposed to another, what makes that person special, different from others?' Hailey asked.

'It is our maker's decision,' I replied.

'But no one person is better than another, why should some people be placed above others in understanding who God is,' Hailey said.

We were all sitting in the living room after dinner. Sarai spoke less this time allowing me to respond to Hailey's questions. The Lord had said coming to God was like threading the eye of the needle. Leaving behind what we knew wasn't so easy after all. We all knew of the fairness that we desired or understood to make us better people. Unfortunately when this fairness was transferred to the spiritual world it became flawed as none of us was perfect in our endeavours. Our fairness was driven only to certain extents that ensured our own safety. When things went beyond this, with the added risks of losing what was ours we became different people. We all wanted a ballad but were unable to fully appreciate what it took to get one. The Lord had said chastisement was not pleasurable to the recipient. However with God's came wisdom, understanding and a freedom that couldn't be surpassed. As man we wanted things to be fair when they worked in our favour but called them unfair when they did not meet our requirements. None of us would wish upon ourselves what the prophets had been through. Yet because of this they were given the grace to fulfill impossible works of God. Abraham had been willing to walk into the forest to sacrifice Isaac and for this he had been given the promise. I couldn't think of anyone who would willingly do the same.

'Yes no one person is better than the other, still it is the maker of the tools that decides what they do. We each have a role to play some look more glamorous than others still each of us has a job to do,' Sarai said, 'I cannot tell what my husband's role is but I know what role he has played in my life and continues to.'

'What of the poor people that are eventually taken away in a tsunami or a baby that is born and dies, what role do they play? Can't you see why many people question the existence of God?' Hailey asked. Sarai had turned on the lamps in the room avoiding the high ceiling floodlights as they made the room too bright and hot. Hailey could see the couple clearly but then now and again it felt as though they were in the shadows. 'I mean can any of us fully understand why this would happen, if we can't then how can we rebuke those people who say God is made up?'

'True. Although I have to say we are always in a rush to condemn faith by our worldly standards,' Sarai said. 'In the spiritual world death is not the worst that could happen to us, perishing in hell is.'

'You do see my point though, that unless one is well versed with what happens in this world that you describe it would be hard to believe in it,' Hailey persisted.

'That is why a true believer is not in judgment of people with no faith or weaker faith. His or her job is to pass on what they know and allow God to show the individuals as he wishes. God teaches us that one person plants yet another may do the harvesting. To each of us is given grace that is sufficient for the task set before us. It is God's will how things work on this journey. Seeking guarantees in faith defeats the reason for having faith. The evidence is in what we hope for.' I said.

Hailey took in a deep breath. I could tell that matters were getting complicated, unreasonable? What did we mean? What were we implying? Our answers were far to close ended and difficult to comprehend. Hailey's understanding of her true self had only just begun. A world driven into self-discovery could only get one so far and then there were doubts and questions that needed answers. She was facing this at present and needed to know.

'I heard what you said but did not understand it?' She said, she would keep asking, that was her job. It was simple we asked to receive, that's how any of us learnt anything.

'Well put it this way faith is walking into a dark cave hoping that there would be light to help you along the way. When you get light, you hope for food, then water and all that you desire to get you safely through the cave. The guarantee is in the hope. In the first instance you hoped for light and you got this. You then hoped for food and you got this. The evidence that your faith is real and working in your favour is in your hope. This hope guarantees your wishes,' I said.

'What if you hope and there is no light and it is just darkness?' Hailey asked.

'Then you keep on hoping and never give up. Part of faith is endurance and longsuffering, perseverance and patience. It is not meant to be easy. Once again there are no guarantees. But because you have faith that God won't leave you in this darkness indefinitely, you just continue hoping until you find the light and the other things that you desire to get you through.'

'Sounds tough,' Hailey said quietly.

'It is tough. That is why the rewards are so great,' I

responded.

'But how does one realize those results if you die even before you see them?'

'That is the thing about faith, it is not just about the here and now but about beyond death. That is why as Sarai said earlier on death is not the worst thing that could happen to any of us.'

Chapter Sixteen

Genoa, Italy. Sarai managed to slide her second arm into the harness tightening the straps that were ideal for holding Luke's weight. The little boy reached for her face, his arms grabbing at her.

'No, don't hurt Mummy,' she said.

'Mummy I think he wants to take your glasses,' Rachel said beside her.

'No, I won't let him because I need them for the sun,' she said.

'Can I have mine too?' Rachel asked.

'Yes you can my darling.' She leaned back into the boot storing the small pack of drinks in the knapsack. Two would suffice for the children. Hailey and herself would have water. Luke could have milk. She added some scones and biscuits and she was set.

'Here hold this darling while I shut the boot,' she said handing over the bag to the little girl. The weight of it made the child put it straight on the floor. 'Is it heavy darling?'

'No I can carry it,' Rachel said.

Sarai smiled down at her, 'Don't worry Mummy knows it is heavy you can put it on the floor while I strap your brother in.'

Hailey came round the car holding Joshua's hand.

'Ancient eh? This is the place for it, I'm thinking something before the middle ages or am I speaking out of turn.' She said.

'Antiquity indeed, the Porto Soprana is no small artifact in these parts.' Sarai said.

'Here give me that bag, I can carry it,' Hailey said taking the knapsack from Sarai as she grabbed Rachel's arm.

'Thanks, looks like we chose a good day out here with the kids. It's quite sunny isn't it? I hope Cephas joins us later, else he would miss out.'

Sarai shut the car and they all mounted the stairs to the Porta Soprana. Its twin semicircular towers were quite remarkable to look at. There was something about them that took one back in time. When they were close enough Hailey placed her hand on the wall.

'Here Joshua, come here and place your hand on this,' she said. Rachel ran from her Mum's side to join them placing her little palm on the wall. It was warm under the iridescent sunlight. Hailey could only imagine how formidable a barrier this would have been in its time against invaders.

'It's hot!' The little girl shouted excitedly to her brother pulling her hand away from the wall.

'No it is not, I can leave my hand on it longer than you can,' the boy said to her.

The women smiled at each other behind their sunglasses. People walked in and out of the famous gates taking pictures of it and wanting others to take pictures of them before it. The location was ideal for those who wanted a picturesque souvenir from the ancient city of Genoa and no doubt the tourists weren't willing to pass on this opportunity. What overlooked the walls of the Plano Soprana was a vast expanse of the city that led into the Ligurian Sea. From these walls it was possible to imagine how easily it could have been back then to spot a flotilla of ship destined for the highly populated ports. Genoa had a unique history that it could boast against other cities for its victories over Venice during a period of wars that had spanned over 125 years. A commercial rivalry that was hard to imagine in the present day and age, had existed between both cities and although Venice had eventually come on top, the Genoese Government had demonstrated their prowess reporting to the imperial powers at the time.

'Can you imagine being around here during that time, when it really served its purpose?' Hailey asked.

'One can't help but imagine once you are here. I guess that is the effect places like this have on us,' Sarai said. She looked curiously at the towers noticing that there were cracks in the stone walls some appearing so natural as if from battle and others perhaps by age. She had been to Genoa before and what had fascinated her on the first visit was learning about the merchants of Genoa. Everyone knew of the merchants of Venice but learning that Genoa also supported this maritime population kindled her interest in the city.

'I'm glad you brought me along.' Hailey said.

'Oh don't think about it we needed the trip ourselves. Well I more than everyone else, so I dragged everyone along. By the way how are you getting on with the article, do you think you have most of what you need now?'

They had driven up the A8 and A10 from Mougins through Cannes and past some famous names such as the Piazza Raffaele De Ferrari into Genoa. Cephas had covered the distance in just over two hours ensuring that they all safely checked into the hotel. Sarai had then popped into Hailey's room mentioning to her that they would have to go ahead with the children, as Cephas would join them later.

'I have to admit it is working out better than I thought it would.'

'I'm glad to hear this.'

'If I have to let you into a secret I would say that this trip doesn't only help me write about you but helps me learn about myself. There is so much that I am discovering about me that I never knew existed before.'

'Great, you should know that you can come back anytime we would love to have you.'

'There is this freedom you have in the spirit which I seek and now value.' Hailey said. This could not be her words, she thought, it felt so bizarre. Who was this new jeu d'esprit? Is this me talking or someone else. I'm a stranger to this person that stands in this splendour. How can I explain this to my friends, colleagues, me? I am shouting within me to wakeup from this reverie. Yet am I spellbound as this new energy flows within me.

Sarai adjusted the hat on her head bending forward to play with Luke in the carry harness.

'It is something we all have to work at. It is only by constant prayer that this can be achieved. Being well off is never enough in life. I had to find out the hard way. Now I live for something more, for a purpose, for God,' she said as she watched Joshua and Rachel run circles around her. She knew Hailey was questioning herself when she talked of freedom. She had been through the same. Where did God fit in one's life when the world challenged your faith? One was left feeling like an alien that cranked up the volume for what the world had periodically moved away from. The comparisons of physical and real rewards against hope, the visible and invisible that fought against each other left us questioning our sanity. Her own journey had required answers for a similar moment to what Hailey was experiencing and she had sought them. In trying to understand her husband she began reading the bible to see this energy that pulled him so deeply from within. She had come across a passage that had shed some light to what was happening. When God had sent Moses to free the Children of Israel God told Moses that he would harden Pharaoh's heart so that his might can be shown by the wonders he would perform on Egypt. Pharaoh had then ordered the taskmasters to increase the burden on the Children of Israel, challenging their faith and questioning them for relying upon vain words. She had recognized herself in this passage. Coming to the Lord always made one feel they voiced vain words especially when compared to the reality of society. Your burden increased significantly as your taskmasters made it clear that God's calling wasn't above one's success in society. A quest that had set out to understand her husband ended up being one of self-discovery. It wasn't her husband she needed to learn about but her own relationship with God.

'I know that you question yourself, I know that you wonder about what you say?' she said.

'Then you can see it, see the changes in me. I have to admit I can barely recognize myself in the mirror these days,' Hailey said.

'Hailey coming to God is not easy. It is very difficult leaving the world behind to follow our invisible God. You would think that it would be easy because he is the almighty. However because you are walking towards his light it then becomes a priority for the darkness to challenge you. In other words putting your trust in hope and faith against what our earthly wisdom demands.'

'I've been asking myself what is happening. I feel wonderful, happy and overjoyed talking to you and Cephas, being in this new place. Yet I know my other world awaits me and it worries me whether I could return to it and be successful with this new person that I have become.'

'That's the thing about the spiritual world we may be meek as sheep yet we can be as wise as serpents.'

'How can we be this?' You need to explain it to me.'

'Do you know I asked the very same question to my husband when he started teaching me about the spiritual world? His answer was to read the bible. He said that was where all the answers lay.'

'The bible?' Hailey asked. She had never thought of it. Her gaze was diverted to the centre of the square that they had walked into. She wanted to run away and hide from this family. If only there was somewhere to hide in this square. She looked at the open windows in the second floor of the rufous building across from where she sat imagining what sanctuary lay beyond. However no hope could be gained from escaping in that direction as the restaurant beneath it and the news stand only a few yards away were an indication that things wouldn't fare any better on the second floor of the building. She turned her attention to birds that loitered in the centre of the small square. They took off as some children ran towards them, gathering again further away and resuming their task of picking at what bits they could find. If only I could be like one of those birds, I'd be free to escape and return as I pleased. She needed to escape. How was it possible that she knew Sarai would say the real answers could be found in the bible? The evidence was there from the moment that she had walked into that church, that cathedral in New York. Things from then on had changed, she rode pillion behind this couple unable to determine her destination. How can I be so different now to whom I was?

'Yes the bible. Believe me when I tell you that I felt exactly the same as you do now. I was screaming internally at myself. Why me? Why is this man in my life? Yet today look at my beautiful children, my home and look at where I am? I am still the same person, only much happier, wiser and living for something, something better and greater than I am. I don't have to force my beliefs on anyone. If they want to hear of God or know him I pass on what I have.'

Hailey was quiet. The spiritual world was pilfering pieces of her old self and she could do nothing but follow to its chant. Had her grandmother not spoken to her in this koan tone resounding riddles that kept the mind bedazzled for days. Her attention was distracted as she waved back to Rachel and Joshua who had each selected a round concrete bollard to sit on as they played freely in the square. If only they knew, I am running into my past in the present as if they are corridors linked by this world that won't let go of me. The essence of the spiritual world was that it existed all around you. She was discovering that faith was a journey that had to be walked without doubt. Sarai was teaching her and guiding her on this path. You followed the light because you believed in it and in everything that came with it. The shelter was God, he was the security and he supplied answers where none could be found.

'Thank you,' She said the words as if she was speaking to herself. She did not know why she said those words but it was all she could think of. She did not know who she was thanking. Perhaps it was Sarai, perhaps it was the invisible God that had brought Sarai into her own life but for whatever reason there was a calmness now that she felt after all the questions and doubt.

Sarai nodded behind her dark sunglasses. My dear girl we have to declare the Lord's name before others in order for him to declare ours before God. This is our responsibility, you will learn of this in time.

'It is one day at a time. None of us has all the answers yet we believe that they would come when we need them.' she said. Speaking of answers where is Cephas, she thought quietly. She hoped he had left the hotel. He knew they had to start out for Portofini if they were to get there before lunch.

She heard the sound before Hailey could ask the question.

'It's mine, its in the bag. Thanks,' she took the phone from Hailey and said, 'hi.'

London. My shadow made a deep indentation in the bath as I climbed into the water. Finally I had just enough warm water to half fill the bath. Autumn was blaring away in the distance with the winter months soon to come. The candle on the window ledge flickered and returned to its wholesome flame. It wavered time and again as the wind blew through the gaps in the windowpanes but held its own. I sank into the water letting my body absorb the warmth it had to offer. *The hole*, as I called my dark cave with candles was not an easy place to be in. However there could be several things said for being alone with no one and no voices for miles.

God was truly amazing.

I did not know how time had flown by. Each day in the hole had made its own chapter in the history of my existence. I could smell the roses of victory. The signs were there in this new found strength and there was now the will to wake up in the mornings without the groans or Cephas's voice to motivate me. I worked my way through time patiently as I waited for that day when I would step out of the hole and make the first journey not as two complete individuals occupying one entity but as myself, one being, spirit and man, Cephas resurrected. We would not achieve perfection because that was only possible after death when one body would rise to be with the father. However we were learning about this paragon by abiding by the words of Christ. If we could succeed in this domain then there was a fair chance that we could share the true rewards of the Lord's greatness.

It was difficult to give a fair account of exactly what had taken place. I did not know how I managed to occupy my mind during the day or at night. I recalled images of men put in isolation in prisons. The world said it changed a person to be in this solitude; they learnt a few things, like how to behave properly in society. They broke down relinquishing aspects of themselves that were wrong. I had seen movies of individuals cast away on deserted islands some lost at sea and others in an age where time had forgotten them. It was customary to lose ones senses eventually, hallucinate as the times got harder. This was different.

I had God.

There was no easy way of ever describing a power great and divine as that of the Lord. He occupied time itself shaping it in all ways that man couldn't. I would think of a time and a place and an instance where I had been in trouble and I would remember that my companion then had been God. I would then switch to another instance when I had been in joy when I had visited one beautiful city and would again remember then that my companion had been God. And then I thought of family, they were the stars that shown brightly in the skies in the darkest of times and through the night with laughs, tears and love given to me to participate in my indoctrination. We were all so different from the smallest to the eldest yet we all shared one spirit, God. Friends, my telamones, some still remained to hand while others had come and gone like the wind in the night. Girl friends, some so stunning that when I looked back I knew that in my short life I too could boast before others because the Lord had been there to make it all possible. And then there were the jobs, the challenges, the colleagues, the managers, directors, and others that had participated in my life. The list was endless but they were all memories that God had given my thoughts to occupy time with. The movies I had seen over the years.

Another myriad, I could play them countless times over and over again and still there would not be enough time in the day, in isolation to bore me. Then the books, I thought of many, those that were studied to learn of mankind, those that were studied to live with mankind and those that were read just for leisure. Working my way through this made it impossible for time to defeat me. If isolation in prison was supposed to break a man mine was allowing me to discover the things that God had given to me. If the books weren't much to go by then there were the meals I had eaten, the different varieties and the countries and restaurants in which I had eaten them. The types of drinks I had drunk, the languages that I could remember and the accents I had heard them spoken in. Then the activities, the sports, I liked. God was truly beyond the understanding of man. I could barely spend an hour in boredom or depression or want, when I had so much of my life lived to the fullest. There was nothing that I had asked for and not received in abundance. Even being in the hole was a welcome break of a difference from being anywhere else. It was my time alone with God and my time to prepare to be resurrected in life to live as spirit and man, as Cephas.

'*It was here that it all begun all those years ago.*'

'It truly was,' I replied.

I could remember the words clearly.

'In every language there is an introduction, the birth of a relationship, first sight a hand shaking activity that is the beginning of a friendship. The spiritual world begins in this way. It is a scene that is set for harmony, peace of mind that allows us the freedom to explore the unknown, the mystery behind the unknown removing all barriers that would otherwise be created by sarcasm, maturity in the flesh, the urgency that comes with responsibility and the impatience that is born with

293

time.'

They were mine and they had started there in the bath and in water. I had decided then that I would truly follow the Lord and I had. I had asked the world to call me a new name as I related events in my life and the name I had chosen was Cephas. I had said it meant nothing but a stone. However I had grown with that name and that spirit to truly understand its meaning and the value that it depicted in my own existence. It was then that the visions started and then that Cephas begun taking a personality of its own, the spirit existing in isolation to the man. However I had been the soliloquist then, relating every event that occurred. Soon it had become evident that Cephas wanted to be a part of it. It had been an incredible journey with many highs and lows but I had held firm on the path.

Finally this, *the hole*, the first stop in my journey to living as one, no more man and then spirit or vice versa but one spirit and man with one identity, Cephas. We were stepping out as one person, spirit and man in perfect unison until the time when the man would be gone for the spirit to seek pastures new. However this time was beyond comprehension so it wasn't worth worrying about at this stage of our existence.

Everything had been set in motion. I would be flying into Washington the next day and then I would spend some time with my brothers, family. I would spend a month and survey the land. The existence of Cephas and I as one after this would depend on what God had planned for me. The four days without light had drawn swiftly to an end as they had started. I had not lost my faculties. I had strengthened them and would never forget this moment with the Lord. I would be on my way the next day and even the hole would just be another memory. I was ready to become one with Cephas. I was ready to see this new light. The timing was perfect; nothing would stop me.

Chapter Seventeen

Genoa Italy. Life was a string of moments, each one carefully carved out and linked to periods of time for us to see the differences in our lives. I was staring at mine now. In another time and place I had been preparing to perform a very similar exercise. I had woken up from the toils of the night before with anticipation for adventure planned for the day. The morning was sunny and inviting back then as the ancient city of Athens that held as much history as anyone could seek reached out to me. Now it was Genoa that called, to be more accurate a little village called Portofini and my family waited.

I quickly splashed water on my face and reached for the white face towel by the sink. I needed to wake up. Sarai had given me a couple of hours respite after the drive down because I had worked until late the night before. I knew I was asking too much of her leaving her alone with three active children but I needed the time to myself and hoped Hailey would help. The light sleep had done me some good and I felt prepared to face the world of adventure that lay before us. I walked back into the large suite and reached for my watch and glasses on the table as my eyes darted briefly to the lamp stand by the bed for my mobile. As I shut the door to the room and walked down the empty corridor I dialed her number.

'I'm on my way darling, I shall see you soon.' I said when she answered.

'Did you get to sleep?'

'For about half an hour or so, thanks for being an angel.'

'We are in the small square as you enter the gates of Porta Soprana. If you can't see us give me a call. Are we still going to Portofini or should I order some lunch?'

'We are going to Portofini but you can get some sandwiches for now.'

'I'll do that darling and see you soon.'

Soon I was down the stairs and walking through the lobby into the quiet street of Via Corsica. The beautiful sun hidden behind the green and yellow leaves that brought autumn greeted me as I navigated a route to the Plaza where my family waited. Today I take in a different part of the deep blue Mediterranean, several seas away from the Saronic Gulf where I had once felt this level of anticipation and excitement. The Ligurian sea extended for miles for as far as the eye could see and driving up it from Mougins into Genoa earlier on that day was a treat that even the children had enjoyed from the back seat of the car. I'm a fool, Lord, truly one. I wasn't so sure when Sarai had suggested we do this yet I felt like a kid in a play shop. The amazing thing was I had been to Genoa before, driven to Portofini with Sarai before yet this time it was different.

It was Hailey. Her presence and questions had evoked memories from my past, stringing a time and place when two instead of one occupied the same space. Then spirit taught man of whom and what it was, the man incapable of believing that he could accept this light into him without fully appreciating the cleansing of his own soul. What made today different was I had those memories still fresh in my mind, yet we were now one, reborn to walk the earth knowing that the man would eventually wither and die away leaving the spirit to carry on for eternity. This was my haeccity. I had adapted to the ubiquitous nature of the spirit and survived the tasks that had been set before me. God had been good to me keeping true to his word and delivering me from whatever I faced in life.

I crossed the road and entered the medieval street of Via Nino Bixio, which led into Via Innocenza my thoughts climbing the walls of the ancient city of Genoa. I spotted an old couple walking together the woman holding on to the man, their backs crouched with age and experience. The man's face was hidden beneath his black hat still they never once looked in my direction. They had seen it all, seen past curiousity and the strangers in their land now they just lived. We all got to this place at some point in our lives. Like life itself the spiritual world had its steps, moments that we all had to experience and when those passed we moved on abandoning the old for the new. It was a confluence of all the parts of a puzzle, the further one delved into it there more apparent the mystery became. Hailey had asked me about freedom, she had wanted to know how one left everything behind. There had been another time and another place when someone else had asked me this same question. How can you be certain, how can you be so sure that what you ask for will happen as you have requested. I had immediately answered by faith. Yet that answer had been incomplete. Faith covered it all yet there were details of how our faith was tested before we truly knew that we would be with God with heart and soul irrespective of what challenge was put before us. Living in the wilderness was one thing but getting past the testing times at the gates of its exit set a precedence for the man we would become. We were offered all things on earth, allowed access to the powers be and if we relented, acceded to this so-called powers be, our dreams perished.

I reached Via Eugenia Ravasco and watched blindly at the people that waited at the bus stop. How had I walked away from work? A plenitude of offers had come, some more tempting than others, one offering me a home with suggestions of a wife if needed. Still I stuck to the rewards of my matutinal spiritual respite. What God had shone me in those early hours of the morning could never be replaced. The visions were my meal and if that was insufficient to keep the sharks at bay then the words of the Lord had come to my rescue. *"Man shall not live by bread alone but by every word that proceedeth out of the mouth of God, Thou shalt not tempt the Lord thy God, Thou shalt worship the Lord thy God and him only shalt thou serve."* These words were easily said when one read them from the bible. However time dictated whether one believed truly in them or appreciated the full nature of what they demanded. I hadn't faltered and time had passed and God had delivered.

I saw them late but their cries woke me from the reverie. The little girl and boy holding unto me as I walked into the small square were mine and they now came to me in reality as they had many years ago in one of my visions. This was freedom, this was what you gained from faith, believing that God would provide in spite of everything, especially the tribulations you faced.

'How have they been?' I asked.

'Am still alive and breathing that should say something,' Sarai said from her seat with Luke standing on her thighs.

'I think they would be tired for the ride down to Portofini.' I offered.

'Thank you darling. I guess I'd be sleeping too in the car. For some reason I feel a little tired myself. Hailey has been my angel, She has helped as you can imagine.'

'I did nothing, they are adorable and besides they were well behaved,' Hailey said from her side of the park bench.

'Thanks Hailey, you both allowed me some sleep.

Now let's see what Portofini has to offer.'

London. The space between two places, that little air gap or hole that allows stray air molecules to flow through. I have no interaction with mankind as I find this space in time. My wounds are weathered from my toils in battle. I have lost this one, knew I would despite my best efforts. It was coming I could see this over the years. Did I want it to happen this way? The Lord said he had to be crucified on the cross for the scripture to be fulfilled, for us his sheep to be saved. He said Peter would deny him thrice. Everything happened as he had said and my point? Some things cannot change, wouldn't because they are written in stone for us to rise up and be those people that we were always meant to be. My parallactic view to this person nears its final journey. I would become Cephas and Cephas me but I would have to lose big in my world for this scripture to be fulfilled.

'I know your type. I see many of you every day. You think you can come in here, tell us a yarn and we should all fall for it. You have no remorse or concern for missing your payments,' the judge said.

'Ma'am to be fair to him he did phone us and adhere to the plan we suggested over the phone so he is making the payments. It is unfortunate that he had missed the court hearing,' the claimant said in my defense almost apologetic for the way in which the judge spoke.

'Do you have anything to say on your behalf,' the judge asked.

'No,' I said.

'You do know that a court order supersedes everything else. It is the law and you have to obey,' the judge said.

I said nothing it was pointless arguing with the

judge. It was her domain, her territory and I hadn't set out to antagonize her. Lord, my home disappears in the distance. In this day and age I had come to understand what Job felt. I had lost everything even falling sick to the point where the face that stood in judgment was unrecognizable to the old one it used to be.

The judge was quiet for a short while as she asserted herself. Perhaps she felt she had been hard on me, even rude but I could tell that my presence irritated her. In any case she had done her duty.

'I will send the bailiffs, you have one more chance to appeal. If you can't win, as I know you can't, be out of the house by 10am tomorrow morning,' her tone a softer version of what it had been before. She didn't want to come off looking like the grim reaper. It wasn't what she had signed up for but it was frustrating to sit in that chair and for anyone to undermine her authority.

I left the courthouse and began walking up the high street. The son of man has no place to rest his head. God had given me plenty. I had seen many kingdoms and traveled many coastlines. I had owned beautiful cars that carried beautiful women in beautiful cities. Every dream I had asked for had come to pass as I desired still I knew that one day I would also ask to follow God. This part of my journey in life was never meant to be easy, still I had come prepared and willingly. No one in their right mind lost all their wealth, their home and any modicum of dignity without feeling a sense of sadness but I wasn't just anyone. I had other things that God had given me to cope with this unjust, I had my visions and the wisdom of his word. The material things in life were not meant to be permanent they were temporal like the carnal body we inhabited. They withered away with time as our bodies did to be replaced by another.

I walked past the local bakery. I would be far from

this place in years to come. I will have everything that a man can dream of and more, however before then I would lose everything.

There was chaos in the apartment when I returned. There were men everywhere. The new towel I had just purchased was on the floor and had been used for a rag to wipe the mud of the gas engineer's boots. The door was broken at the lock as the handy man worked craftily to change it. Already signs had gone up on the main door, EVICTED. I had been thrown out, kicked out of my home because of the path I had chosen, because of the promise, the contract that had to be fulfilled in spite of the loss.

'Sorry mate, as you know we gotta do our job,' the man said. He had a pensive look in his eyes, expectant. He had done this plenty of times and expected a certain level of hostility. None was forthcoming. Now we are one, I thought. There is no more Cephas and man, two bodies, with one that listened to the jibes of the world that forced it against the spirit of God within. I have accepted Cephas by walking this path fully. I've lost it all Lord, the car, the house, the girl and any self dignity that was afforded me. This is my journey, this is my path, this is the only way to learn about you. I have left the restraints of the world behind unaided by anything. It was never my decision, no not at all. I could not have given myself this strength to walk away from what had taken a lot out of me to build. However your grace surpasses it all, and by it only would I survive through this. 'Be not afraid stranger, for I won't hit back, or tear your arms to pieces. I would stay quiet and move out as you demand. My name is Cephas and I am complete,' I thought.

'You can come back for all your things but you cannot live here after tomorrow. We usually clear people out as soon as we get the court order. In your case we would allow a couple of days for you to pack I know that it is not easy,' the man said.

'Thank you,' I replied. Thank you for allowing me to walk away with all my bones intact. Thank you for my resurrection into the being that completely serves my God. You are a good messenger even though you bare these sort of tidings.

I walked into the room and began packing. I would have to leave without most of my things as I had nowhere to put them. Still there were no tears as the chanting had begun. Lord we have had some good times and some tough times in this house still I know one day I too would have my own place that you would grant me. Longsuffering was the testimony of the journey for all those who wished to follow Christ. No one was better than his master and so no one expected to be treated better than his master was. It was amazing how one's life could look so different when it was stripped off any dignity that made it worthwhile. I picked up my bible beneath my pillow. I may leave all behind but the word of God would follow me for the rest of my days. I opened the book to Psalm 23 and read,

"the Lord is my shepherd, I shall not want. He maketh me to lie down in green pastures: He leadeth me beside the still waters. He restoreth my soul: he leadeth me in the paths of righteousness for his name's sake. Yea, though I walk through the valley of the shadow of death, I will fear no evil: for thou art with me; thy rod and thy staff they comfort me. Thou preparest a table before me in the presence of mine enemies: thou anointest my head with oil; my cup runneth over. Surely goodness and mercy shall follow me all the days of my life: and I will dwell in the house of the Lord forever."

You have indeed restored my soul Lord and prepared a table before my enemies. As I stand for the last time in this place that I once called home I know that what awaits me is your house to dwell in forever.

By noon the next day I was driving away in a friend's car and watching as a busy Saturday started a new journey in my life. One day people would understand and see the truth of why all was lost. One day they will know what it takes to dwell in the house of the Lord. All is not lost, I told myself, far from it. On the contrary plenty has been gained. The Lord has made me stronger for I am not dead. I have lost everything but I have me and we shall see what happens next.

Portofini, Italy. 'What was the hardest thing you had to do in life? What was the worst moment you ever faced where your faith was truly put to test?' Hailey asked, her eyes bore holes through us. It was evident that as her time drew near for departure back to her world, she wanted some form of closure. Something to tell her that she wasn't dreaming that we were human and could be broken like everybody else. If only she knew that it was by grace and not strength that one walked the spiritual world her life on this path could have been made easier. Still we all had to walk the path to learn and understand the word. We all had to bear the cross to know our strength and wisdom was none existent in the spiritual world. This place belonged to God.

I glanced at Sarai. She was as beautiful as she had looked in the vision before I met her. Her long black hair ran to her shoulders, the top part of it just hidden beneath the brown hat she was wearing. Even behind the large dark sunglasses any man would watch, stare to see and dream of the emollient features possessed by the woman behind the face. No, this wasn't a dream, I was looking at my wife. If I increased the periphery of my vision I would be looking at the family that she had made for me. The Lord had granted me other visions, he had said three children, two boys and a girl, I had them too. There was Mougins to think about the French Riviera only a few heartbeats from the Italian Riviera and so many miles away from the past. A plane, cars, contract and loving my hobby, my job of being a writer, I had dreamed and God had provided. I had hoped with faith and God had not forgotten. If only Hailey knew how difficult it was to answer her question she won't have asked it.

'It is difficult to answer that question because with God a thousand days can feel like one day and one day like a thousand. Every time a good thing replaces a bad thing it makes the bad thing look as though it never happened and it is then hard to effectively measure how difficult that time was. The truth is I cannot really answer your question because with faith there are no worst moments. There are just moments linked to form a journey, a story and your path to God.' I said.

Portofini was truly a gem hidden away from the world. You were enveloped by the reverie you felt, and the need to emblazon its unique personality. There was warmth were one needed it to be, beauty were the eyes desired and the jilting sounds that heralded thoughts you hoped you had experienced and never forgotten. In places such as this it really wasn't what you saw that made your day it was what you felt. I was the peregrine that visited the high cliffs of this beautiful coastline and returned to earth knowing that I would do this over and over again without regret or fear. This was my spiritual odyssey and this was the path that God had placed before me.

'I have a confession to make,' Hailey began. 'I am at the end of my article. You have both been so kind and I know that what lies ahead for me is a journey of new discoveries but I think I have what I need now to complete Sarai's article. I can't tell you what an experience it has been since I met you. My whole life is different, I feel different.'

Sarai nodded. 'I remember when I was a little a girl I used to watch my Mum pull her hand away from a hot pot and place it in her mouth. When I grew up and had the same experience the next question I used to ask myself is would I rather avoid the hot pot altogether or be burnt at least once just so I can feel as my mum did? The funny thing is my personal response to this question changed as I grew older in life with personal experiences. At one time in our lives we would rather avoid this burn because we can't cope with it. Eventually we learn that we need this burn for us to know that we can cope with it. I don't know why Cephas brought God to my life in this way but one thing is for sure I need God to know what life is.'

'I won't leave out anything. I shall write freely irrespective of the confines of my magazine. If anyone is as inspired as I have been on this journey then I would have done my job,' Hailey said.

'We are waiting. Still you haven't left yet so let's enjoy what this fine little village has to offer us,' Sarai said and smiled.

Mougins, France. Sarai watched as the little girl combed the hair of the doll on the floor beside her. She was in a world of her own and saying all the things that little girls did when they played house. Perhaps that was the world she needed in order to find rest from her morning efforts. It was a lot easier being the director than the manager, you oversaw what happened yet you didn't have to chase people. Instead you chased those who managed people and because they were often more concerned about their careers than the work itself they chased you instead. It was time to take a break from the computer and tend to the bills and junk mail that came through the door. There were a few letters from people wishing to sell property and then she saw what looked like a parcel. She immediately picked it out. She pulled off the strip of tape at the top of the envelop and cut through to pull out the magazine within. She was about to put it amongst the other pile of junk already building up by the side of her desk when she saw her picture in the front page.

'Me? It can't be,' She whispered quietly afraid to disturb the little girl in the corner. She opened the magazine and began searching until she reached the centre and saw the headlines. It was another picture of her and a series of shots taken from her house. The title read, *The House of Abba by Hailey Wong.* It was her story, a four page article that told several details of her life. She ploughed through the pages briefly scanning the words some of them, hers that she had forgotten. Hailey talked of her, of the children and of Cephas. She talked of a family, a mysterious family that had come together because of God. She had ended the article saying that it was only befitting that she called it the House of Abba because this family lived and dwelt in a mystery that only God could explain.

Sarai jumped to her feet and picked up Rachel. 'Let's go and look for your father and brothers. It seems he isn't the only famous one in this house, Mummy is too.'

The child responded blindly to her mum's excitement. She didn't have to know why. If Mummy was happy then so was she.

It was difficult engaging in a game of wits when the competition was a child. I was stored away in one of the spare rooms that I had converted to a playroom for the children as I tried to make the game I played more interesting than it really was. Luke sat in his chair watching as I taught Joshua how to use the console of the game hoping that one day he would be good enough to give me a challenge.

'Daddy I'm winning, I just scored a goal,' the boy said.

'Yep, you are better than me,' I replied. Sooner or later the boy would really know how to play and then I would have some real competition.

'Have you guys been here all afternoon?' Sarai asked as she walked in.

'That's how long it takes to get into it. You know these games are addictive. I can't help myself.'

'Well I have got something for you to see. Looks like I'm the famous one in the family now darling,' Sarai said waving her article before me.

I diverted my gaze from the screen before me briefly to look at what she referred to.

'Well, what does it say, don't keep us guessing, do tell O ye famous one.'

'This beautiful lady of elegance, a mysterious woman who dwells in the finer parts of the French Riviera is convinced that all that she owns was given to her by God. I am left with no other option but to call this family '*The House of Abba*' because in everything that they do or say there is an inference to God.' Sarai said.

'She really wrote that?' I asked without taking my eyes off the game.

'She did and there's plenty more with pictures of me and the house.'

'Let me take a look,' I said taking the magazine off her.

It was all there as Sarai had read. It was in print, the House of Abba. I looked at Hailey's words and the picture of Sarai in silence and wonder. Many would read this article and deliberate about the people within it. Many would recognize themselves in it and wonder how it all happened, little would they know of what it had taken to find this dwelling. Athens seemed like a hundred years ago yet that was where I had met Hailey and that was where the spirit had taught me of the resurrection. Yet for that to be complete there had to be an exodus. There had to be a demarcation from the old to the new as I left my past to seek this family in my visions. Hailey had given the perfect description to our new dwellings. We lived in the House of Abba. It was the Psalm all over again dwelling in the house of God after the many passages that got one there.

'You're a star my darling,' I said looking into Sarai's eyes.

'Thank you,' she replied with a smile that spoke volumes of her accomplishment.

The End